Captain Costain Chooses a Wahine

Golden-skinned Leilani stood in the darkest corner of the *Sea Eagle*'s hold, her large, dark eyes glowing with fear of what was to come.

She'd had no chance to explain that it was all a mistake—that she was not a prostitute, but an *alii-nui*, a princess of royal blood. She'd been forcibly herded here with five other young girls to service the crew of thirty-six, along with three officers. Now the handsome young Captain, Mark Costain, was about to exercise his privilege of first choice of a *wahine*.

"Pick me, Captain," cried one of the girls. "Am I not pretty?" The others swarmed about him, echoing her words.

Leilani decided her only hope of escaping rape at the hands of every sailor on board was to be selected by the Captain. He might at least listen to her plea.

"Captain," she said softly, bringing her supple golden body close to him.

"Now the silent one speaks to me!" said the stalwart, blackhaired Captain Costain.

With one hand, Leilani touched him lightly on the shoulder, in a spot known only to the *alii-nui*, a spot that controlled his energy flow. By redirecting this flow, she was subtly, secretly redirecting his sexual desire.

"I—I choose you," the Captain said thickly.

Leilani knew from his eyes that she was now in more danger than ever.

Savage
Rapture_____

Paula Moore

A Dell/James A. Bryans Book

Published by
Dell Publishing Co., Inc.
1 Dag Hammarskjold Plaza
New York, New York 10017

Dell ® TM 681510, Dell Publishing Co. Inc.

ISBN: 0-440-07743-5

Printed in Canada

First printing—September 1978

PART ONE

Chapter One ————————————————————

THE LONG, HIGH wave rolled powerfully up
the beach, boomed with surf thunder, then fell
back into the ocean with its energy dissipated
into millions of frothy, luminous bubbles. A
cold full moon hung over the dark water, paint-
ing a streak of silver along the wet sand of the
shore and softly lighting the waving palm trees
outside a small, grass house.

Sleeping on matting on the floor inside was
one of the loveliest sights in this tropical garden
of beauty. Fourteen-year-old Leilani, daughter
to the daughter of King Kamehameha the
Great, was nude, a condition as natural to the
Hawaiian of 1840 as to a fish or a bird. Half
of Leilani's body was in the shadows, dark and
mysterious, and the other half was touched by
the silver nightglow of the full moon.

Someone moved outside the house.

"Hurry, hurry," a voice urged.

Bare feet crept over the sand.

"Hurry," the voice said again. "She must be moved to the *heiau* before the moon crosses the rim of the crater."

"*Pupule!*" another voice replied. "Crazy one! Do you think I don't know what must be done?"

"But we must hurry. There is little time left."

Their excited whispering could be heard inside the house, but there was nothing Leilani could do. Today had been the *wahine* luau, the feast of becoming a woman, and for the first time she was allowed to drink the *okoleohao*, a powerful Hawaiian liquor. It had left her groggy and incapable of resisting.

There were more whispers, and the sound of a tapa curtain slowly drawn open.

"She sleeps now," a voice said.

Leilani tried to get up. She sensed she was in danger, but could do nothing about it.

"It is good that she sleeps," another voice said. "Perhaps we will have no trouble with her."

With a great effort Leilani forced herself to sit up, trying to understand what was happening. "What is it?" she asked drowsily. "What do you want?"

"Quickly, she wakes! Cover her with the mat!"

"Help!" Leilani shouted, but her voice was immediately muffled as a grass mat was dropped over her head.

Powerful arms lifted her up, and although she

kicked and tried to force her way out, she was a prisoner. The mat was drawn more tightly, and she felt as if she would suffocate. She panicked and tried to scream.

"Careful with her," one of the voices said. "You know what will happen if she is marked in any way."

"She will not be marked," another voice answered. "Look, the moon nears the crater of Pele. We must hurry."

Pele?

Leilani was suddenly cold with fear. Pele was the goddess of fire! Those who still believed in Pele followed the practice of offering human sacrifices. The victims were young virgins on the threshold of womanhood. Leilani was a virgin, and only today she had celebrated the feast of womanhood. Also, as the daughter of a daughter of Kamehameha the Great, she was of royal blood and would make an ideal offering to Pele.

Who were these people? Did they worship Pele? Was she being taken to be sacrificed?

Leilani renewed her struggles, but she was subdued by a cloth held over her nose and mouth. She inhaled something with a strong, rather pleasant scent, then she felt her head spinning and everything went black.

When Leilani opened her eyes a short time later, she found that she was in the *heiau*, the temple which was once used in the worship of ancient gods. Gods like Pele. She was tied to four posts in the position of a sacrificial victim with her arms and legs stretched out on a soft mattress of tapa, laid over a cushion of fragrant flower petals.

Two girls hovered over the mattress—Leilani thought they were about her age; they wore masks of brilliantly colored bird feathers so she couldn't be sure. Their naked bodies had been bathed in oil, and they glistened like gold in the flickering light of a coconut lamp.

"Why am I here?" Leilani asked in a frightened voice. "Am I to be sacrificed to Pele?"

The girls didn't answer her. Instead one of them produced a glass flask of amber-colored oil, which glowed as it caught the reflection of the coconut lamp.

"Why won't you answer?" Leilani asked. "Am I to be sacrificed to Pele?"

The girls began silently applying the oil. It felt warm and sensual, and as their hands spread it over Leilani, her body seemed to glow like the coconut lamp, too. There was a warm, pleasureable sensation as her skin reacted to the soft touch of the young girls' probing fingers.

The masked girls gradually rubbed the oil over her arms, shoulders, stomach and legs. Then one girl eased up to her firm uptilted breasts, and the soft hand caused her nipples to harden quickly. Although she was still frightened, an involuntary moan of pleasure escaped from Leilani's lips. This feeling was intensified when the other girl moved her hand up to the inside of her thigh to the junction of her legs,

and spread the warm oil in that secret place
which was now most sensitive.

Then the girls stopped and began a soft,
musical chant. Their voices were soon joined
by many others outside, and Leilani realized
that a crowd had gathered to witness whatever
was about to happen.

Could there be that many Pele worshipers?

The girls slowly withdrew and Leilani was
left alone. She struggled again to free herself,
but this time there seemed to be more than the
ropes restraining her. The anointing by the girls
had generated strange, frightening, but excit-
ing sensations in her body. There was a vague
sense of pleasure, but even stronger was a
frustrated yearning she had never experienced
before, a yearning she did not yet understand,
and that kept her lying there waiting for something else . . . for something more. Her body
had been awakened and now needed to be satisfied.

As the chanting outside grew louder, a drum-
beat began. There were drums of various types,
from the large, bass kind made of huge, hol-
lowed-out trees, to very tiny drums made from
small branches and struck with twigs. Together,
they created a rhythm which perfectly
matched the pulsing in Leilani's body.

The tapa curtain was drawn open again, and
a man approached her. He was covered with a
brilliant red and yellow feathered cape, and
crowned with a high crested helmet of the same
colors. He held his arm crooked so that the cape

covered his face and she couldn't see who he was. She knew that he was a man for the cape was open below his waist, and she could see the fullness of his manhood.

"What is it?" Leilani asked fearfully. "Who are you?"

The man suddenly threw the cape aside and Leilani screamed. He was wearing a large, grotesque mask, with a mouth full of boar's teeth, and red eyes staring out over a demonic nose.

But, frightening as the mask was, Leilani was even more terrified of what protruded between the man's legs. It seemed to thrust out at her like a weapon, large, gleaming wickedly from the oils similar to those with which she had just been anointed.

The beating of the drums grew louder, and the man began to dance with savage vitality as if responding to them. He drew closer and closer to her until, with one great leap, he towered over her. Then he slowly lowered himself until the hideous mask was only inches from her face. She could hear his breathing and feel his hot breath on her, and then she sensed his swollen, rearing manhood was poised just above her.

"No!" she pleaded. "No, please."

The man paid no attention. With one powerful lunge, he drove himself into her. Leilani felt a great, blinding stab of pain, and she cried out.

The masked man began to thrust in and out with the same rhythm as the drumbeats, and

Leilani suddenly felt a return of the intense sensations she had experienced earlier when the girls were anointing her. But this time her whole body was dominated by it. This was the mysterious *something more* she had yearned for.

But no! She would not let her body submit. She must resist such domination; she began struggling against him. She cried out again for him to stop. He ignored her, and the pace of his thrusts grew faster, and in spite of herself, she responded, moving with him, helping him to drive deeper and deeper inside her.

Her body was actually taking him joyfully. But before she could attain the full satisfaction her body was seeking, the man above her let out a groan, gave a few faster, more frenzied thrusts, then stopped with an exclamation of pleasure. She wanted him to go on, but she somehow knew it was over. He slowly pulled free from her, then stood up and looked down at her for a second before turning to leave. Leilani's body was left aching for fulfillment, longing for release . . .

The drumming outside stopped and the chanting slowly began to fade into the distance. Leilani could tell everyone was leaving. But what about her? Was she to be left here? Was she to remain tied up all night?

As if to answer her the two masked girls turned and took off their masks, revealing her two closest friends, the twins Kamala and Malaka.

"You!" she said, with great relief. "But what is this?"

The girls laughed. "It is the ceremony of the Alii-Nui," Kamala said. "You are the grand-daughter of Kamehameha the Great, and you are the Great Princess."

"But my mother is the Alii-Nui," Leilani said.

"Still, did you not become a woman today?" Malaka asked. "It is the custom that girls of royal blood become Alii-Nui when they reach womanhood."

"And as a woman, you must know a man," Kamala said. "Did you enjoy it?"

The girls untied Leilani as they talked, and she sat up and began rubbing her wrists and ankles. She hadn't been tied tightly enough to stop circulation, but her struggles had caused the binding to cut into her skin.

"Yes," Leilani said. "I suppose I enjoyed it, but I was frightened, too."

"I know," Malaka said. "You thought you were going to be thrown to Pele. Pele, don't eat me," she mocked, laughing.

"Did you know such fear at your ceremony?" Leilani asked.

"We are not Alii-Nui," Malaka said. "Only the Alii-Nui undergo such a ceremony."

"It was an impressive ceremony," Leilani said. "But you knew of it and I did not."

"Yes," Kamala said, laughing. "Once when you visited us, I thought you would see the mask, for I was working on it even then."

"But I threw a tapa over it and took it out,

saying it was a coconut," her sister added. "And you never guessed."

"Who was the man who was with me?" Leilani asked.

"We don't know," Malaka said. "Nobody knows. He was chosen by a secret meeting of the *kahauna*, the tribal priests."

"Then they know who he was?"

"No, not even they know. Ten were chosen. They drew in secret from a jar of ten stones. Nine black stones, one white. The white stone was the one, but no one could tell what color stone they drew."

"Perhaps someone saw," Leilani suggested.

"If they tell, the penalty is death," Kamala replied. "We were warned of that as we prepared for your ceremony.

"It was very well organized," Leilani said. "Except . . ."

"Except what?"

Leilani wanted to convey that it had left her frustrated, unfulfilled, but she didn't know how to explain.

"Except I was frightened," she said instead.

Chapter Two

LEILANI ATTENDED NOT one but two schools.

In the morning she spent four hours at a mission school run by Marcia Grimsley, wife of Reverend Jebediah Grimsley, who had been sent to Hawaii by the American Board of Commissioners for Foreign Missions in 1823. She spent two hours there studying religious subjects and the other two hours on reading, writing, and arithmetic. Leilani was a very bright girl and a quick learner, but that was not exceptional in her culture. The Hawaiian population, with the help of the missionaries, had become literate in a mere twenty years. Never in world history had an entire ethnic group made such stunning gains in education. Yet it was merely a by-product of the missionaries' main work of spreading the word of God, and even if they had realized that they had helped to accomplish something unparalleled in history, it would have meant little to them compared to their religious work.

But learning the skills needed to adjust to a rapidly changing world meant that the Hawaiians were in danger of losing contact with their old culture, which was being left behind. So in the afternoon, when she came out of the mission school, Leilani went to another school run by her mother, Lakiolani, who was the Alii-Nui, a title meaning great princess and high priestess.

Leilani's mother was very big, weighing close to three hundred pounds. Although her rolls of fat now hid most of her former beauty, her eyes, nose and mouth still showed how she had once looked.

"Some of our ways are changing," Lakiolani told Leilani. "And it is good that these ways change, for we have long been a people who, like the wind, could find what is true. If things do not change, they may wither away."

"What things have changed?" Leilani asked.

They were sitting on the grassy flat top of a cliff which overlooked the ocean. Leilani held a flower as they talked, occasionally sniffing its fragrance. In contrast to her mother, she was slender, and as graceful as a palm leaf stirred by the breeze. She had high cheekbones, not prominent but well accented, and her large, sparkling eyes, with eyelashes as beautiful as the most delicate lace, had a sexual quality she was not yet aware of. She was wearing a silk skirt and a lei of flowers, but her swelling breasts, golden globes of perfection, were bare.

"Many of the *kapus* we once had are no more. Once a girl child was put to death if she was the first born. That is no longer done. Once there were many human sacrifices, but not now —even though you thought you were to be fed to Pele." She laughed and went on with the lesson. "Once it was necessary for the Alii-Nui to eat much to become a very big woman so that all who saw her would know that she is the Alii-Nui"—she patted her stomach with amusement—"but now this is no more. You, my daughter, may stay as slender as the palm, for by your wisdom will they know you are the Alii-Nui. These things have all changed, and it is good they have changed."

"What things have not changed?"

"The powers which have been transmitted through our ancestors for one hundred generations. These powers we still have."

"Makua Grimsley does not believe in these powers. He will not speak of them. He says his God does not approve," Leilani said.

"Reverend Grimslely does not understand what he cannot see," Lakiolani explained. "Now, you must learn this:

I am the Alii-Nui, daughter of Lakiolani who is the daughter of Leilani, who is the daughter of Lakiolani, who is the daughter of Leilani, and thus it has been for one hundred generations."

Leilani repeated the chant, then learned many other things. Finally, when the lesson was over for the day, she kissed her mother, took off her skirt and lei, and dived from the cliff into the clear blue water over fifty feet below.

Leilani swam with swift, sure strokes until she was more than a mile out, far beyond the outer reefs. She then rolled over on her back and lay floating in the soothing water. Her blue-black hair spread around her like silken seaweed, and the ocean seemed to warm the golden skin of her body as if she were being gently caressed.

Come to me, Leilani thought. Her eyes were closed, and she didn't speak with her lips, but she thought the words and they were given flight by her mind and went across the sea to summon her friends.

I am the Alii-Nui Leilani, daughter of the sea. I summon you, Mahimahi, come to me.

Leilani had floated for less than a minute when she felt a gentle nuzzling against her thigh. She looked down and saw the sleek, grinning face of a dolphin staring at her with large, expressive eyes. She reached down and caressed him. He was much bigger than she was, and he floated peacefully nearby, allowing her to put her arms around him to hold herself up. She liked the warm, friendly feeling of him.

It had been three years since Leilani's deflowering ceremony when she became a woman, and now at seventeen, she had nearly completed her training as an Alii-Nui. She was learning an entirely new aspect of living, a secret known to very few. The rites and practises had been shrouded in mystery for ten centuries, even from others in the same culture. Alii-Nuis were the result of selective in-breeding and developed a complex intraculture to unlock mysteries which had puzzled human beings for eons. But the amazing truths they discovered were completely unknown outside the narrow confines of the direct line of descendants. When the last Alii-Nui died, the secrets would die with her, except for a few unpublished and unauthenticated reports. The missionaries, who were responsible for recording much of the history of Hawaii, learned nothing. The Hawaiians kept it from them, knowing they would become upset. And they were never curious anyway about what they considered to be primitive pagan behavior. If they didn't believe in something, they were simply not interested in recording it. So they missed the great secrets of the Alii-Nui.

Leilani learned how to control the total resources of her mind, to use the major part of the brain that others never develop. She mastered the martial skill of kola-kola, an art more deadly than karate and more secret than kung fu. But most of the time was spent in developing the power which was recognized as mankind's most potent—sexual power. If a skillful woman knew exactly what she was doing, she could use sex to dominate any man.

Leilani learned the complete sexual makeup of both the male and the female body. Long before science gave them a name, the Alii-Nui had understood the neurology and physiology of the erogenous zones, along with many secret stimulations of these parts of the body known only to them. Complex sexual techniques were developed, and Leilani grew into a total sexual being.

Leilani learned to be at one with the Universe, and how to read signs and omens in nature. She was at home in any water, and could read the ocean just as her ancestors had done one thousand years earlier when they navigated their canoes across 2,500 miles of open sea to discover the Hawaiian Island chain. Their feat was amazing because the Hawaiian Islands were the most isolated land mass in the entire world—and Leilani was one of their descendants. They found the islands by reading patterns in the ocean currents. When a wave bursts on the shore of an island, it starts an echo conveying the shape and size of the island which moves back for thousands of miles across the ocean. It is nature's radar, and Leilani could read this pattern as well as her ancestors.

But she understood more than the currents of the ocean. There were the creatures who lived in it as well: the shark, the whale, the sea bass, and Leilani's personal guide, the Mahimahi or dolphin.

Leilani could talk with the dolphins—they understood each other at a much deeper level than even that between human beings and very intelligent pets. She treated the dolphins as if they were equals.

That day when she lay in the ocean resting against a dolphin, Leilani sensed her tenderness and a great sexual energy, and she realized she had just finished mating.

She closed her eyes and concentrated on the patterns forming in her mind. As she thought of the dolphin, it was almost as if she became one with it . . .

She was a beautiful female, swimming smoothly through the water, diving to find a cool stream, or darting up to wrap herself in the blanket of a warm current. Now a flash of silver catches her eye, and she picks up the high-pitched clicking of a big male, sleek and powerful and ruler of the sea through his strength and intellect.

The male flashes by once, rubbing against her, finding that part of her which is responsive, and playing on the erotic chords of her body in a skilled symphony of sexual foreplay. She begins to return the rubbing and nuzzling until the male moves himself into position with a powerful stroke of his tail. He opens the skin flap which covers his genitals, then completes the mating, the joining of male and female, the universal language of all living creatures . . .

Leilani's mind bridged the gulf with the dolphin, and there, floating lazily in the water, she suddenly knew and enjoyed the white heat of orgasm. In that instant, in a sudden cosmic insight, Leilani realized that all mankind was spawned from the ocean.

Chapter Three ———————————————

SOMEWHERE IN THE forest which climbs the volcanic hills of Maui, a nightbird whistled quietly for its mate. A whispering breeze fanned the palm trees, rustling the fronds and sending shadows across the moonbeams.

Leilani came out of the dark forest like one of the shadows, and moved quickly across an open glade onto a projecting cliff which overlooked the ocean, shimmering now with soft silver reflections under the moon. Three ships stood at anchor just off Lahaina, three enchanting silhouettes from the world beyond the sea. Leilani often came at night to stare at the yellow lights which peeked through the windows of the great cabins like promises of gold.

"I knew I would find you here," a voice said quietly.

Leilani jumped at the unexpected interruption, then looked around to see a familiar sallow-faced young man. He was Calvin Grimsley, the son of Reverend Jebediah Grimsley, the missionary. He had washed-out blond hair, light blue eyes and pimples. He was about twenty years old.

"Calvin," Leilani said, smiling at him, "What are you doing up this time of night? I thought all *haoles* slept at night." *Haole* was the Hawaiian word for people who were not natives of Hawaii, but especially whites.

"My father and mother do sleep at night," Calvin said, moving closer to Leilani. "That is why it is possible for me to come here."

"Why do you come? Do you like to see the ships at night as I do?"

"No," Calvin said.

Calvin stared openly at Leilani's nearly nude body. She was wearing a lava-lava, or wraparound skirt, and a lei of flowers. The lei rested across her swelling breasts, just covering the nipples. Leilani often dressed this way, but now, under Calvin's severe stare, she began to feel extremely self-conscious.

"Why do you make of yourself an abomination before the Lord?" Calvin demanded suddenly.

"What do you mean?"

"You do not clothe your body, but parade it in its nakedness, so that you might incite lascivious thoughts in others."

Leilani folded her arms in a vain attempt to shield her breasts. Calvin was making her extremely uncomfortable, not by his criticism, but because she sensed there was desperation behind it.

A girl's laugh, carrying a great distance as sound sometimes will over water, reached them from one of the ships.

"There are girls with the sailors," Calvin said, and his tone condemned them. "My father will not like that. He doesn't approve of such things. The sailors of those ships will burn in the eternal fires of hell for what they are doing. It is a sin, for it is written in Ezekiel: *I will do these things unto thee, because thou has gone a whoring after the heathen, and because thou art polluted with their idols.*"

"Calvin, why does God give you such disquieting thoughts?"

"Because He wants me to be a good Christian," Calvin answered. "And He wants you to be a good Christian, too."

"I am a Christian," Leilani said. "I have been baptised by your father."

"That isn't enough," Calvin said. "We must work every day to try and do what God would have us do."

"I do try," Leilani said.

"No," Calvin retorted, "you are the Devil's handmaiden, and even now you tempt me as our Lord was tempted."

"What do you mean?" Leilani asked, aware of the growing tension in Calvin's voice and his heavier breathing.

"I'm talking about *this!*" Calvin suddenly yelled, pulling her lei apart with his hands. The flowers fluttered to the ground, and Leilani's breasts and nipples were exposed to his challenging eyes. "And this!" he said, jerking her lava-lava off so that Leilani now stood completely naked before him. She was proud of her body and felt no shame, but as she looked at Calvin's face, she became very uneasy. She now saw what she had heard in his voice—his burning lust.

"Calvin, what are you doing?" Leilani asked, edging back, ready to run.

"You are the Devil's handmaiden. I know that you have been sent to tempt me with your flesh," Calvin cried, pointing contemptuously at her while he undid his pants and let them drop to the ground. Now he, too, was naked, and in the soft moonlight, Leilani saw the swelling proof of his lust.

"Calvin, I'm not tempting you," Leileni said in a frightened voice.

"Oh, yes! Oh, yes! Oh, yes, you are, you are!" Calvin shouted, and he walked toward her as if he were driven crazy by desire.

"Calvin, get away," Leilani cried.

"You have been sent to draw me into the sin of fornication," Calvin said. "And I say to you, I am weakened by this devil lust. I will let you have your way, the Devil will get his due."

"No," Leilani said.

Calvin grabbed her and pulled her to him. He thrust his erect manhood against her, and though he didn't penetrate her, he did touch the most sensitive part of her, starting sensations which she knew should have been pleasant but which merely added to her fear.

"Come," Calvin said in a strained voice. "I can no longer fight the Devil's will. I will do as you, his handmaiden, bids."

"No," Leilani cried, "leave me alone!"

"Your flesh shall know my flesh, you harlot!"

Leilani strained and twisted free of Calvin's grip, then took a few running steps and dived over the cliff and into the ocean, fifty feet below. When she bobbed back to the surface, she looked up at the cliff and saw him standing there, silhouetted against the moon.

Calvin waited, for a long time, just staring down at the water. Finally he turned and walked away.

Chapter Four ───────────

THE SUN WAS still an early morning orange just above the sea when Reverend Jebediah Grimsley began waking his family. But Calvin had been back only two hours, and he rolled over and went back to sleep.

"Mrs. Grimsley," Jebediah said. "Could some illness have befallen Calvin? He seems disinclined to rise."

"Calvin, the Lord does not love a lazy man," Marcia Grimsley told her son as she shook him awake again. "Please be up and about. Breakfast will soon be ready."

Reverend Grimsley looked in a few minutes later to make sure Calvin had got up this time, and then he walked down to the beach. He went to the beach every morning at sunrise, and had for twenty years, missing only once when he nearly died from fever.

Even though he was only going to a quiet,

secluded part of the beach, he felt it necessary to dress fully for the occasion. He wore a pair of striped pants which were too short for his long legs, and to large for his small waist. The pants were held up with suspenders which passed over a white shirt with frayed cuffs and detachable collar, and under a well worn vest. His jacket was a black claw-hammer type which he kept buttoned whenever he was about in public. A tall, stove-top hat completed his outfit and made his skinny, six-foot two-inch frame appear even taller and leaner. He had a hawklike nose which might have seemed less severe with a beard, but as Jebediah considered facial hair a vain affectation, he was clean-shaven.

As he strolled along the beach he saw a boat coming ashore from one of the ships. It was full of girls who were being taken back to the fort at Lahaina, where they were already serving time for prostitution. The sight of them angered him and he vowed to speak with Governor Kekuanna about them. Getting Governor Kekuanna to stop it would be difficult, because Jebediah was certain that the governor must have given his permission. But it was God's will that it be stopped, and Jebediah was determined to be the instrument of that will.

When Jebediah returned to the house, Marcia already had the breakfast on the table. It consisted of sweet potatoes and salt-beef, both products shipped from California. Like most missionaries, they spent their lives barely subsisting on substandard food from America, while all about them fresh meats, vegetables, and fruits were readily available.

Marcia brushed back a loose strand of blonde hair from her face and sat at the breakfast table to hear the morning grace. She was thirty-six years old, and her face showed the strain of her life. Cheeks which had once been rosy with health were now sallow. Eyes, once bright and laughing, were now dull and hollow. A mind, which had been inquiring and challenging, had succumbed to the dominance of her husband's iron will. Each day connected to the next, and then to the next, in an endless chain of service to her husband, and to the God that her husband perceived, so that she had nothing left for herself.

Except memories. In a small corner of her heart she had memories of a past vitality, life, and even passion. Sometimes she retreated to them in the still of the night, and in the privacy of her own thoughts. It was these memories which had sustained her when it seemed to her that she was about to cease to exist . . . to drift away into nothingness like a quick cloud on a sunny afternoon.

"Did you not hear me, Mrs. Grimsley?" Jebediah asked.

Marcia looked up and suddenly realized that her husband had been speaking to her. "I'm sorry," she said easily. "I was in prayer."

"I said I saw a sight which disturbed me this morning," Jebediah repeated as he chewed on a tough piece of salt-beef.

"What did you see?"

"There are girls being taken on board the ships," Jebediah said.

"Surely Governor Kekuanna's policemen can observe such law-breaking," Marcia replied.

"I am certain that they do observe it," Jebediah said. "That is why I am afraid the governor is a party to it."

"What are you going to do, Father?" Calvin asked. "This is an abomination, and cannot be tolerated."

"It does me good to hear you speak with concern over this," Jebediah said. "I shall not feel in the least apprehensive about turning my church over to you when you return from the seminary."

"What are you going to do?" Marcia asked.

"I will speak with the governor," Jebediah said. "And if that does no good, then I shall see King Kamehameha the Third."

"Why don't you just go see Kauikeaouli right away?" Marcia asked. "Why even bother to see Kekuanna? If he is behind this as you suspect, he won't do anything to try and stop it."

"Because King Kamehameha the Third isn't in Lahaina now," Jebediah said. "He's in Honolulu. And I fear he is going to stay there for a long time. There is talk of moving the capital there."

Chapter Five ————————————

THE ADMINISTRATION BUILDING in Lahaina was a curious blend of cultures. It was European gothic in its construction, large and substantial. But its openness and sweeping roofline were definitely Hawaiian. It was the seat of the government for the island of Maui, and when King Kamehameha III was in Lahaina, the seat of government for all of Hawaii.

Jebediah had to go through the appointments secretary to seek an audience with Governor Kekuanna. The secretary took his name and invited Jebediah to sit down and join all the others who wished to see the governor that day.

The others, Jebediah noticed, were nearly all white, and most were merchants or sailors. It had been much simpler when Jebediah arrived twenty years ago. There was no governor then, and anyone could speak to the king at any time.

There were, of course, certain rules to be followed, such as not touching the king's person or standing on his shadow. But getting to see him was very easy.

Jebediah settled back to wait. He would wait all day if necessary, and if he didn't see the governor today, he would come back tomorrow. He sighed and began concentrating on the Psalms, passing the time by reciting them in his mind.

A short, fat, prosperous-looking man came into the office and left his card with the governor's secretary. He spoke to a few of the others, then came and sat in a chair next to Jebediah, greeting Jebediah warmly. His name was Angus Pugh, and he was a doctor, a wealthy landowner, and a merchant.

To a casual observer, Dr. Angus Pugh and Jebediah Grimsley would seem to have nothing in common. Pugh was well dressed in the finest clothes, and had the bearing of a man of wealth, whereas Jebediah wore only those clothes which were sent to him from the rag collections of the missionary barrels in America. But the two men actually had a lot in common, for Dr. Angus Pugh had also been a missionary at one time, and had come to Hawaii with Jebediah and ten other missionaries and their wives. Of that original group, four were dead, five left the mission to become businessmen in the islands, and two had returned to the United States. Only Jebediah remained true to the original oath of commitment.

"Jebediah, it is good to see you," Angus said, holding out his hand. "What brings you to the governor's office?"

"I wish to take up a certain matter with the governor," Jebediah replied. "The girls of Lahaina are visiting the ships. This is wrong, as you well know, and it must be stopped."

"Of course it's wrong," Angus agreed. "But there are already laws against such things. What more would you have the governor do?"

"I would have him enforce those laws as he is supposed to," Jebediah said.

"Why, I believe he does, Jebediah. I myself have visited the fort on frequent occasions, and have seen the jail filled with girls who violated this law."

"It is those girls, I fear, who are visiting the ships," Jebediah said. "This morning, as I took my walk, I saw a boat loaded with girls. They had been whoring with the sailors on the ships, there was no mistaking that. And as I watched, the boat went straight to the fort where the girls climbed onto the ramparts and disappeared inside. That is something they wouldn't do without the approval of the fort authorities."

A ship's officer sitting near Jebediah and Angus heard them talking. He was bald, and wore an eyepatch over one eye. It was difficult to guess his age; he could have been anywhere between thirty and fifty.

"You, sir, are a goddamned troublemaker," he growled.

"I beg your pardon, sir?" Jebediah replied,

shocked by the man's language and the fact that the man would address him in such a way.

The bald man spat a stream of tobacco juice into a nearby spittoon and wiped his mouth with the back of his hand.

"I said you're a goddamned troublemaker. We had it good here 'til you goddamned Bible-thumping pissants started changing things around. You'd best be careful, sir, or you'll find yourself in a war one of these days."

"In a war, sir? With whom?"

"With every man jack sailor afloat," the bald man replied. "I'd daresay a broadside from a gun deck of thirty-two-pounders would just about level this town."

"And you would threaten such a thing just to have your way with sin?" Jebediah challenged.

"Me? Why, no, sir. But I do give you fair warning. Leave be the issue of the girls. 'Tis none of your business."

"But it is my business, sir," Jebediah insisted. "For it is the Lord's business, and I am His agent."

"Then you 'n' the Lord better get out of the way when trouble comes."

"The Lord's word is mightier than all your cannon, sir," Jebediah said resolutely.

"Makua Grimsley, you may see the governor now," the appointments secretary said.

"Thank you," Jebediah replied. He excused himself to the sailor and Angus Pugh and went into the large room which served as the governor's office.

The governor was a big man, and he sat in a chair near a window and smiled a welcome at Jebediah as Jebediah entered, but he didn't rise. He wasn't wearing a shirt, and his breasts and stomach hung like pouches. He scratched his bare chest.

"Makua Grimsley, my friend, it is good you come to see me. But I am a very busy man with many things to do, and cannot visit with you for a long time. What is it you want?"

"Thank you for seeing me, Governor Kekuanna," Jebediah said. "I have come on a grave matter."

"Speak."

"I fear that the laws which were made by the great Kapiolani, concerning the sexual visits of the girls of Lahaina to the ships, are being violated."

"When my police catch such girls, they place them in jail," Kekuanna said.

"But, Governor, it is from your jails that the girls are taken."

"Why do you say this?"

"I saw it with my own eyes this morning," Jebediah said. "As is my custom, I took a walk along the beach as the sun rose. And while walking, I saw a longboat come from one of the ships in the harbor. The boat was filled with girls, and the girls were returning to the fort."

"This is very bad," Governor Kekuanna said. "Who were the girls?"

"I'm afraid I don't know," Jebediah said.

"They were too far away and I was unable to identify any of them."

"What about the *haole?* Do you know who they were?"

"No."

"The ship? Do you know which ship the girls came from?"

"I don't know that either, I'm afraid," Jebediah admitted.

Governor Kekuanna smiled. "Reverend Grimsley, what do you want me to do? You do not know the girls who did this thing. You do not know the *haole* who did this thing. You do not know the ship who did this thing. What do you know?"

"Perhaps," Jebediah said, realizing that he was in a weak position, "you could instruct your policemen to show more resolve in enforcing these laws."

"Perhaps," Kekuanna replied.

"And I will be more observant if I see a future violation."

"Mahola, Makua Grimsley. Thank you for coming to see me. Aloha," Kekuanna said.

Jebediah, realizing that his interview had been terminated, started for the door. But just before he left the room, he tried one more time.

"Governor Kekuanna, I know King Kamehameha the Third has great faith in you, and trusts you to do the right thing. He is, as you know, one of my flock, and listens also to my counsel. I hope it is not necessary to discuss this matter with him when he returns."

"It will not be necessary, Makua Grimsley," Kekuanna said. "I will take care of everything. Goodbye now."

"Goodbye," Jebediah answered.

Angus Pugh was ushered into the governor's office right after Jebediah left. The governor greeted him warmly, then offered him a chair near the window.

"Thank you for seeing me, your excellency," Dr. Pugh said.

"We have important things to discuss," the governor said. "Not small things, such as Makua Grimsley and his problem with the girls who go to the ships."

As Angus leaned back in his chair, he caught a glimpse of Jebediah through the window. Jebediah was even then shouting at a young girl who was strolling down the street with bare breasts, and Pugh could see others on the street turning to watch.

Jebediah was regarded as a joke by many people. He was singlehandedly trying to save the world, and his zealousness knew no bounds, his condemnation no mercy. He attacked sin with the same enthusiasm he had when he stepped off the boat so long ago.

They had all been enthusiastic then, Pugh recalled. For he had been one of the Lord's chosen as well, and had come to the islands armed with a medical degree and a certificate of ordination, ready to do battle with Satan for the heathens' souls.

But Pugh had changed over the years. The

hard edge of his faith had been eroded by contact with the easy habits of the natives. The issues became less clear, the goals more cloudy, until he was no longer able to be the rock of faith necessary for a missionary's work. He abandoned the calling and went into business, lending some truth to the spoken Hawaiian saying, "When the missionaries came, they had Bibles and the Hawaiians had land. When they were finished, the Hawaiians had Bibles and the missionaries had land."

Angus Pugh had grown wealthy in business and land speculation, as had many others who once had followed an evangelical calling. Only Jebediah Grimsley, of all the people Pugh knew, had maintained the strength of his faith. Only Jebediah Grimsley had never succumbed to the slightest temptation of material things.

Angus Pugh couldn't help but have respect for a man who so steadfastly stuck to his principles. And he never failed to feel guilty for his own straying away.

"I have talked with my friends," the governor said. "They will do as I say."

The governor's voice brought Angus back from his wandering thoughts. "Good," he said. "But they must remain quiet until we are ready to move. A revolution of this type must depend on secrecy. No word must get to Honolulu and the king."

"After we make the revolution, I will be the king," the governor said smiling.

"No," Pugh said. "If we replace one monarchy with another, then we will have accomplished nothing."

"We would accomplish much," Kekuanna said. "We would make me king!"

"No," Pugh said again. "We could never count on the support of America if we made you a king. Americans don't like kings."

"What do they like?"

"They like freedom," Pugh said. "We must draw up a declaration of independence, just as the Americans did during their revolutionary war. We must make it appear as if there are only the highest moral motives involved."

"After the revolution, will we kill the king?"

"No," Pugh said. "After the revolution it will not be necessary. The king will have no power. He will be like everyone else."

"The Alii-Nui?"

"The Alii-Nui, too, will be like everyone else."

"No," Kekuanna said. "The Alii-Nui have powers which are great. They have *mana* from the gods."

Dr. Pugh laughed. "Kekuanna, perhaps I wasn't successful as a missionary, but I did hope to rid your people of all their foolish superstitions. There are no gods, there is just God. And the Alii-Nui are people, no different from anyone else. They have no strange powers."

"You don't understand, Dr. Pugh," Kekuanna said. "My people have great fear of the Alii-Nui, for the power of the Alii-Nui is strong."

"Tell your people that such fear is mis-

placed," Dr. Pugh said. "And have everything
in readiness to strike quickly when the dragoons
arrive to help us. Soon, my friend, we shall es-
tablish the Republic of Hawaii. And you will
be its new leader."

"Fine, fine," Kekuanna said. He smiled broad-
ly. "I know who I shall be," he said proudly.
"If I cannot be king, then I shall be George
Washington. George Washington the Second.
The American people like George Washington,
don't they?"

"Yes, my friend," Pugh said, laughing. "The
American people like George Washington."

After Pugh left, Kekuanna's appointments
secretary came in to talk with him.

"He will not help us with the Alii-Nui,"
Kekuanna said. "He does not understand."

"What shall we do, Excellency?"

Kekuanna put his hand on his chin and
looked through the window, striking a thought-
ful pose as he had seen the king do. "If the
revolution is to succeed, then the Alii-Nui must
die. Tell the others."

"Yes, Excellency." The secretary started to
leave, but Kekuanna called him back. "Yes?"

"I shall be George Washington the Second,"
Kekuanna said. "How does that sound?"

"That sounds very good, Excellency," the secretary replied easily.

Chapter Six————————————————

LESS THAN A mile from the administration building on board one of the three ships lying off Lahaina, a man came up on deck and walked over to the railing. His name was Mark Costain, and he was a tall man, thirty-two years old, strongly built, with thick, black hair, cut short. He was wearing a dark blue jacket, cut away to show a white vest and white pants. The buttons on the jacket were gold, and there was a faint mark on the shoulders to show that he had worn the gold epaulets of a naval officer at one time.

Mark's face had a white scar from the slash of a saber blade, and he rubbed it absentmindedly as he leaned against the rigging of the *Sea Eagle* and gazed at the beautiful, lush shoreline of Maui. He was the captain of the *Sea Eagle*, a three-masted schooner which was recorded in *American Lloyd's Universal Standard of Shipping* as an armed merchant ship. It had handsome tapering masts, two gun decks of thirty-two-pounders, and swivel guns fore and aft.

Mark was a graduate of the United States Naval Midshipman program and had received his training aboard naval vessels. By the time he was twenty-six, he was the youngest ship-o'-the-line commander in the Navy, and nearly everyone who knew the handsome young man predicted a great future for him.

He was ambitious with plenty of drive, and he intended to reach the top and become an admiral. To achieve this, he volunteered for dangerous assignments in the hope he would become well-known. He had asked for, and received, the most dangerous assignment then available to a naval commander—trying to stop the slave trade. It was not against the law to own slaves, but it was illegal to import new blacks from Africa for the purpose of selling them into slavery. Shippers, however, continued to carry slaves and were still making millions of dollars from it. So much money was being made that some shippers were wealthy enough to buy themselves out of any trouble. Thus it was that when Mark captured a ship belonging to one of the wealthiest slave dealers in New England, the man soon got it back by buying off a powerful official. After the ship was released Mark Costain, the young naval officer with the brilliant future, was cashiered from the navy for "dereliction of duty, gross misconduct, and mistakes in judgment."

The ship's company had been called to attention on deck for the ceremony, and Mark was ordered to report, in full uniform, before the fleet commander. As the drums rolled, the fleet commander cut the epaulets from Mark's shoulders with his own sword. As the blade flashed from one shoulder to the other, it left a slash on Mark's cheek, and he stood there, unflinching as the blood ran down his face.

"I'm sorry, Mr. Costain," the commander apologized. "If you will see a civilian doctor and have that wound attended to, I'll personally pay the cost, as the navy no longer will."

"That won't be necessary," Mark muttered angrily between his teeth.

The wealthy slave dealer who had brought about Mark's dismissal from the service also prevented him from getting an officer's berth on any merchant ship. Twice Mark sailed under an assumed name as an able-bodied seaman because he could find no other work.

Then a group of adventurers, who had heard of Mark's dismissal and knew of his seamanship and leadership ability, offered him a special job—to command a ship taking guns and equipment past the Spanish Caribbean Fleet to support a revolution in Cuba. Mark accepted, and for six months he was an active revolutionary. On three occasions he engaged Spanish ships in battle.

The Cuban revolution against Spain collapsed, as had so many earlier uprisings, and Mark found that he had to flee to California to avoid charges of international piracy.

He didn't bring a fortune away from Cuba as he had hoped. He did bring a case of recurrent malaria, however, and wherever he went now, he had to take with him a supply of quinine to fight the fever.

Mark's reputation preceded him to California, and once again he was approached by representatives of a revolutionary group. This time people representing a dissident movement in Hawaii wanted him. Mark had no other job prospects, so he accepted their offer and was given command of the *Sea Eagle*.

His instructions were to proceed to Lahaina and then wait for further orders, and with the crew already mustered, he did just that.

The *Sea Eagle* had anchored off Lahaina for three weeks, and was already arousing curiosity. Most merchant ships, even those classified as armed, didn't have the firepower of the *Sea Eagle*. In fact, there were very few capital battle ships in the world which could match her in firepower. As for speed and maneuverability, Mark decided he had never handled a better ship. They had left San Francisco late in the day, with a brisk, easterly wind seeming to hurry the sun through a slate-colored sky. The *Sea Eagle* pointed her bow for Hawaii. She was so fast that she had a lift that slammed the ship across the waves instead of merely plunging it through. They made the 2,400-mile run in ten and a half days.

"Cap'n, we're going ashore for girls," Ben Hall, his first mate, said, interrupting his memories. "Do you want us to bring you one?"

Ben Hall was a bald-headed man with an eye-patch covering the empty socket of an eye that had been ripped out during a slave uprising on a slaver. He spat a stream of tobacco over the rail and waited for Mark's answer.

Mark thought of the girl he had had the night before. She had been young and beautiful, with a strong back that never tired. He had never known any girls with a fondness for sex to match the Hawaiians.

"Yes," he said. "Bring me another one."

"If that damned preacher has his way there won't be any girls available," Hall said.

"What preacher?"

"His name is Grimsley," Hall said. "I saw him in the administration building today." Hall laughed. "I think I frightened him enough to keep him out of our hair though. I suggested a broadside from a deck of thirty-two pounders would put an end to the existence of this miserable little town."

"Fool!" Mark spat. "You're going to jeopardize this entire operation with your loose tongue."

"Don't worry, I didn't give anything away," Hall replied. "What do you say I bring us back a bottle of that Hawaiian whiskey, too?"

"Bring two bottles," Mark told him. "But

don't bring the same girl I had last night."

"What's the matter, wasn't she any good?"

"Certainly she was good," Mark said. "But I have a rule. There are too many women in the world to have the same one twice."

"What was the girl's name? Maybe I'll take her for myself."

"Her name was Malaka."

Malaka wasn't free to be with either of them. Calvin Grimsley had found her first. At that moment he was putting his clothes back on, his back to her. Only moments before he had been in the grass with her, flesh against flesh, losing himself in her plump, eager body. Now, though, with the overwhelming pressure of his sex drive eased, he could think again of modesty, and the Lord, and he wouldn't let her watch him dress. When he had finished, he turned back and saw that she was still naked, lying in the same place, with her legs spread open.

"Cover yourself. You are an abomination before the Lord."

Malaka laughed. "We are the same," she said. "We fornicate, we sin."

"You have sinned," Calvin said. "And you will burn in the eternal fires of hell."

"Will you?" Malaka asked.

"No," Calvin replied. "For it is written: *If the wicked turn from his wickedness and do that which is lawful and right, he shall live there-*

by. I have but to turn from my wickedness, and I will be saved."

"If I turn from my wickedness, will I be saved?" Malaka wanted to know.

"Yes," Calvin said. "But only I can save you. For I have the keys to the Kingdom, and you cannot enter the Kingdom unless I open the door for you. Do you want to enter the Kingdom of the Lord?"

"Yes," Malaka answered, smiling at him. This was great fun for her—like a game. It never occurred to her he could be serious.

"Then you must kneel before me," Calvin ordered. He pointed at the ground in front of him. "Get down on your knees, you miserable sinner, and confess your sins and beg for forgiveness."

Malaka got on her knees as she was instructed, and Calvin placed his hands on her head. "You are a miserable sinner," he said.

"I am a miserable sinner," Malaka repeated.

"You are guilty of wantonness and fornication with a messenger of the Lord."

"I am guilty of wantonness and fornication with a messenger of the Lord."

"Do you want forgiveness?"

"Yes."

"Are you sorry for your sins?"

"Yes."

"I, Calvin Grimsley, forgive you your sins. Oh, Lord," he began to pray, "I can walk with sinners and yet not sin, consort with harlots and yet not fornicate, because I am doing your work. I have gone whoring among the heathens and become as a heathen so that I can tell them of your glory. Though my blood runs hot, and my flesh knows hunger, I have the strength to resist the pleasure of these whorings, because I am working to spread the praises of your name. And now I ask that you take the soul of this miserable sinner I am about to send you into your bosom. Amen."

Calvin moved his hands from the girl's head down to her neck. He began to tighten his grip.

"What are you doing?" Malaka asked, suddenly frightened by the game.

"Fear not," Calvin said, "for I am giving you the gift of eternal life. I am sending you to dwell in the House of the Lord."

"Help," Malaka tried to call. But it was a weak cry. His hands were too tight, and already the death rattle had started in her throat. She was soon lifeless in his hands.

Calvin dressed Malaka's body in her muumuu, then dragged her to the edge of the cliff and threw her over. The body hit a large rock just at the breakwater, and bounced into the sea. It was swept toward the shore with the first wave, then carried out to sea as the wave receded. Calvin watched for a moment and saw the girl's body disappear.

He turned innocently and started back toward his parents' house, but he was startled to see his father coming up the path toward him. His heart beat violently. Why was his father coming? Did he know that Calvin had just become a fornicator? A whoremonger who had known the flesh of a female?

"There are more girls being taken to the ships," Jebediah said as he joined Calvin at the cliff's edge.

"Can the governor not stop this evil?" Calvin asked, reassured that his father knew nothing.

"The governor can, but he will not," Jebediah replied.

"What will you do?"

"It may be necessary for me to travel to Honolulu to see the king. The king will be angry that his rules are being mocked, just as the Lord is angry that His laws are not being obeyed."

"But the Lord will forgive His children, won't He?" Calvin asked anxiously.

"The Lord will judge His children," Jebediah answered sternly. "For He is a God of judgment, and the whoremongers will know His wrath."

Calvin felt a twinge of fear and nearly said something to his father. His fear at that moment was not that he had done evil by killing Malaka, but that he might have misinterpreted his mission when he fornicated with her.

Suddenly the sound of music came up from a village in the valley on the hillside opposite their house—hauntingly beautiful, a rhythmic chant catching the sound of the surf, the rustle of the palms, the moan of the wind.

The smell of roast pork was in the air, and it was rich and succulent, and Calvin's mouth watered at the delicious aroma.

"Heathens," Jebediah cried. "Sinners . . . lost children. Oh, Lord, tell me. Are all my years to be spent here in vain? Will these heathen sinners never learn the glory of Your word, and give up their old evil and sinful ways?"

"What is it, Father?"

"It is a luau for Hula-hula, the one they call the god of fun. It is a blasphemy in the eyes of the Lord," Jebediah said. "Come, we will put a stop to it."

Jebediah rushed angrily down the hill, followed by Calvin. When they reached the center of the village all the villagers were dancing and singing. A young girl, naked except for a lei of flowers, ran to Calvin and put a lei around his neck.

"Welcome, Makua Grimsley and son," one of the men shouted joyously.

"Remove that vile trapping of the Devil!" Jebediah roared, pointing a long, bony finger at the lei around his son's neck.

The music stopped and the village grew silent. Calvin broke the lei and let the flowers slide off the string and fall to the ground. Jebediah looked around accusingly, his eyes glaring red in the reflection of the fires that had been lit as part of the rejoicing.

"Are you the same people who come into the Lord's church on the Sabbath?" he asked. "Are you the same people who have pious looks and pious words for the Lord? Are you the same people who say you are Christian?"

"We are good Christian people, Makua Grimsley," the man who had welcomed them said contritely. "You know we are good Christian people."

"I do not know that you are," Jebediah said sternly. "And God does not know that you are. I am angry and God is angry that you have done this thing."

"Makua Grimsley, it is but a luau," the man said. "It means nothing."

"Nothing? You worship idols, when the Lord says, *Thou shalt not make unto thee any graven image, or any likeness of any thing that is in heaven above or that is in the earth beneath, or that is in the water under the earth: Thou shalt not bow down thyself to them, nor serve them.* He commands that you shall not worship idols."

"But we do not, Makua Grimsley."

"Then what is this?" Jebediah asked angrily, pointing to a small altar with several figures prominently displayed.

"They are our old gods," the man said. "We do not worship them anymore, but we have brought them to the luau of Hula-hula that they might have fun."

"Idolators!" Jebediah shouted, angrily brushing the statuettes off the table.

There was a mumble of disapproval from several of the villagers, but it died quickly. Jebediah fixed them all with his steely gaze.

"I would suggest," he said, "that you all return to your homes now, and there fall upon your knees and pray to God and beg His forgiveness."

There was an uneasy, challenging silence for several seconds. Jebediah didn't back down or even flinch, but stood there staring at them. Finally, one or two of the villagers turned to go. Within a moment they all started to leave, and soon the center of the village was empty. Even the fire, built in the pit where the pig was roasting, was left unattended, and it seemed to roar and crackle all the more loudly in the silence.

"Come, Calvin," Jebediah finally said. He brushed his hands as if ridding himself of contamination. "We have done a good day's work in this place."

Calvin followed his father back to the house. He didn't mention that he had picked up one of the idols. It was a small bird, wearing a crown. It was delicately wrought and very pretty, and seemed to be made of pure gold.

Gold, Calvin knew, was very valuable. Perhaps Angus Pugh would give him money for it. His father had no use for money, but perhaps Calvin could find a way to spend it.

For the Lord, of course.

Chapter Seven———————————————

THOUGH JEBEDIAH GRIMSLEY broke up the celebration, it was but one of many being held that night. All over the islands Hawaiians held luaus to Hula-hula. It was a celebration that was held often and it had absolutely no religious significance. It was for fun and nothing more, though Jebediah Grimsley couldn't understand that, for he had no sense of fun or humor. Even Christmas was considered frivolous by this grim man, and apart from marking the birth of Christ, had no meaning for him.

In the village where Leilani lived, about three miles up the coast from the Grimsley house, the Hula-hula luau went on far into the night. The pork was eaten, the *okoleaohao* drunk, and music made from tamping the ends of hollow bamboo reeds against the ground, together with flutes and drums, filled the air. The night was full of laughter, singing, and echoes of happiness. Beautiful girls with skins of flashing gold, dressed in grass skirts and flower leis, danced passionate and erotic dances.

In a clearing near the fire two men grasped two long bamboo poles, one at each end, and started beating the poles against the ground, then snapping them open and closed like two large pincers. They did this faster and faster, until the poles were opening and closing so fast that they made a blur against the ground.

Leilani leaped into the clearing and began dancing in a wild, powerful display of energy, with graceful and fluid movements. Her bare feet flashed up and down in intricate steps, while moving ever closer to the bamboo poles. Finally, at the peak of her dance, she leaped in and out of the poles as the two men continued to slam them open and closed. One error, one missed beat, and her ankles would have been smashed, but Leilani continued her dance untouched, her feet flying in and out with perfect timing.

Then, with a loud shout, a warrior began twirling a long sword inches above the ground. Leilani left the bamboo poles and leaped toward the flashing blade, moving in and out, missing the keen edge of the saber by only a split second.

Someone tossed her a short length of bamboo with fire burning on either end, and Leilani began twirling it so quickly that the fire made a blazing circle, and she moved the ring of fire between her legs and passed it around her body.

Then, while twirling the fire baton, she moved once more toward the whirling saber blade of the warrior.

There were cheers and laughter to greet Leilani's performance, and finally the warrior twirling the blade grew tired and begged for an end to the dance.

Leilani's mother was lying on matting, eating pork and watching the dances. Leilani, when she finished her dance, went over to sit beside Lakiolani.

"You dance well, my daughter," Lakiolani said. "When I was young and small, I, too, could dance, though never as well as you."

"I love to dance," Leilani said. "That is why I have no wish to become a very big woman like you."

"It is no longer the law," Lakiolani said. "But many men like large women. And to be large is to have much respect as the Alii-Nui."

"But you said by my wisdom I shall be known," Leilani said.

Lakiolani smiled. "And so you shall, my daughter, so you shall." Lakiolani's smile vanished. "And now I must call on that wisdom, for I fear something evil is in the air."

"What?" Leilani asked quickly.

"I have spoken with my omens, and they tell me there are bad men who would make war against our king, and against us. Have you heard nothing of this from your omens?"

"No, mother," Leilani answered, ashamed that she had not.

"Who will war against us?"

"George Washington," Lakiolani said.

"Do you mean America?"

"Some will be *haole*, but it will not be America who makes the war," Lakiolani said. "It will be George Washington."

"But George Washington is dead. He was a great man and was the first President of the United States of America," Leilani said.

"This is not the George Washington who is dead, but one who lives," Lakiolani explained. "It is a Hawaiian George Washington."

"I have never heard of a Hawaiian George Washington," Leilani said. Leilani didn't ridicule her mother's insistence that their enemy was George Washington, nor did she try to make light of the premonition. Lakiolani was an Alii-Nui of many years, and was a very wise woman. If she had such a premonition, then there was indeed danger.

"Tomorrow," Lakiolani said, "speak with Mahimahi and find out the truth of this thing. Perhaps Mahimahi knows more."

"I will speak with my friends of the ocean," Leilani promised.

A few young men strolled by the matting where Leilani sat with her mother. They smiled at Leilani, hoping she would choose one of them for sex, but Leilani waved them away with a tiny move of her hand, and they left, disappointed.

"Now," Lakiolani said, "I sleep."

Leilani kissed her mother on the forehead,

then went into her own sleeping room and lay on her matting. The noise had died down outside now, because the hour was late, and the revelers were either asleep, paired off for sex, or drunk.

Leilani went to sleep quickly, and while she slept, the dolphin came to her in a dream . . .

"Leilani," the dolphin said. "Leilani, come to me. I have news of great importance."

"Can you not tell me now?" Leilani asked.

"No. You must come to me in the sea."

"Is it about the war my mother fears?"

"Yes," the dolphin said.

"Tell me."

"No. You must come to me, Leilani. Lei . . . lan . . . iiii!" the dolphin seemed to yell, and the sound filled her mind . . .

"Eeeeeeee," a night bird screamed, and Leilani sat up in her bed and looked around. The dream returned to her at once, and she stood and walked to the window and looked out toward the ocean. Out there, one mile out, Mahimahi waited for her.

Leilani looked into her mother's room and saw that she was sleeping, then started for the ocean to meet the dolphin. Once outside, she noticed that several of the celebrators were still lying on the ground where they had passed out, drunk. The fire where the pigs were roasted had just about died down, and only the glowing of the coals and the rich smell of cooked pork remained to recall the great feast.

As Leilani started toward the water, she saw

her friend Kamala walking around, looking at the sleeping bodies.

"Kamala, why are you walking around looking at everyone?" Leilani asked.

"I'm looking for Malaka, my twin," Kamala said.

"Perhaps she went to the ships again," Leilani suggested.

"No. She wished to attend the ceremony tonight. We spoke of it."

"Perhaps she did, and has coupled with someone."

"Perhaps so," Kamala said with a shrug of her shoulders. She yawned. "There are many in my house tonight and I have no mat," she complained.

"You may sleep on my mat," Leilani said. "I must go for a swim and speak with Mahimahi."

Kamala thanked her, then stood watching for a moment as Leilani hurried on to the ocean's edge.

The dark water rolled in ceaselessly, and as she looked out over it she could see occasional splashes of white froth as waves spilled over long before crashing against the shore.

"Mahimahi," she called softly. "You have sent for me and now I come to you."

Leilani stepped into the water. The ocean had trapped the sun's heat during the day, and now it gave back its warmth to her as she swam out to the dolphins.

When Leilani was far beyond the reef, she

rolled over on her back and called to the dolphins.

None came.

She closed her eyes and concentrated hard, trying to summon her friends, but still none came.

You have called me, yet you do not come, she thought. Why is this?

After several minutes, a dolphin glided up beside her. Leilani reached for him, and felt the dolphin's fear.

"Why are you afraid?" she asked aloud, puzzled.

The dolphin stayed with her for several moments, but apart from a vague sense of fear, Leilani received nothing from him. The dolphin then broke free and swam away.

Leilani was puzzled. She had learned nothing. She still didn't know who George Washington was. She still didn't know what danger they were in from a war. There was nothing she say tomorrow if her mother should ask.

Suddenly, overwhelmed by an urgent sense of danger, Leilani screamed. "*Mother!*" She had been looking out to sea the entire time she was in the ocean, and now as she cried out, she turned to look back toward the shore. An orange glow lit the sky above the village, and as a wave lifted her high in the water she saw that several of the houses were burning. Her village was on fire!

Leilani swam back as fast as she could, then

raced across the beach and up to the village. She heard crying from women and children, and in the light of the flames, she could see a few people, dazed, frightened and confused. There were several bodies scattered about, and those who had been sleeping off their drunkenness on the ground a short while earlier would never wake. Most had been decapitated.

"Alii-Nui Lakiolani!" Leilani screamed. "Where are you?"

Leilani ran through the village, passed the burning houses and the fallen bodies, until she reached her own house at the end of the square. It, too, was burning, but it wasn't the flames which brought grief to Leilani.

There, on a pole in front of the house, was the large, severed head of her mother. The pole was marked with the *kahili* of her mother, the feathered scepter which symbolized her position as an Alii-Nui.

Leilani fell to her knees beneath the pole and wept. Then through her tears, she noticed for the first time the pole beside her mother's. It, too, was marked with a *kahili*, only this *kahili* belonged to her. On top of the pole was the skewered head of Kamala.

Whoever killed Lakiolani had found Kamala sleeping in Leilani's bed and assumed she was Leilani, an Alii-Nui. That was why Kamala was killed, she realized.

The dolphins, by calling Leilani to sea in the middle of the night, had saved her life.

Chapter Eight————————————

BOTH WHALING SHIPS left with the morning tide. After they left, only the *Sea Eagle* remained anchored off Lahaina.

The longboat carrying the girls back to shore had just left, and the girl with whom Mark had spent the night blew him kisses as the boat pulled away. She, and the others who were riding with her, laughed at some remark, and their laughter rolled across the surface of the water like an intrusion in the early morning calm.

Mark rested his arms on the quarterdeck railing and leaned over, looking across the bay at the city. He had left his bunk and the girl who was still sleeping in it one hour before sunrise. Now he stood on the quarterdeck as the sun lifted out of the water, and breathed the fresh air, scented by the perfume of the flowers ashore and spiced with the tangy salt of the sea.

The girl he had been with during the night

was good, as were many of the others he had made love to in his life. He had never known the love of a woman, though he had made love to many. He could not remember one woman out of the hundreds he had known, however, who had made a deep impression on him.

In the drunken tales of smoked-filled bar-rooms ashore, and in the quiet conversations of ship wardrooms at sea, Mark's prowess with women had become legendary. But in the privacy of his own thoughts, he often asked himself if there shouldn't be something more. He could claim the affection of no woman, only the warmth and excitement of their bodies when they shared his bunk at night. There was something empty about that.

Mark's attention was caught by a pall of smoke hanging in the sky about three miles upshore. It wasn't boiling up as it would have been if it were a big fire, so he didn't take it very seriously. He was actually seeing what was left of Leilani's village, though he had no way of knowing that.

The longboat was returning to the ship, and Mark noticed that there was someone in the boat who wasn't a member of the crew.

"Mr. Hall, the spyglass, please," Mark said, holding his hand out toward Hall who had just come on deck.

Hall handed the glass to Mark, and he sighted on the boat, then slid the instrument shut and handed it back to Hall.

"Who is it, Cap'n?"

"It's Dr. Pugh," Mark said. "I have a feeling our waiting has come to an end."

"Good," Hall said. "I've been achin' to throw a few rounds of iron at that town and its pissant preacher."

The boat pulled alongside and rubbed against the hull of the ship. A jacob's ladder was lowered for Dr. Pugh. He climbed aboard with some difficulty, then stood on deck for a moment, puffing and wheezing from the exertion.

"You have some news for me, I presume, Dr. Pugh?" Mark asked.

"Yes," Dr. Pugh answered. "I had hoped to postpone things until we got our company of dragoons here from Honolulu. They are well armed and trained, and have been held in readiness. But something has happened to force our hand."

"What?"

"The Alii-Nui were killed last night. Kekuanna took it on his own. That's what the smoke is that you see," he added, pointing up the coastline.

"Who did you say was killed?" Mark asked.

"The Alii-Nui," Dr. Pugh replied. "They are very powerful people in Hawaiian society. They are a cross between royalty and priestesses. The Hawaiians ascribe certain magical powers to them. And because they do, it was feared that they would prevent the revolution by some sorcery. Despite my assurances that there was nothing to fear, Kekuanna had them killed."

"You mean they actually believe these people have powers, like witchcraft?" Mark asked.

"I'm afraid so," Dr. Pugh said. "They are still quite primitive, actually. And now, unfortunately, our hand has been forced."

"What do you want me to do?" Mark asked.

Dr. Pugh walked to the ship's rail and pointed to three buildings in the city. "Those are the arms warehouses and the king's troop billets," he said. "Train your guns on them. If you do not see white flags raised over them by eight o'clock this morning, open fire and continue to fire until the white flags go up."

"Anything else?"

"I hope the threat of your guns will be all we need," Dr. Pugh said. "But if it comes to it and you have to fire on those buildings, then we will be at war. And if the king returns with his army from Honolulu before we can get our reinforcements in, we will be outnumbered five to one. Our only hope is that we can bluff them before they can mount an attack against Kekuanna and his police."

"How many shore batteries are there?" Mark asked.

Dr. Pugh took a piece of paper from his pocket and spread it open for Mark. The positions of all the shore batteries on the island were pinpointed.

"It looks as if there are only three that can come to bear on us," Mark said, looking at the map. "If we have to open fire, we must neutralize those guns first."

Dr. Pugh let out a sigh. "You are the warrior," he said. "I'm merely a businessman."

"Then, for God's sake, man, tell me why you are getting involved in such as this?" Mark asked.

"Because I am a businessman," Dr. Pugh replied. "With a republic, I would have the power to effect laws which would be more favorable to business. Laws which would build a future for Hawaii. As long as we remain a monarchy, we will never get too far from the Stone Age."

"Yeah? Well if you want my advice, you'd better pull out of it now," Mark said. "Because if the king makes a fight of it, we don't have a chance."

"That's what I'm afraid of," Dr. Pugh said. "Unfortunately, it's too late for that. We're committed." Dr. Pugh went back to the jacob's ladder and climbed down into the longboat. "Remember," he called up as they started toward shore, "if you see no white flags by eight o'clock, open fire."

"I will, Dr. Pugh. You can count on that, at least."

"Good luck, sir," Dr. Pugh called.

"And to you, sir," Mark replied. Mark watched for a moment or two, then turned away from the rail. "Mr. Hall," he called.

"Aye, sir."

"Call the men to stations."

"Aye, sir," Hall replied. "All hands, all hands, man your battle stations," he shouted.

The thirty-six men of the *Sea Eagle*'s crew began preparing for battle. The port covers were opened and the ugly black snouts of sixteen cannon poked through on the upper and lower decks. Those men who had shoes removed them. Their hair was tied back, and their shirts were stripped off.

"Cap'n, you want the guns on the larboard manned?"

"No," Mark said. "We've no threat from the sea."

Shot and powder were brought into position and placed behind each gun. Breeching ropes, which secured the heavy guns, were checked to be sure they could withstand the guns' recoil and prevent them from slamming all the way across the deck when they were fired. Sponges were laid in to swab the barrels before recharging. A charge of gunpowder in a cannon which still had flaming bits of residue from the previous round could cause a premature explosion. Mark had seen it happen once when they were engaging an armed slave ship. An over-anxious gun crew tamped a charge of powder in an unswabbed barrel, and the resulting explosion killed four.

At approximately ten minutes to eight, Mark climbed into the rigging and examined the targets with a telescope. He saw no white flags, nor any activity there. He looked down at his men standing by their guns, staring intently toward shore.

"Mr. Hall, aim on the three shore batteries," he said.

Hall repeated the order, and the guns divided into three sections, each section aiming at a shore battery.

"Mr. Hall, light the matches," Mark ordered quietly.

The captain of each gun-crew reported to the firebox where glowing coals were kept burning, and lit the long, specially designed matches. They would use these to touch off the guns when the time came to fire them.

At about five minutes to eight, Mark saw a flash of light and a puff of smoke from all three shore battery positions. Three cannon balls were fired toward the *Sea Eagle*. One whistled through the rigging, missing Mark by only a couple of feet, and the other two splashed noisily in the water nearby. The thunder of their firing rolled across the water a few seconds later.

"The sons of bitches are firing on us!" one of the men shouted.

"What did you expect, sailor?" Mark shouted back. "We are about to fire on them."

"Shall we open up, Mr. Costain?" Hall called up.

"Commence firing, Mr. Hall!"

The gun captains held the slow-burning matches to the touch holes, and the guns boomed and jerked back against the breeching ropes.

Mark checked on the accuracy of the guns through his telescope.

"Gun captains, lay in your adjustments!" he ordered. Elevation soundings were shouted by the individual captains to their crews. There was such a noise that an outsider would have wondered that any sense could be made, but the gun-crews responded instantly. The barrels were swabbed and reloaded.

The short batteries flashed again, and three more cannonballs screamed toward the ship. One whizzed high in the rigging, cutting rope and dropping a stay to the deck. Another splashed in the water, but the third slammed through the ship's rail and raked along the deck, tearing up the planking and smashing with a loud crash into the base of the mizzenmast. Screams told Mark that someone had been injured.

"Fire!" Mark shouted, and once again the guns roared.

This time he saw several rounds slamming into their targets. The shore battery on the left and the one in the middle were both destroyed. Only the shore battery on the right was relatively undamaged.

"All guns bear in on the battery to the right!" he shouted.

The *Sea Eagle's* gun-crews were able to reload and fire again before the remaining shore battery could answer, and Mark saw several rounds score a direct hit, totally destroying the gun.

"Good job, men!" he shouted. "Now, train the guns on the buildings."

"Cap'n, look," Hall called up.

Mark looked where Hall was pointing and saw white flags fluttering from the three target buildings.

He snapped the spyglass shut and came down from the rigging. "Stand by your guns a while longer, lads," he said happily. "But it looks as if we just won our war."

The men answered with loud cheering and hurrahs, and from every gun-crew, bottles of whiskey appeared.

Leilani had watched the bombardment of the shore batteries from the streets of Lahaina. She was wearing a plain shift of tapa instead of the colorful silk she normally wore. She heard many people say that the Alii-Nui Lakiolani and her daughter Leilani both were dead, and she felt it would be safer to let people believe this for a while, so she tried to remain as inconspicuous as possible.

When the white flags went up above the government buildings, the governor's police began cheering, then started rushing through the streets arresting anyone who wouldn't swear allegiance to Kekuanna, who now called himself George Washington the Second.

"*Auwe,* you were right, mother," Leilani murmured to herself when she heard the name. "It is a man named George Washington who has brought this evil on us."

A crowd of people rushed by, laughing and cheering. "Long live the Republic of Hawaii!" one of them shouted loudly.

"Long live George Washington the Second!" another answered.

People continued to rush through the streets, cheering and shouting praises of the revolution. But to Leilani, even the most boisterous supporters seemed to be pretending, as if they were frightened not to show enthusiasm.

Leilani saw an old woman crying, and she started toward her, intending to comfort her. But two policemen reached her first.

"Why are you crying?" one of the policemen demanded.

"Because the Alii-Nui are dead. The king has been overthrown. The old way is gone."

"You should rejoice over this," the other policeman said. "Now you have a new government under the rule of His Excellency, George Washington the Second."

"I would rather have the old government under the king," the old woman said.

"She is not of the proper revolutionary spirit," the first policeman said. "Let us arrest her."

"Leave her alone," Leilani shouted.

"What? Who are you?"

"Never mind who I am," Leilani replied. "Go, old woman. These evil ones will bother you no more."

"Let the old woman go," the other policeman

said. "Look at how beautiful this girl is. The sailors on the ships would pay a good price for her, don't you think?" The policeman smiled broadly, showing a broken tooth.

Broken Tooth's friend returned the grin. "Yes," he said, "I believe you are right. For someone who is as beautiful as this girl, the sailors would pay much. We would win the governor's favor if we captured this one."

"That is true," Broken Tooth said. "But before we give her to the governor, perhaps we should take her to the mountains and try her ourselves."

"Yes, yes," his friend agreed eagerly. "After all we wouldn't want to give the sailors someone of inferior quality."

"No, that wouldn't be right," Broken Tooth said, laughing evilly at his friend's joke.

Broken Tooth lunged toward Leilani. She leaned slightly to one side, and Broken Tooth's rush carried him past her. She stuck out a leg to trip him, then helped him fall with a quick chop to the back of the head.

Broken Tooth's companion tried to grab Leilani, but she took his arm and flipped him high in the air. Broken Tooth got up and saw more policemen in the distance. He shouted for them to come, and Leilani found herself facing four well-muscled policemen, all carrying menacing war clubs.

Broken Tooth smiled at her wickedly. "Now we will see how skilled you are."

Leilani tensed for a fight, then realized that

it would be useless. She would not be able to hold them off for long, and she faced the possibility of being badly hurt. She shrugged her shoulders and held out her arms, giving herself up.

"Now, shall we try her?" Broken Tooth's friend asked.

Broken Tooth leered at her. "No. We will send her to the fighting ship which helped us win our revolution. There, all the sailors will take their turn with her. We will see how much spirit this little one has then."

The policemen laughed at Broken Tooth's remark as they dragged Leilani away. She tried to remain calm, ready to deal with whatever was going to happen next.

Chapter Nine————————————————

MARK HAD THE ship's company mustered at attention on deck, and the ship was cleaned and made ready for a visit from Governor Kekuanna, who now called himself His High Excellency, President of the Republic of Hawaii, and General-in-Chief, George Washington the Second.

His High Excellency came alongside in a double canoe, sitting in a sedan chair on the connecting deck.

"Pipe him aboard, Mr. Hall," Mark said.

Hall gave the signal and the boatswain's pipe whistled.

"Aloha, aloha, aloha," His High Excellency said as he stepped aboard. He was wearing a high hat, striped pants and a wing collar, but no shirt.

"Welcome to the *Sea Eagle*, His High Excellency, President of the Republic of Hawaii, and

General-in-Chief, George Washington the Second," Mark said, barely able to keep a straight face as he pronounced this title.

"I have come to thank you for helping to secure victory," said George Washington the Second.

"If you'll excuse me for saying so, you haven't won much of a victory yet," Mark said.

"It was a great victory," His High Excellency protested.

Mark laughed. "Really? We knocked out a few shore batteries and your police ran roughshod over a few civilians. But King Kamehameha is in Honolulu with his army. When he returns, you're going to have to fight the second round of this little match."

"Exactly," Dr. Pugh said. Pugh had come on board with His High Excellency. "That's why we have something for you to do that is very important."

"What?"

"You must go to Honolulu and pick up the dragoons which we have armed and trained, and return here with them."

"You think these dragoons can do the trick for you?" Mark asked.

"Yes," Dr. Pugh replied. "They are all professional soldiers—American, British and French mercenary troops. They will be more than a match for the king's army."

Mark rubbed his chin thoughtfully. "There's one little problem," he said.

"What?"

"Suppose someone has already gone to Honolulu to warn the king?"

"All the more reason for you to move quickly," Dr. Pugh said.

"If you see the king returning from Honolulu, you have my permission to sink his ship," said His High Excellency.

"Is the king's ship armed?"

"No," Dr. Pugh said. "Not really. His men are armed, but there are no cannon on the ship."

"I won't fire on an unarmed ship," Mark said.

"It may not be necessary," Dr. Pugh said. "I know King Kamehameha. He's a very methodical man. He will take a few days to assess the situation, then he will get organized before he returns. That will give us enough time to prepare a welcome for him."

Mark sighed. "That means we must leave immediately. I think the men were planning on a victory celebration."

His High Excellency smiled. "You may have your celebration, Captain," he said. "I have brought everything you need."

"Hey, look!" one of the men shouted.

Another canoe pulled alongside the *Sea Eagle*, and six beautiful girls came aboard. Roast pork, fish, fruits, *poi*, and liquor was also passed up to the eager sailors.

"You see?" His High Excellency said. "Your men may still celebrate our fine victory."

"Very well," Mark said. "Gentlemen, if you will excuse me then, we'll get underway."

There were six girls in the ship's hold. The six of them would be expected to service the thirty-six men and three officers of the *Sea Eagle*. Leilani didn't know any of the other girls, and she sat in a dark corner, hoping none of them would recognize her. But as they talked, she no longer feared recognition, because she realized they were all from other islands, brought to Maui on board the whalers and dropped off at the fort. Kekuanna did a brisk business in supplying girls to the ships that plied the islands.

Leilani learned she was not the only unwilling girl to be taken to the sailors. If the governor got requests to supply more girls than he had willing and available, then he sent his police out to round some up from the streets. The girls would be taken to the ships and raped, and then they often joined the governor's other girls as part of his regular business.

"Who are you?" one of the girls asked Leilani.

"I am Kalama," Leilani said.

"Have you been brought here against your will?"

"Yes. Is there no way I can escape?"

"No," the other girl said. "The sailors will have their way with you."

"What will happen?"

"Much, much fornication," another girl said. "If you are lucky, the captain will choose you."

"Why is that lucky?"

"Because then you have only the captain to

fornicate with. If you are left for the sailors, many, many men will take their turn with you."

"Who is the captain?" Leilani asked.

"He is a man named Mark Costain," one of the girls answered. She rolled her eyes and smiled. "He is very handsome and a good lover. He will choose me again, this I know."

"No," another girl said. "It is well known that *haole* Mark Costain never chooses the same girl twice. It is said that no girl can satisfy him more than one time. He will choose another."

"I suppose you think he will choose you?" the first girl said.

"Yes."

"Perhaps he *will* choose me again."

The others laughed. "Do you think you are better than all the girls he has ever known?" one of them asked.

"Perhaps I am. He liked me very much. I know this."

"He will not choose you, so do not think that he will."

There was a great deal of shouting on deck, and Leilani heard a strange, rattling noise.

"That is the sound of the chain as the anchor is being raised," a girl said. "Soon now, the Captain will come and choose, and the argument will be settled."

A red-headed, freckle-faced sailor stuck his head in and grinned broadly.

"Are you girls getting along all right?" he asked.

"Who are you?" one of the girls asked.

"Mike Fitzpatrick, second officer of this ship," the grinning sailor answered. "I'll be seeing you girls soon, right after the captain makes his choice."

The girls grew anxious for the captain to come, but there was much to do to get the ship underway, and it was a long time before he appeared on the orlop deck. And then he came as a conqueror, examining his prize by the flickering light of a lantern.

Leilani looked at the man who had aroused such excitement in the other girls. He was a handsome man, but she felt nothing in her heart except anger and sorrow. She would not be moved by his good looks.

Mark walked around the hold and held the lantern over each girl. They all smiled at him, and turned first one way and then the other, trying to entice him. With a few of them, he held their face closer to his lantern to get a better look.

Leilani sat on a coil of rope, and refused to stand for his inspection. Surprised, Mark looked over at her.

"Do you not want me to look at you?" he asked. "I may select you for my bed."

"I am not a pig to be selected for cooking," Leilani cried.

Mark laughed. "I agree, you certainly aren't a pig." He held his lantern up close to her, but she turned her head away.

"Costain, was I not good for you before?" the

girl who had bragged of being with him asked.

"Yes," Mark said. "Yes, you were very good."

"Then you want me again?" she asked eagerly.

"No, I think not," Mark said.

"Then me, perhaps?" the girl who had argued with her suggested.

Leilani realized that there would be an advantage in going with the captain. If she were left to the men, she would have no chance to explain that it was a mistake, that she shouldn't be there. Perhaps the captain would listen to her.

She decided to make him choose her.

"Captain," she said quietly.

"Oh. Now you decide to speak to me," Mark said. He smiled arrogantly, confidently. "You wish me to choose you, do you? But I say to you, it is my choice to make, and I will make it."

Leilani looked at him with cool, appraising eyes. She reached up and touched him lightly on the shoulder. With her Alii-Nui knowledge, she found a secret spot from which a strange heat emanated. The heat was, she knew, his life energy flow. By redirecting this flow, she could arouse immediate sexual desire. She applied just the right pressure between her thumb and forefinger. It was subtle, so subtle that no one realized what she had done.

Such an act was dangerous, she realized, for she might be stimulating in him a desire so strong that even he would be unable to control it. But she knew that she had no choice. She had to go to his cabin if she was to have any chance at all.

Mark felt a sudden surge of desire for her that he couldn't resist. He had never before reacted to a girl so quickly and overwhelmingly.

"I—I choose you," he said thickly, oblivious to the sexual entreaties of the others.

Leilani started up the ladder in silence.

"Cap'n," Fitzpatrick said as Mark followed her, "may I turn the men loose for their pleasure now?"

"Yes," Mark said. "How have you arranged it to prevent fighting?"

"By lottery, Cap'n," Fitzpatrick answered. "It's all fair and square."

"See that no one abandons the watch," Mark cautioned.

"Aye, Cap'n," Fitzpatrick said.

Ben Hall joined them at that moment, and he laughed. "By god, I'd like to see that pious bastard Grimsley's face now. I told him we'd broadside his town, and we did."

Hall and Fitzpatrick were still laughing when Mark led Leilani into his cabin. It was the first time Leilani had ever been on any vessel other than the native outrigger canoes or the island boats. She was amazed by the size of the cabin and by the huge bed. It was large enough to have accommodated her massive mother in comfort. Two people would have plenty of room for making love.

"Do you like it?" he asked.

"It is very large," Leilani said cautiously. She crossed the cabin and looked through the open porthole. The moon was already shimmering on the surface of the sea. She hadn't realized that night had fallen since she was brought on board. No light from outside had filtered through to the orlop deck.

"Are we far out to sea?" She asked in a voice that reminded Mark of tiny, golden bells.

"We are in the Kolohi Channel," he said.

Leilani looked back at him. Her skin, already golden, was shining as if lit from within, catching the subtle reflections of the lantern hanging overhead.

"I must speak with you about something," she said. She poured Mark a glass of whiskey and held it up to him. The whiskey's amber color glowed softly in the lamplight. Leilani realized that this was the room with the yellow lights she had seen from the shore. This was the room with its promises of gold. The thought seemed to mock her now.

"What do you want to talk about?" he asked, taking the glass from her.

"I am not like the other girls," Leilani said.

The captain loomed over her, smiling. "That's certainly true!"

"No. I mean I did not wish to come on board your ship."

"I'm sorry," he said, "but you had no choice. My ship was the only one in the harbor."

"You do not understand," Leilani said. "I did not want to go on any ship. I do not want to fornicate."

"It's too late." He took a drink and stared at her over the rim of the glass.

"I thought I could talk to you. I thought I could appeal to you as the captain of this ship."

"Are you a virgin?" he asked.

"No, I am not," Leilani said.

Mark grinned. "Then it shouldn't matter to you."

"It matters to me with whom I make love," Leilani said.

His answer was to reach out and jerk on the tie which held the lava-lava in place. It fell to the deck, leaving Leilani completely nude. He caught his breath at what he saw. Leilani had never looked more beautiful. Her golden skin shone over her swelling breasts and full thighs, and looked dark and mysterious where her perfect curves were half hidden in shadows. Her eyes had a strange sexual look.

"My God, you are beautiful," he said, his tongue thick with passion.

"Please, captain," Leilani replied as calmly as possible, "I don't wish to do this."

"Get on the bed," Mark commanded.

Leilani stepped back toward the door, and Mark grabbed her by the shoulders and flung her on the bed. The back of her knees struck its edge, and she fell on the mattress. Mark stood ready to push her down if she tried to get up, and he began taking off his clothes.

"Captain, please," Leilani cried up at him, "there are other girls on this ship who want you to make love to them."

"I don't want any of the other girls," Mark said as he stripped off his shirt. His chest was broad and covered with dark hair, and as his arms stretched, Leilani could see the knots of muscles bulge, gleaming under the lamplight.

"But surely, Captain, you would prefer someone who is more willing?"

"I don't need someone who's willing," Mark growled. "I only need someone who is available."

"Captain, please," Leilani begged.

Mark refused to listen to her. When she sat up, he pushed her back down, then he bent over her and kissed her, trapping her mouth with his own. She felt his manhood against her leg.

Leilani had never been kissed. Kissing was not common to her people, and though she had heard of it, the thought of it had always repulsed her. But when she felt his lips over hers, she was amazed at the sensations it evoked. Her head started spinning, and then she felt his tongue, first brushing across her lips, then forcing her lips open and thrusting inside. It was another way of entering her, she realized, and she felt a warmth spreading rapidly through her.

For a moment the sensations so overwhelmed her that she stopped struggling, and Mark quickly put his hands on her body. One big hand covered a breast and gently caressed it and then moved further down. His hand was so hot that Leilani looked down, fully expecting to see a red mark on her breast. She saw only the hard little buttons of her nipples.

His hands moved gently across her smooth, golden skin, spreading fire wherever they went, and though she continued to resist, she was now struggling against her own feelings as much as against the man over her.

Leilani couldn't account for what she was feeling. It was a sexual response, and that in itself wasn't new to her. But this was much more intense than she had ever felt before. There was as much difference between what she was feeling now, and what she felt in the sexual games she controlled, as there was between a soft afternoon shower and a violent, ripping typhoon.

"You are the most beautiful woman I have ever seen," Mark said thickly, as his hand finally reached between her legs. The heat and dampness of her desire belied her struggles, and he smiled at her when he realized it.

"No," Leilani said one last time, though her body trembled with fire under his touch.

Then, with her legs spread wide, her hands held, and no other means of defense against him, she felt him move over her, his manhood hard against her. He thrust deeply into her. Leilani gasped loudly, and scratched his bare back with her fingernails. But he ignored her, overwhelmed by his desire as he thrust into her again and again. He moved his mouth over hers, stifling her cries with smothering kisses and a darting tongue, which moved in and out of her mouth in perfect rhythm with that other part of him invading her body. Slowly her struggles ceased, and she began to give herself up to him as he moved deeper and deeper into her.

Lightning struck Leilani: once, twice, three times. She felt an orgasm of pleasurable violence, with a force more powerful than anything she had ever before experienced.

Then, all at once, it was over for Mark. His body went rigid. A hissing, groaning sound escaped from his lips. And as pleasurable convulsions racked his body, Leilani could feel them enter her own. His manhood strained inside her and then slowly slackened. But when he rolled off her, she still felt the hugeness of him. He lay to one side breathing heavily for a few moments. He spoke very quietly.

"What is your name?"

"Leilani."

"Are you from Maui, Leilani?"

"Yes."

He lay quietly beside her, and Leilani knew that he wanted her to talk, but she remained silent, wondering about her own feelings.

"What is wrong?" he finally asked.

"I did not wish to do this," Leilani said. "You raped me."

"Are you going to try and tell me you didn't enjoy it?"

"Who would enjoy rape?"

"You don't rape harlots," Mark said. "The governor was paid for your services."

"The governor's police kidnapped me," Leilani said. "I was brought to your ship against my will, and you made love to me against my will. That is rape."

He sat up and looked at her. "Are you serious? You mean you aren't one of the regular girls who visit the ships?"

"I am not," she said. She pulled herself up proudly. "I am Leilani," she told him.

The captain sighed. He got out of bed and pulled on his pants and shirt, then turned to look at her. "I am sorry, Leilani," he said. "I have never had to find unwilling girls for my bed in the past, and I wouldn't have started with you, had I known you spoke the truth. But, madam," he added with a grin, "it did not appear to me as if you were unappreciative of my lovemaking."

The captain's insolence angered Leilani, and she wanted to find a way to put him in his place. He obviously thought she should be grateful to him. He stood over the bed with a satisfied expression and pushed his shirt tail in as he looked down at her. "But you shouldn't worry, for you are perfectly safe from me now," he said jokingly.

"How do I know that?" she asked seriously.

"Because I never bed the same girl twice."

"Never?"

"No."

"Why not?"

"If you must know, there are too many women in the world to waste time making love more than once with the same girl. I want to make a new discovery each time."

"What if you found a woman you loved?"

"I do not believe there is such a thing as love," he said.

"Of course there is love," Leilani insisted.

He smiled. "For silly young girls, and boys not yet over puberty. But for me, a man of the sea, there is no such thing as love, and there is no time wasted on one woman. Now, if you'll excuse me, I must make my rounds. I recommend that you stay in my cabin. If you go on deck, the others are likely to think you are fair game, and have sport with you."

Leilani stood up and walked over to him. She knew that he was conscious of her nudity, and her closeness, and she was sure there was still some interest, even though he had just made love. She smiled at him and put her hand on his shoulder, applying pressure in that secret spot known to the Alii-Nui.

"I—I have to go now," he said.

"I know," Leilani replied. "You've no time for the same girl twice."

He gripped Leilani's wrist as if to remove her arm from his shoulder, then, as if controlled by a force outside of him, he pulled her to him and kissed her again.

This time Leilani was ready for the kiss, and

she opened her mouth on his, and ran her tongue across his lips, and thrust it inside his mouth.

His hands started moving over her body again, and though his touch aroused the same sensations as before, this time Leilani felt that *she* was in command. The heat in her loins was a controlled fire, her feelings were channelled into a measured response. *She* was now the master.

When she knew that he was no longer able to stop, she pulled away from him.

"I believe you said you must make your rounds, Captain?"

"The rounds can wait," he breathed. He began to pull off his shirt.

"Surely, Captain, you don't intend to bed me again?" Leilani teased. "After all, didn't you tell me there were too many women in the world to waste time with one?"

"I—I must admit that I don't understand it," Mark said. "But I must have you again. Why is that? And why do I feel that I . . . have no choice?"

Leilani smiled and lay back on the bed, letting her breasts rise and looking at him with that strange sexual look he found so inviting. Her smooth, golden body lay as if ready, and his manhood rose as he pulled off his pants. His senses were charged with a sexual stimulation greater than any he had ever known.

"Captain, does it look like I'm raping you?" Leilani whispered as he came to her.

"My God, what is this?" he mumbled, pulling her to him, caressing her breasts, feeling between her legs as if his desires were completely out of control. Leilani gave a short laugh of victory as he entered her.

Chapter Ten

WHEN MARK LEFT the bed much later, he had a worrying feeling that this girl had somehow reversed the roles on him. It was unsettling for his male pride, and his old insolence with her was gone. He stopped at the door and looked back at her. She smiled at him, a loose, confident, almost insolent smile.

"I have work to do," he said, feeling he must find some excuse for leaving her.

"So do I," Leilani answered.

Mark had no idea what she meant, but he gave it no thought. He wanted to forget her. When he stepped outside he saw one of the sailors sitting on a pile of spare canvas. The sailor was eating a piece of meat and drinking from a bottle.

"You aren't in line for any of the girls, Sanders?" he asked.

"I was first in line," Sanders replied, grin-

ning widely, his teeth broken or missing. "I
guess they figure a man my age can't do much
damage to 'em, so they let me go first, without
a lottery even. And, as one time will do me for
the night, I let the young'uns get in line for
the second time."

The second time. Mark thought of the un-
precedented "second time" he had just had with
Leilani, and for one instant, he was tempted to
go back in. But he was firm with himself.
"Sanders, keep an eye on my cabin for me, will
you?"

"Aye, Cap'n, I'll look after yer wench for
ye," Sanders said with a chuckle.

What was it about this girl? Was it a sense
of guilt? It certainly wasn't a pleasant feeling
thinking that he had forced himself on her.
But, he reminded himself, the girl's response
had shown that she had enjoyed what they did.
There was no need to feel as if he had victimized
her. Especially in light of their second time
around. Why, then, was the girl still bothering
him? She was merely a physical release for
him. . . . and she had served her purpose. There
was no need to concern himself with her again,
so why couldn't he forget her?

As Leilani dressed, she thought happily of the
way she had evened the score with the captain.
It had been easy to break down his facade of
superiority, to ridicule his boast that he would
bed no woman twice. It was satisfying to see

the insolent smile replaced by a look of confusion.

Leilani told herself there was only one reason she had made him come to her a second time—to teach him a lesson. She told herself that, and it gave her great satisfaction to believe it. But in the part of the heart which accepts no lies, Leilani knew the truth. She had made him come to her because she wanted him.

Mark climbed the ladder to the deck and looked around. It was night, and they were running with trimmed sails, though there was enough canvas to maintain headway. Kanole, a big Hawaiian who had become a part of Mark's crew, was at the helm.

"Where is Fitzpatrick, Kanole?"

"He is with a girl," Kanole answered.

Mark checked the ship's course and glanced at the set of the rigging. Kanole was a skilled, experienced seaman, and the ship was properly trimmed and on the right course, taking advantage of a slight so'easterly wind.

Mark was miffed that the crew had abandoned their stations, but he knew there was little he could do about it. On a United States Naval ship, he had absolute authority over well-disciplined seamen. Here, he was forced to operate with a crew of deserters, rummies, pirates, and cutthroats. They were all skilled seamen, but without discipline or loyalty. If he intended to get anything out of them, he had to let them know what they stood to gain personally, and he had to overlook some of their work habits.

Mark leaned against the rail and looked at Kanole. Kanole, like most Hawaiians, was a big man. He was well muscled and probably weighed well over two hundred pounds, Mark figured.

"Kanole, you are from Maui, aren't you?"

"Yes."

"Why did you join the revolution?"

"Dr. Pugh said if I would help, he would give me much land."

"Tell me about the Alii-Nui of Maui," he said after a moment.

"They are very powerful," Kanole said. "They can make magic and weave spells."

"Do you really believe that?"

"Yes."

"Do you think it was necessary to kill them to make the revolution?"

"Yes," Kanole said. "For if they lived, they could stop the revolution."

Mark laughed.

"I speak the truth," Kanole said.

"How do you know they have magic? Did you know them?"

"Yes."

"I was told they weighed three hundred pounds apiece," Mark said.

"Lakiolani was a very big woman," Kanole replied. "She was the mother."

"And the daughter? Did she weigh only two-hundred fifty pounds?" Mark asked with a laugh.

"No," Kanole said. "She was slender and very beautiful to the *haoles*. I, myself, like women bigger than Leilani."

"What?" Mark asked, feeling a strange chill down his spine.

"I said I like my women bigger."

"No. I mean the name," Mark said. "What was the name you used?"

"Leilani," Kanole replied.

"Leilani," Mark repeated thoughtfully. "I imagine that is quite a common name for Hawaiians?"

"No," Kanole said. "On Maui, it is forbidden for any but the Alii-Nui to use the names Lakiolani or Leilani."

"Yes, but . . . no, it couldn't be," Mark murmured to himself. He hurried back to his cabin.

"She's still in there, Cap'n," Sanders said cheerfully. "Ain' nobody tried to go in, either."

"Thanks," Mark grunted. He opened the door and stepped inside. "Leilani," he called.

There was no answer.

Mark looked around his cabin. There were few places to hide and he checked these. There was no sign of the girl who had said she was Leilani. He stuck his head back out. "Sanders, I thought you told me she didn't leave."

"I swear to ye, Cap'n. I've not taken my eyes off the door once. An' she ain't come out."

Mark checked his cabin one more time, then

started back on deck. "Mr. Hall!" he shouted. "Mr. Hall, on deck at once!"

He shouted several more times, and a few moments later, Hall joined him on deck, pushing his shirt tail into his trousers. He had left his eye-patch behind, and a puffed, red socket stared at Mark.

"What is it, Cap'n?" Hall asked.

"Turn all hands to," Mark said.

"Cap'n, are you serious? Three-fourths of the crew are drunk, and the rest are with the girls. If we turn them to now, I'm afraid we're going to have a mutiny on our hands."

"If we don't turn them to now, we're going to have them dead," Mark said. "The Alii-Nui is on this vessel."

"The who is what?"

"The girl," Mark said. "The girl I was with. Her name is Leilani. She is Alii-Nui of Maui."

"Cap'n, have you gone crazy with Hawaiian whiskey? If you expect me to turn the men out because of some notion—"

The words choked in Hall's mouth as Mark pulled a knife from his waistband and put the point to Hall's throat. "Turn them to, Mr. Hall," he said. "Or you'll not have a tongue left with which to issue the order."

"Aye, sir," Hall murmured.

"And the girls," he said. "Get them up here, too."

It took several minutes to get the crew on deck. There was a lot of grumbling and cursing, and not a few threats. Some of the drunken men were incapable of moving, and they were dragged to the deck by their friends. The five girls stood near the rail.

"There are only five of you," Mark said. "When we started, there were six. Where is the other one?"

"You are speaking of Kamala," one of the girls said. "She went with you."

"What did you say her name was?"

"Kamala."

"Do any of you know her?"

The girls looked at each other, then back at Mark. "We met her only tonight. She told us her name was Kamala."

"She told me another name," Mark said.

"Well, who is she?" Hall asked impatiently.

A shout came from high above them. "I am Leilani!" They all looked up to see Leilani high in the rigging.

"It is the Alii-Nui!" Kanole said. He dropped to his knees and touched his face to the deck. "Alii-Nui, forgive me. I am not one of those who killed you."

There were a few snickers from the assembled men, but even they sounded a little uneasy.

"Look!" Leilani cried down to them. She pointed out to sea. "At my command, I can raise an army from the sea to destroy you! Mahimahi!" she shouted.

At her shout, more than a score of dolphins broke the surface of the sea near the ship.

The five girls dropped to their knees, and there were shouts of fear from the sailors.

"Shoot her!" one of the sailors cried. Another, who was armed, fired at her, but missed.

"The bullet passed right through her!" a hysterical sailor shouted, though, in fact, it had passed through the sail sheet near her.

Leilani leaped from the rigging in the mainmast to the mizzenmast, then down to the deck, landing lightly on her feet. Two sailors grabbed for her, but she did a quick twist, then flashed both arms out savagely, slashing the knife edge of her hands across their throats. They fell, gurgling, to the deck.

"Stop her!" Mark commanded.

Leilani picked up the fire box and ran to the powder locker. "Captain Costain, put your boats over," she called to him.

"Get away from there, you fool!" Hall shouted. "That's gun powder. You want to blow us up?"

"Yes," Leilani answered, smiling. "I am going to destroy this ship. If I destroy it now, there will be no soldiers coming from Honolulu to help Kekuanna. Now, get your boats over quickly if you wish to live."

"Cap'n, what are we going to do?" one of the men shouted.

"We are going to put the boats over," Mark replied, watching Leilani.

The sailors who had been drunk sobered quickly, and even though they were still con-

fused and close to panic, they managed to swing
the two boats over very quickly.

"Get in them," Leilani ordered.

They rushed to obey. It didn't take long
for everyone aboard the *Sea Eagle* to scramble
down into the two boats, and then the deserted
ship was adrift in the open sea. The boats were
quickly pulled away from the ship by anxious
rowers.

"Are you going to kill yourself just to destroy
this ship?" Mark yelled through cupped hands.

"She can't die, Cap'n. Didn't you see that ball
pass through her?" one of the sailors asked
fearfully.

"The ball struck the sail," Mark said. "I saw
it."

"What is she doing now?" another asked.

They soon knew. Leilani tossed the firebox in
on the kegs of gunpowder, then she dived into
the water and swam away with fast, powerful
strokes. Within a few seconds, the bowels of the
Sea Eagle were ripped open by a tremendous
explosion. The masts collapsed onto her burning
decks. Another explosion blew out the hull and
water began rushing in. In less than a minute,
the ship slipped under the sea, and nothing was
left of her except bubbling water, and a few
floating, sizzling pieces of charred timber.

"Where did the girl go?" Hall asked.

"Back to Maui, I suppose," Mark said.

"How far is it?"

"To the closest point of land, I make it about ten miles."

"She'll never make it."

"She'll make it," Mark said confidently.

"You're damned right she will," another said. "She's a witch. She's got magic powers."

"No," Mark said, laughing. "She has no magic powers. But she is quite a woman. Quite a woman, indeed," he added, and his mouth set in an almost wistful smile.

"What'll we do now, Cap'n?" one of the men asked.

"Gentlemen, my suggestion now is that we head for Molokai and take the first ship out of there. The revolution is lost, and I don't want to be around here to see what happens next."

Chapter Eleven

WHEN THE TWO boats from the *Sea Eagle* reached the island of Molokai, they were expected. Debris had washed ashore from the wreckage hours before the boats made it, and the islanders, who were skilled at reading the messages of the sea, knew that a large ship had sunk. By now, also, there had been news of the revolution on Maui, and the residents of Molokai, islanders and *haole* alike, were anxious for a full account.

Although the crew of the *Sea Eagle* had agreed among themselves before landing that they would say nothing about their ship's mission, or the way it was destroyed, word soon leaked out. Freely flowing whiskey and beautiful but curious girls loosened the tongues of the sailors, and within a short time the news had spread through the island.

"Leilani returned from the grave to avenge her death!"

The sailors, who normally rejected the Hawaiians' superstitions and legends, were confused by what had happened, and expressed their bewilderment.

"I see ole' Peters put a ball right through 'er, I did. The ball passed through 'er body like it warn't nothin' more'n a cloud."

"She teched off the powder locker, then dived inter the water 'n never come back up. 'N here's the strange part. She knowed she wasn't goin' ter come up. It was lak as if she lived under the ocean."

"She come onto the ship in the body of a dolphin. 'N after she'd done her hell to the ship, she changed back into a dolphin. I wouldn't believe this, but I seen it with my own eyes."

The stories were told and re-told, exaggerated and embroidered, then spread via the island boats to all the other islands. Soon everyone knew of Leilani and her feat, and she became a genuine heroine.

Search parties went to look for her, but she was nowhere to be found. Her village was combed, all of Maui was searched, people were questioned, but no one had seen her.

Many claimed to have seen her body though, and that only added to the mystery. Further investigation was out of the question, because the bodies of Lakiolani and the girl thought to be Leilani had already been disposed of in the way prescribed for an Alii-Nui. The flesh had been baked away from the bones and the bones scattered. That prevented any desecretion of their bodies but it also made positive identification impossible afterward.

Governor Kekuanna, in the meantime, had managed to save his own position so that he achieved a personal victory in the midst of defeat. When he realized that the revolution was lost, he quickly arrested many of the conspirators who had formerly been his allies, and threw them in jail. He also freed the king's troops, and replaced the revolutionary banner, which flew over the government houses, with the Royal Standard of King Kamehameha III.

Governor Kekuanna sent word to Kamehameha III that he had pretended to cooperate with the rebels and had, as a ruse, set himself up as George Washington II, in order to find out who was the revolution's leader.

"Tell the king I achieved great success in thwarting the rebellion," Kekuanna told the king's messenger. "I learned of the plans, and then offered my services in order to protect the king's interest. I have discovered that the principal traitor seems to be Kanole, a distant cousin of the king, who would himself be king. He was aided in his rebellion by an American ship captain, named Mark Çostain. Costain is a soldier of fortune, preying on others. He was forced to leave the United States Navy and flee America, because he was charged with international piracy. He also tried to start a revolution in Cuba, and that proves his guilt."

Kekuanna was asked about the story that the ship was destroyed by Leilani.

"The story is entirely false," Kekuanna said, laughing. "It was one of my most trusted servants who destroyed the ship. I sneaked her aboard, disguised as a whore. I cannot tell you her name, for to do so would put her life in great danger. Leilani, unfortunately, was killed, along with her mother, Lakiolani, when the traitor Kanole raided their village on the night before the attack. The reported sightings of Leilani since that time have been false hopes stirred by the people's genuine love for their king and Alii-Nui, and their eagerness to believe in the possibility that Leilani may have survived."

Governor Kekuanna provided the king with a list of names of the foreign mercenaries who were waiting in Honolulu to participate in the rebellion. He said he had cooperated partly to get these names, and thus he had prevented a counterattack by the rebel forces.

King Kamehameha III may not have fully believed Kekuanna's story, but it was politically expedient for him to do so, just as it was economically advantageous to turn a blind eye toward Angus Pugh's involvement. Therefore, the Republic of Hawaii under George Washington II had a history of less than two days, and within a week after the revolution, life on the island had nearly returned to normal.

All that remained to remind people of the revolution was their sadness over the death of

Lakiolani, and the belief, which couldn't be suppressed, that Leilani had somehow come back from the dead to avenge her murder and then had returned to her grave once her revenge was complete.

"It is blasphemy to say that she has returned from death," Jebediah Grimsley told his wife as they sat at breakfast. "Yet many say this. I am forced to remind them frequently that only our Lord has risen from the grave."

"Have you forgotten, husband, that our Lord also raised Lazurus?"

"Would you compare the Lord's miracle in raising Lazarus with the sacrilegious murmurings of heathens over a false prophet?" Jebediah asked.

"I make no such comparison, husband," Marcia said simply.

"I would hope not," Jebediah said. "For to add the sin of blasphemy to your sin of adultery would make you truly miserable in the sight of the Lord."

Marcia bit her lip and looked down. Tears welled quickly in her eyes, and she blinked several times to try and fight them back.

"Husband, can you not forgive and forget that which is passed?" she pleaded.

"It is not my forgiveness you should seek, woman," Jebediah said. "You should seek the forgiveness of the Lord. And it is just for this reason that I cannot forget. I must remember, for every day I pray to the Lord that he will grant you salvation, despite the terrible sin on your soul."

"Oh, please, husband," Marcia begged. "Do not torment me so."

Jebediah pushed his breakfast plate back and stood up. He walked to the door, took his hat from a peg and put it on, then turned to look at his wife.

"The torment is of your own making," he said.

There was no rancor in his voice when he spoke. It was, in fact, agonizingly calm, and that was what Marcia found most difficult to take. His ignorance of her pain and his total lack of personal feeling mocked their marriage.

"Do not forget your sins of the flesh," Jebediah went on. "Your soul was in terrible jeopardy when you came to me. I have not added to that burden."

Jebediah walked out, and Marcia remained at the breakfast table, fighting back her tears, and remembering how it had been as a young girl in Salem, Massachusetts.

She was the eldest daughter of Reverend Marcus Tremaine, and at sixteen she was said to be the most beautiful. She had deep blue eyes that sparkled when she laughed, and a natural flirtatious way about her which caught the attention of the boys.

Marcia liked to laugh, and she did so often, even though she was constantly reminded by her mother and father that so much laughter was unbecoming a lady, and an invitation to the Devil to work his ways with her.

Marcia Tremaine didn't believe that. She couldn't see how anything as innocently enjoyable as laughter could be a sin. There were other things she couldn't understand, either. Why, for example, should she have to hide her beautiful long blonde hair under a black headdress? Nor could she understand why, when speaking to boys, she was expected to look at the ground and talk in monosyllables. And what was the harm in pinching her cheeks to make them glow rose-red?

Marcia had seen nothing wrong with these things, so she did them all. She laughed, she let her hair hang in saucy, golden curls, and she made her cheeks look red. And, most scandalous of all, she stared at boys when she spoke to them. She liked to do that because she knew that boys found her pretty, and she enjoyed watching their expressions when they looked at her. She could tell when a boy wanted her, and she liked that feeling. It was most obvious in the face of young Joseph Priddy.

Joseph Priddy was a nineteen-year-old printer's apprentice, who rented a small sleeping space in the attic of Reverend Tremaine's house. He slept and ate there, and Marcia saw him every day. Joseph practically melted every time he looked at Marcia, and she delighted in his reaction and made a game of teasing him.

She wasn't certain when the game started.

Joseph had lived there for four years, and when Marcia was only twelve, he took very little notice of her. But by the time she was fourteen, she began to blossom into a young woman, and several times she caught Joseph giving aching, sidelong glances toward her. Always, when he was thus caught, Joseph would look away with a flush of embarrassment.

Marcia enjoyed the situation. If she could sit in such a way as to show a turn of her ankle, or move her body to display the curve of her bosom, she would do it, just for the delight of the game. But by the time she was sixteen, it was no longer a harmless game to her. She found that she looked forward to the chance encounters as much as Joseph did. And though they never talked about anything important and never touched each other, they were carrying on an affair as lustful and as wanton as if they were actually sleeping together.

The situation reached a boiling point one hot, summer's night when Reverend Tremaine, his wife, and Marcia's two sisters attended the regular Wednesday evening prayer service. Marcia didn't go. She was excused because she had wrenched her ankle during the day and was in bed with her foot on a pillow. The pain had long since stopped, but she had used the accident to avoid the interminable service.

Joseph was supposed to work that night, but when he reported to the shop, he found that the printing master had a summer cold and it was closed. Joseph returned to his room.

"Mother, is that you?" Marcia called when she heard footsteps on the stairs. She put the pillow quickly back in position under her ankle so as not to give herself away.

"No," Joseph said. He came to the door of the bedroom and looked in. "It's me."

"Joseph, don't look in here," Marcia said, as if she were truly scandalized. "I'm in my night-dress."

"I'm sorry," Joseph said, looking quickly away.

Marcia laughed. "I don't know why it should be so wrong to see a girl in a nightdress, though. They are certainly as modest as the clothing one wears during the day. And as warm," she added, fanning herself slightly. "Perhaps it is just the idea that this is what a girl wears to bed."

She said "bed" in a suggestive tone, knowing full well the effect it would have on Joseph. Then, still fanning herself, she undid several buttons at the neck, realizing that in so doing she was exposing the rising mounds of her breasts to Joseph's view. "Whew," she said. "It is warm in here."

Joseph blushed, looked quickly away, then started to leave.

"Oh, Joseph, don't be such a silly goose," Marcia said. "No one is here but us." She smiled and patted the side of her bed. "Come in and sit with me for a moment. It is so lonely with every-one gone."

Joseph paused for a moment and then recklessly did as she suggested. He looked at her, and his eyes started at the neck, then traveled down the smooth skin until he reached her breasts.

Marcia saw something in his eyes then. Something that both frightened and thrilled her.

Joseph reached for her.

"No," Marcia said, leaning away from him. "Don't do anything, Joseph, please. You are frightening me."

"I—I want you, Marcia. I want you very much," Joseph said thickly.

"Joseph, no, please, no."

He put his hand on her shoulder. "Marcia, I've waited years for this. Don't deny me now."

"Joseph, what are you doing?" she asked, more frightened than before. The game was becoming serious. She was losing control, and it was confusing her.

Joseph leaned down and kissed her. He touched her mouth with his, and Marcia marveled that the kiss could be so wonderfully tender, yet so frighteningly urgent.

"Joseph . . . no . . . please . . ."

"We must, Marcia, can't you see that?" Joseph said. His voice was pleading and yet strangely unhappy, as if he was aware that what they were doing would be the ruin of them both. But they had no choice now. Their desires were in charge, sweeping away all barriers, forcing them together against their will.

Marcia made a strange animal sound in her

throat, but whether of passion or fright even she couldn't be sure. She closed her eyes and waited for Joseph to make the next move, longing desperately for it, yet still afraid. She could no longer trust her own body to keep her out of trouble. She realized she should resist him, but she knew she would not, because she was no longer in control.

Joseph stretched out on the bed beside her and put his arm around her. He kissed her again, this time pressing against her, pulling her body against him. She could feel the hardness of his muscles, and a rapidly spreading warmth growing from within. Her mind told her it was wrong. Her body told her it was what she needed.

Joseph grew bolder at her lack of resistance. His kisses became more demanding, and Marcia felt the tip of his tongue darting across her lips. She opened her mouth instinctively and Joseph's tongue stabbed inside, changing the warmth to fire. Then, because they were lying so close together, and her sleeping dress was of thinner material than the one she usually wore, she felt the sudden growth of his maleness. It aroused her as she had never been aroused before. Eager hands pulled at the hem of the gown and clutched at the buttons of trousers. With a passionate sense of freedom, Marcia felt for the first time in her life the warmth of a man's naked body against her own. The white heat rising in her created a sticky pent-up feeling, and there was urgent craving in her loins for more than a mere touch. And when, finally, Joseph moved his hard and demanding body over her soft and yielding thighs, she was ready to receive him.

She let out a low whimper of pain as he found her, and then a sharper exclamation as she felt him thrust into her. It was painful as he opened her up, but the pain was soon mixed with the most intense pleasure she had ever known. Gone was all pretense of caution and game-playing. She felt only a hunger to be satisfied, a need which was being completely fulfilled. He thrust her by his manhood up to the stars, and she cried when at last it was over, but only because it was over.

She and Joseph had become frequent lovers after that, sometimes even risking detection in the middle of the night when Marcia's needs would reach the point that she would climb silently into the attic and go to him in his own bed.

Such recklessness was not without consequence, however, and within a few months Marcia realized that she was pregnant.

She was terrified, because she knew that pregnancy wasn't a condition which could be hidden indefinitely. Finally, contritely, she confessed to her father, crying and praying for his forgiveness, and for the forgiveness of God.

Reverend Tremaine was very angry. That his daughter would dare to disgrace him in this way was more than he could accept. He would never forgive her, nor would he allow her to continue to live under the same roof with her sisters, for fear that she might contaminate them with her evil. He would, he said, have to rearrange her life so that she was punished and forced to live decently.

Joseph went to Reverend Tremaine and asked that he be allowed to marry Marcia. He and Marcia were in love, he said. Marcia begged her father to agree.

Reverend Tremaine responded with an outburst of rage, and he threatened to have Joseph put in prison for life for statutory rape if the boy ever saw Marcia again. Then he contacted Joseph's employer and explained what had happened. Joseph was dismissed from his job and forced to leave town.

Marcia hoped Joseph would come back for her, and when she heard sounds in the night, she would hold her breath and pray that it was Joseph. But it never was.

Finally, more than a month after Joseph left, and just as Marcia's pregnancy was beginning to show, Reverend Tremaine came home with a tall, gangling young man named Jebediah Grimsley.

"It is the work of the Lord," Reverend Tremaine said. "Reverend Grimsley has petitioned for a position as missionary to the natives in Hawaii. But their acceptance of him is contingent upon Reverend Grimsley being married. He therefore needs a wife before next week. You, woman, will need a husband to provide a father and name for the bastard child you are carrying in your polluted womb. You will marry Reverend Grimsley, and you will go to Hawaii with him. That way your evil influence will be removed from your sisters, your family will be spared some of the disgrace you have brought them, and by being a wife for Reverend Grimsley, you will be serving the Lord."

"Yes, Father," Marcia said, thinking of Joseph.

"This means, of course, that we will never see each other again. Do you understand that?"

"Yes, Father."

"Good. Then I won't have, I hope, any foolish crying and carrying on when you leave. You made your own bed, woman, and now you must sleep in it."

"Yes, Father."

Marcia's mother began crying.

"Still your tears, woman," Reverend Tremaine ordered.

"I can't help it. To think that I will never see our little girl again," Marcia's mother said. She dabbed at her eyes.

"She is no longer our little girl," Reverend Tremaine said coldly. "She is the daughter of Satan. I can only hope that a lifetime of contrition with the likes of Reverend Grimsley can save her soul from damnation."

Marcia and Jebediah Grimsley were married and left soon afterward for Hawaii. Jebediah made no move toward Marcia on their wedding night, or on any other night. Once, during the voyage out as Marcia was remembering the moments of passion she had shared with Joseph, she heard the bed sounds of Angus Pugh and his wife making love in the tiny cubicle next to theirs, and she tired of waiting for Jebediah to make the first advance. She reached for him.

"No!" Jebediah said sharply, slapping her hand away.

"What is it?" Marcia asked. "What is wrong?" She was surprised by his reaction.

"I have taken a vow before the Lord," Jebediah said. "A vow of celibacy."

"But, Jebediah, we are married," Marcia insisted.

"We are married in the spirit, woman," Jebediah said. "But we will never be married in the flesh."

Marcia's baby was born as the ship made its way up the western coast of South America. Jebediah named the boy Calvin, and swore to take special pains to bring the child up in such a way as to help it overcome its sinful birth. And he tried to make Calvin a living example of his evangelical zealousness and dedication to fighting the Devil.

But Marcia was alone.

Chapter Twelve

AFTER LEILANI TOUCHED off the explosion aboard the *Sea Eagle,* she swam toward Maui. But she had no sense of triumph from what she had done and struggled against the heavy burden of guilt which lay on her.

She had failed. That was how she saw it. Never mind that she had destroyed the ship and thwarted the revolution. She had failed because she had not prevented the trouble from starting in the first place.

Her mother had sensed the danger and had tried to warn Leilani. But she had enjoyed the privileges of being an Alii-Nui without accepting any of the responsibilities. She was too caught up in the joys of sex and the pleasures of living, and never realized there was danger threatening them.

Now Lakiolani and the others were dead. And Leilani, who had not understood the signs, believed that she was to blame. In fact, and this worried her most, she had received only one sign—the one which caused her to swim far out to sea to save her own life. She felt she had failed the hundred generations of Alii-Nui who had come before her. Lakiolani had died before completing Leilani's education, and therefore secrets which had been preserved for one thousand years were forever lost. Leilani was painfully aware that they were lost because of her.

The guilt weighed heavily as she swam toward Maui, and she wondered if she should return. Could she face the people she had failed?

No, she could not.

Then what could she do about it?

The water was warm and inviting, and it would be easy, so easy, for Leilani to stop swimming now, to let herself sink quietly into the sea.

"Mahimahi, I'm coming to you," she said softly.

She slid beneath the waves and swam deeper and deeper with smooth, powerful strokes. The water grew darker and darker until she was far below the surface.

Here I will die, she thought.

With the realization that she was about to die, Leilani stopped her mind from functioning so that there would be no struggle to stay alive. She felt no fear, no pain, no remorse. There was only a calm acceptance of her fate.

She waited to die, and as she waited, the division between reality and hallucination began to disappear. She could see other people—her mother, her father, Malaka, Kamala, villagers she had known, and, strangely, Captain Mark Costain. She didn't know if they were mere illusions, or if they were from the world beyond life. Whatever they were, they were all beautiful, and each one seemed to glow with some inner light. Then Leilani heard music! The ocean this deep was dark blue, and the color itself seemed to be emitting beautiful, melodic chords. She wanted to ask the people if they, too, could hear the music, but though she tried, she couldn't get their attention.

Mark Costain was playing a flute. Leilani was certain that he would be interested in hearing blue, so she tried to call him to her, but when she looked at him she could hardly believe her eyes. There were bright yellow colors splashing from the end of the flute, and the colors sparkled and danced as they hung there.

Leilani saw Kamala. Beautiful Kamala with her golden body, oiled as it had been for Leilani's Alii-Nui ceremony, was making love with the bright drops of color! Kamala was leaning over backwards, her hands holding on to her ankles. Her hips were thrust forward, and the color was moving in and out of her. It was a solid, three-dimensional color, and the thrusts were deep. Leilani could see Kamala as her stomach swelled slightly with each thrust.

As Leilani watched, some of the color came

to her. She knew why it came, and she spread her thighs appreciatively. The color entered into her, and she gave herself to it and felt it course through her body. She was swept with washes of color, and the blue sea chanted the song of love as she came to ecstasy in wave after wave. There seemed to be one unending climax—or were there several, one after the other?—with the peaks and valleys so close that she couldn't distinguish them. Her whole body seemed to dissolve under the pressure of such immense pleasure.

How was she doing this? She was aware of remaining in a state of climax as she drifted through the sea. It was as if she had been able to retain the feeling of ecstasy that usually lasted only a short time and then was gone. Now she lived at that peak of feeling, only it was greatly multiplied, shattering her personality into several parts, each with the sensations of the whole.

Leilani looked at the other people from her new perspective. She knew who she was now. She had moved into the aura of the sea and breathed fresh life into it—life spawned by her pleasure. Leilani became as the sea, a part of everything. Now she was part of the manhood of Mark Costain. Odd, she didn't feel as if the penis were in her, she felt as if she were a part of it. She could feel the throbbing of the veins, the rushing of the blood, and the tightening of the skin as it grew larger. She felt her temperature rising and a drop of pre-coital fluid. While she could feel all this, she was also the stiff protrusion in the soft, smooth vagina of Kamala, with whom Mark was about to make love. There was warmth and moistness there like a touch of the sea. The nerves twitched with a sense of awareness and anticipation. Leilani felt the head of Mark's manhood as it entered, proudly rearing within the juices and forcing its way deep inside. It felt hard and huge. Leilani now was not only experiencing a climax but living it. From this new perspective, she was able to feel the lovemaking of these two lovers throughout her entire body. When the driving penis finally erupted in a hot spurt, Leilani felt herself being shot into the tunnel of love, skidding along like a board on a surf, cascading off the walls of the innermost part of love's playground.

The two lovers were spent, so Leilani, living this ecstasy full time, felt herself leaving them, and she found two others and became a part of them. She felt again the fullness of total lovemaking, climbing to the peak with each of them as they reached their climaxes, one after the other, then she left them when they were drained, to go on and on, with no end to the pleasure in a state of perpetual ecstasy. Among the lovemaking masses, only she seemed to be fully aware of what lovemaking meant, and only she therefore was able to stay at the peak of pleasure.

Eventually Leilani drifted through the sea to make herself whole again after the shattering effects of the climaxes, and then she returned to her body. When her personality was whole again, she felt herself falling deeper and deeper into the sea. She tried to stop herself, but she couldn't. Soon all the colors, the music, and the people were gone. She was in a violet ocean now. She looked for the sky, but there was none. There was only the soft, warm, purple velvet of the deep.

Leilani felt as if she were sinking further and further until she reached the bottom. There, she was swallowed by a tiny fish and deposited on a grain of sand. She slowly drifted without mind or body, and time had no beginning and no end . . .

When Leilani awoke, she found herself lying across a hatch cover, part of the flotsam from the ship. She felt something nudging her leg, heard high-pitched clicking sounds, and saw two dolphins circling their makeshift raft.

She sat up and looked around, and saw she was very far out to sea with no idea where she might be.

"Why did you save me?" she asked.

At the sound of her voice, the two dolphins began clicking excitedly, and leaping from the water in great delight.

"I know," Leilani said. "You are happy that I still live."

The dolphins jumped and clicked again, and Leilani laughed at them in spite of herself.

"Very well, Mahimahi. I shall live. But first, I must find land. Do you know where land is? No? Then I shall use the way of the ancient ones, and read the water."

Leliani looked at the sea and caught a wave pattern, which indicated an island to the southeast far away. It was good that an island lay in that direction, because the wave swells and the ocean current seemed to be carrying her that way.

A strong wind came up on the second day Leilani was on the raft, and she made rapid progress. In fact, though she didn't know it, she was being swept southeast at a little over a hundred miles a day. Gentle rains provided her with water, and flying fish flopped onto her raft often enough to supply her with food. Mahimahi kept her company and gave her strength and courage, and after ten days, she sighted the island.

It was not an island that she knew. It was very small, shaped rather like a fish hook, no more than three miles long and slightly over a mile wide. The fish-hook shape gave it a protected bay.

Leilani rolled off the raft and swam ashore. She picked her way across the beach by stepping on rocks, and left no footprints in the sand. If the island was inhabited by people who were unfriendly, she wouldn't alert them to the fact that someone had landed.

There was ample vegetation on the island. Many types of trees, some with fruit and some bearing nuts, climbed the slopes of the volcanic mountains which rose imperiously over the island. There was a low-lying mountain ridge with two rather prominent hills at one end. The ridge had the form of a woman sleeping, and the twin hills were her upthrust breasts.

Leilani explored the island thoroughly and quietly, but found no signs that others lived here. There was, she quietly rejoiced, a great variety of birds, but she found no springs of fresh water, though there were many rock basins which caught and preserved the almost daily rainfalls. No one else lived here, but the island was habitable. That made it perfect for Leilani. Her sole desire now was to spend time meditating over her failure. If she was to spend the remainder of her life in total isolation, then so be it.

Leilani found a depression in the rocks, and with palm fronds, she fashioned a shelter for herself with an opening toward the sea. There was a coconut tree nearby which not only provided coconuts for her but gave her a lookout tower, should one be needed.

Leilani saw a bird's nest on a rocky crag above her, and she scrambled up to it. A large bird was just approaching the nest, and it screeched angrily, then wheeled away as Leilani scooped out two of its eggs.

"Don't fret so, bird," Leilani called. "You have four more eggs which I shall leave, and they will make fine children for you."

Leilani dropped lightly down from the rock, and placed the eggs under a coconut shell to keep them from being stolen by another predator. She started a fire, and with the other half of the coconut shell, boiled some water. Then she dropped the eggs carefully into the water and leaned back to watch the flames crackle and enjoy the peace of her new home.

Chapter Thirteen

CALVIN GRIMSLEY SAT in the back room of Angus Pugh's trading post and held the small golden idol in his lap. It was wrapped in tapa cloth, and he held it close to him, as if afraid someone might try to grab it from him.

Calvin was there in God's service. At first, he wasn't sure what was expected of him, but after much prayer as to how best to serve the Lord, the answer came to him one day as words on the wind.

"You must become my messenger," the voice said.

"But am I not already your messenger?" Calvin had answered. "Do I not spread your word, telling all who will listen of your Glory? Do I not confront the Devil who walks the streets as a roving lion, seeking whom he may devour?"

"I require much more than that," the voice replied. "Calvin, is it not true that you have lusted after the flesh of Leilani and the other native girls?"

Calvin fell to his knees in contrition. "But I have not been guilty of the sin of fornication," he said.

"You have been guilty of a lust for the flesh," the voice replied. "But now, verily, I tell you, you can cleanse yourself of that guilt."

"How?"

"By saving the souls of sinners and fornicators, and sending them to me."

Calvin was on his knees in the sand when the way was shown him, and with tears streaming down his face, he gave thanks.

That night Calvin had gone "whoring among the heathens" to do the work which he now knew was his. First, he had looked for Leilani, but when he couldn't find her, he saw Malaka and asked her to have sex with him. She agreed, and afterward, after he had killed her, he felt a spiritual uplifting of his soul. It was wonderful! There was absolutely no guilt whatever.

But new problems had sprung up in Calvin's campaign to save the souls of the heathen girls. Despite their seemingly immoral ways, Calvin discovered that the island girls were not as promiscuous as he had thought. They treated sex as a natural, pleasant interlude, but they wouldn't have sex with just anyone at anytime. Calvin had been unsuccessful in finding even one more girl's soul to save after the one success with Malaka. He knew there was work he should be doing among these girls . . . sins to commit and then atone for, and souls to save. But try as he did, he found no one willing to have sex with him.

He prayed and transcribed long passages of the Bible to try to relieve the terrible lustful pressures which began building up inside him, but nothing helped. So, in the quiet of the night, in the dark of his house, long after he heard the deep breathing of his mother and father and knew that he was no longer able to fight it, Calvin discovered the sin of Onan. He knew that it was better to plant his seed in the belly of a whore than to cast it on the ground, but the belly of a whore wasn't available free of charge.

Then he remembered the golden bird. If he could sell it, he could use the money it brought to visit the governor's whores. His blood quickened as he realized that there were more souls he could win. He rejoiced as he thought of all the work left to do. So he took the bird to Angus Pugh's trading post and now sat in the back room, waiting for Dr. Pugh to finish with a customer out front.

The curtain parted a moment later and Dr. Pugh came into the store room. Pugh went over to a shelf and started to fill a pipe for himself. When he had been an active missionary, Pugh had preached against the sins of tobacco, but now that he had left the ministry, he often smoked, even in public.

"Well, my boy," Pugh said as he held a candle to his pipe and began drawing on it until smoke wreathed his head, "what can I do for you?"

"I have something I wish to sell," Calvin said cautiously.

Pugh laughed. "You have something you wish to sell?"

"Yes, sir."

Pugh pointed at Calvin with the stem of his pipe. A string of spittle stretched from his lip, glistened in the light, then broke. "Does your father know that you are entering the world of mercantilism?" he teased.

"No," Calvin said quickly "Dr. Pugh, you mustn't tell. You must promise you won't tell."

"Well, I suppose I can be counted on to keep your secret," Pugh said. "Now, let's see what you have there."

Calvin pulled the tapa cloth to one side, and showed the little bird to Pugh. "This," he said. "It's gold, isn't it?"

Pugh's mouth dropped open in surprise, and he reached quickly for the little bird. "Where did you get that?" he asked.

"I found it."

"Found it, where?"

"Here, on the island," Calvin said, not wanting to say that he got it from one of the native villages. Pugh might guess the rest and then he might be in trouble. "Will you buy it from me?"

"Buy it? Yes, yes, of course," Pugh said. "I'll be glad to buy it."

"And you won't tell anyone?"

"No. I'll not tell a soul," Pugh promised. He looked at the bird with suppressed excitement. "No, sir, you can count on that. I won't breathe a word of this to anyone."

"How much money will you give me for it?"

"I'll give you fifty dollars," Pugh offered.

"Fifty dollars?" Calvin's face broke into a wide smile. Fifty dollars would buy him a hundred visits with the governor's whores. "I'll take it," he said.

Pugh went into the other room for a moment, then returned with the money in his hand. He gave it to Calvin, then took the bird and looked at it lovingly.

Calvin started for the back door, then stopped. He looked around just before he left.

"Remember," he said. "You'll not tell my father?"

"Not a word," Pugh promised.

After Calvin left, Pugh rummaged through some books until he came across a large, green-bound volume. It was dusty, and he brushed it off with his hand, then looked at the title:

The Voyage of the Golden Hind and the Lost Drake Treasure.

He sat back and thumbed through the pages until he found what he was looking for. He began to read:

> *After raiding several Spanish settlements, Drake captured a Spanish ship, the Caca-fuego, and stole its cargo of gold, silver and jewels. He planned to return to England*

*through the Straits of Magellan, but feared
an attack by the Spaniards if he sailed
south, so, loaded with treasure, he started
across the Pacific Ocean.*

*At one point in the Pacific, Drake thought
he saw sails, and as he realized his ship
would make a rich prize, he took the
choicest items from his treasure and placed
them in a chest which he buried on an
island. He called the island Sleeping Lady
Island, so named because of a distinctive
ridge of hills which looked like a lady
sleeping. Drake intended to return for the
Treasure, but it was fourteen years before
he was able to get another expedition together, and he died of dysentery on that
voyage before the destination was reached.*

*To this date, no one has found the mys-
terious Sleeping Lady Island, though many
have tried.*

Then followed an inventory of the pieces in
the treasure chest—a treasure which Angus Pugh
knew would be worth several hundred thousand
dollars if it could only be found.

He ran his finger down the list of items until
he came to the one which made his blood race
with excitement.

*The Thorncrown Bird. One of the few
pieces of treasure which was English in
origin, it had been created by a goldsmith
to depict a well-known English legend. The*

English robin's red breast is said to have come about when a small bird plucked a thorn from the crown of Jesus as he was on the cross. A drop of blood from the thorn stained the bird's breast red, and so it has remained. The Thorncrown bird, like the bird of legend, is an English robin, made of gold. It is approximately three inches high, and is wearing a crown of thorns on its head. Just behind the left foot, the goldsmith put the initials "ER" in honor of Queen Elizabeth, the reigning monarch at the time.

With trembling hands, Pugh turned the little bird up and looked behind its left foot.

It was there—ER!

"My god," he said, scarcely able to believe what he was seeing, "this is it."

He realized that some natives must have taken a prolonged canoe trip since Drake's time, and found the Thorncrown Bird. That meant that the island was somewhere in these waters. The legend was true, and Pugh was holding the key in his hands.

It was an awe-inspiring thought.

Chapter Fourteen ─────────────

MARK DECIDED IT would be best for him to leave the islands as quickly as he could, and Kanole, because he was the one falsely charged with leading the revolution, asked to go with him.

There were two whalers at anchor off Kaunakakai, but he had no wish to sail aboard a whaler. He heard that there was a merchant ship at Kaluapapa on the other side of the island, so he and Kanole trekked across to try to sign on.

The ship was there, just as they had heard, and it lay quietly in the protected waters off Kahiu point. The sight of an ocean-going ship never failed to move Mark, and he stood quietly for a moment, looking at it, just enjoying its lines.

"Is something wrong, Captain?" Kanole asked.

"No," he replied. "I was just looking at the ship. It's beautiful, isn't it?"

"Not as beautiful as the volcanoes of Maui," Kanole said.

Mark put his hand on Kanole's shoulder. "I know how you feel, Kanole. I, too, am a man without a country." He smiled. "You and I, Kanole, we shall be our own countrymen, and no one shall come between us. We are citizens of the sea!"

Kanole returned the smile. "You are right, Captain."

"But you'd best not call me Captain," Mark warned. "For if we can sign on aboard this ship, I certainly won't be a captain. I will be lucky to be a ship's officer."

"There," Kanole said, pointing to an islander beaching his canoe, "I will ask him to take us to the ship."

"Fine." They walked out of the trees and down the small hill onto the wide beach. Kanole hailed the islander, and in the Hawaiian tongue, asked if he would take the two of them to the anchored *haole* ship. The Hawaiian agreed, and Mark and Kanole rode through the surf out to the ship. The ship was named the *Mary Luck*, and her port of registry was Norfolk, Virginia.

As they went on board Mark was met by a man so small that his head came up only to Mark's chest. The man had a sneer on his face, and he kept one hand on the butt of a pistol and the other on the hilt of his sword. Mark could sense at once that his evilness more than made up for his lack of size.

"Captain Jason Roberts at your service, sir," the little man said. "Who might you be?"

"I am Mark Costain, of late captain of the armed merchant vessel *Sea Eagle*, now sunk. This is Kanole, one of my best men."

"Mark Costain?" Captain Roberts said. He rubbed his chin for a moment as if thinking. "Haven't I heard your name? Yes, and the Hawaiian, Kanole. I've heard his name, too."

Mark sighed. "I won't hide it from you, Captain. My friend and I were engaged in an unsuccessful undertaking, which now necessitates our leaving the islands for a while."

"I see," Captain Roberts said. "And you want to buy passage, is that it?"

"No, not exactly," Mark replied. "That is to say, we do want passage, but we want to work for it. I'm afraid we have no money."

"Work, you say?"

"Aye, Cap'n."

"You'll be wantin' an officer's berth, I expect," Captain Roberts said.

"I've sailed before the mast. I can do it again if need be," Mark said. He adjusted his legs easily to the rolling deck of the ship.

"Won't be necessary," Captain Roberts said. "I've heard of you. You're a damn good seaman from what they say. I could use a good man to help with this crew of wharf rats. I'll tell you what I'll do. I'll make your man Kanole an able-bodied seaman, and you can be my first mate."

"Hey, what the hell? What about me? You

ain't plannin' on makin' that son-of-a-bitch first mate o'er me?" a big man exploded angrily.

"I'm the captain of this ship, Pigg," Captain Roberts retorted. "And I'll make the appointments. Mr. Costain is my new first mate. You will be my second officer. Any more complaints and you'll be a deck hand."

The man named Pigg suddenly pulled a knife from the waistband of his trousers and tested the point with his finger.

"Ain't gonna be first mate iffen he is dead," Pigg taunted. "How 'bout it, Mr. Costain? You think you kin handle Big Pigg? Iffen you cain't, then you'd best start sayin' your prayers, 'cause ole Big Pigg is gonna cut yer heart out."

Mark stripped his shirt off quickly and wrapped it around his left forearm. A pelt of black hair stood out against his bare, muscled chest. His skin, bronzed by the sun, now glistened with a sheen of sweat from the tension. He held his arm, padded with his shirt, crooked in front of him, then automatically reached for the knife he carried in his waistband. It wasn't there, and he remembered then that he had lost it when the ship went down.

"I need a knife," he said calmly.

No one made an effort to help him except Kanole, who reached for the knife in the waistband of the sailor standing beside him.

"What you think you're doin'?" the sailor asked, putting his hand down to protect his knife. "Git yer hand away."

Kanole took the sailor's arm in his powerful

grip and forced the sailor to his knees. The sailor let out a surprised yelp of pain. Kanole reached with his other hand and easily slipped the knife out of the waistband, then flipped it toward Mark. It flashed once in the sun, then stabbed about one half inch into the planking on the ship's deck, quivering rapidly, making a tiny swishing sound as the handle moved back and forth.

Mark pulled it from the boards with a snap, and assumed a stance similar to Pigg's. He was crouched a little, right arm out, blade projecting from across the upturned palm between the thumb and index finger, with the point moving back and forth, slowly and hypnotically.

It was obvious that the fight would not last long. Both men were going to try for a quick kill. Neither wished to prolong it.

Pigg danced in, lightly for a heavy man, and raised his left hand toward Mark's face to mask his action. He feinted with his right, the knife hand, outside Mark's left arm as if he were going to go in over it. In the same movement, when Mark automatically raised his left arm to block, Pigg brought his knife hand back down so fast it was a blur, and he went in under Mark's arm.

The knife seared Mark's flesh like a branding iron along his ribs, and opened a long gash in the tight ridges of muscle. The cut began to spill bright red blood down his side and over the belt of his trousers. Mark brought his left hand down sharply, almost by reflex, and he knocked away the knife which Pigg was now holding with an air of careless confidence. He jabbed quickly with his right hand, sending the blade of his knife into Pigg's diaphragm, just under the ribs.

They stood that way for a few moments, Mark twisting the blade in the wound, trying to make certain his stab was fatal and struggling to stay on his feet in spite of the pain burning across his ribs. Pigg watched the world dim around him in surprise. Finally, he began to collapse, expelling a long, life-surrendering sigh as he did.

As he felt him going, Mark turned the knife, blade edge up, letting Pigg's body tear itself off by its own weight. He cut deeply along the ribs, disemboweling him. When Pigg hit the deck, he flopped once or twice like a large fish gaffed from the water, then lay still while the contents of his opened stomach stained the boards.

For several seconds, everyone remained quiet and still. Then Mark staggered back to the rail and leaned against it, breathing heavily. The fight had not been physically exhausting, it was over too fast. But it had totally drained him emotionally. He looked into Pigg's face. The eyes of the fallen seaman were open and unseeing, and still registered surprise. Pigg had not had time to know fear or to feel much pain.

"Mr. Costain," Captain Roberts said as calmly as if nothing had happened. "Please have the sailmaker prepare a shroud. I believe Pigg would prefer to be buried at sea. We will get underway in one hour."

"Aye, sir," Mark replied breathlessly. He felt along the cut in his side and tried to estmiate how serious it was. He examined the blood on his fingers.

"Mr. Costain, I'm the ship's surgeon, Doctor Quince, at your service, sir," a rather stout man of about fifty said. "If you'll come along with me, I'll have a look at that side."

"See to it here, Surgeon," Captain Roberts called from the quarterdeck. "We've no time for a leisurely tot of rum on the orlop."

"Aye, Cap'n," the surgeon answered easily. He examined the cut and probed at it, then began tearing strips of cloth into bandages. "Not much to it, lad. It'll be a mite sore, but that's all."

"Thanks, Surgeon," Mark said.

"Tinker," the surgeon said to a black youth of about fifteen who stood nearby, watching the examination. "Be a good lad and run to my cabin to fetch back a tot o' rum, will you?"

"Aye, Surgeon," Tinker answered, darting away.

The surgeon laughed. "You'll find the rum as good here as on the orlop deck. And I've a good deal to dispense. For medical purposes, of course."

"Of course," Mark said, smiling. "Tell me, Surgeon. How are you fixed for quinine?"

"Do you have the malaria chills and fevers?"

"Aye, on occasion. I had ample quinine on

board the *Sea Eagle,* but it lies at the bottom of the sea now."

"We've none aboard," the surgeon said. "None of our hands suffer from the disease. Perhaps we can raise a ship en route and get some from her. Where did you pick up the disease?"

"In Cuba, I'm afraid," Mark said.

"I'm sorry we don't have any," the surgeon said. "If you get an attack, you'll just have to weather the storm. Quinine doesn't do anything but help you through anyway. It doesn't cure the malady."

"That I know," Mark said. "But the chills and fevers, without quinine to help, can be pretty bad. I've known men to go out of their head."

"Right you are there, lad. But if you get an attack, we'll do what we can to ease you through it with the rum aboard. Speaking of rum, here's my boy with some now."

Tinker handed the jug to the surgeon, who put it on the deck beside him as he finished bandaging Mark's wound.

"Is Tinker your slave?" Mark asked curiously.

"That he is," the surgeon replied. "I won him in a poker game in Norfolk, thinkin' I would be doin' the lad a favor by givin' him his freedom. But he insisted on comin' with me. He's a smart lad, 'n' would make a good ship's surgeon some-day if you could get sailors to take their doc-torin' from a black. There you are, lad, all ship-shape," the surgeon said, finishing up.

"Thanks," Mark said.

"Just take a tot o' this to clear your mind," the surgeon said. He gave Mark one drink of rum, then took two for himself, closed up his bag and, with a smile, left Mark.

"Can you see to your business now, Mr. Costain?" Captain Roberts shouted.

"Aye, Cap'n," Mark answered.

He sent men aloft and walked around on deck to make ready to get underway. Suddenly a block and tackle pawl slipped from one of the uppermost arms and swung down from the end of a rope toward his head.

"Sir!" Tinker yelled, at the same time diving for Mark. "Look out!"

Tinker hit Mark just above the knees as the heavy pawl whistled by and crashed into the deck with a burst of splinters. Mark fell on his wound and cursed.

"Are you all right, sir?" Tinker asked, helping Mark to his feet.

Mark got up shakily, and, seeing the damage to the deck, he knew at once what had happened.

"Well, Tinker, I guess I owe you my life," Mark said. "I want to thank you."

"You, Tinker," Captain Roberts called before Tinker could answer, "come here."

"Aye, sir," Tinker said. He started toward the captain with the speed of someone who had been long at sea.

"You'll be getting five lashes for striking an officer," Captain Roberts said.

"Captain Roberts, sir," Mark said in total disbelief, "He saved my life!"

"I know that, Mister Costain, I saw it. That's why he's getting off so lightly."

"But you can't be serious, sir."

"Mr. Costain, you have much to learn about me, sir. I do not make jokes. And I will not let a man-jack of my crew go unpunished for striking an officer, regardless of the reason, though I am not without mercy. Thus the extenuating circumstances in this case dictate that I give him only five lashes for what is normally a much more severe penalty."

"But . . ." Mark started.

"It's all right, Mister Costain," Tinker said. "I'll take my due, sir."

Mark slammed his hand against the mast and walked away in disgust.

"Punishment will commence at four bells of the evening watch," Captain Roberts said.

Preparations continued to get the ship underway, and finally the time for departure arrived.

"Loose the topsails," Captain Roberts ordered, and Mark repeated the order in a loud voice.

The topsails filled, and the *Mary Luck* began to move.

"Loose the forecourse and the mainsail."

The canvas rose in the wind, and the ropes began singing through the blocks as the sheets filled. The *Mary Luck* heeled over to starboard, and with wind-puffed sails, began moving quickly across the bay, heading for open water.

A strong wind took hold of the ship and moved it through the water at a steady pace. But there was still an immense amount of business to be done, and Mark continued to stroll about the deck, looking up at the rigging. Every few minutes he would notice something undone, and he would send a seaman scurrying up the mast to crawl out on one of the arms to make some minor adjustment.

"Mr. Costain, lay a course of east by sou'east, sir," Captain Roberts ordered.

"Aye, sir," Mark replied.

Mark set the course, then with a sextant began estimating their exact position. He saw Tinker clearing the decks of the litter and he felt compelled to talk to him.

"I'm sorry about what happened," Mark said.

"The cap'n has a taste for the whip," Tinker replied. "If it hadn't been for this, it would have been for somethin' else. I'm glad it's only five lashes, 'n' not fifteen." His eyes lit on the sextant. "Mister Costain, are you good at navigation?"

"I sure am, lad," Mark answered. "I could chart a course to the stars if there were sea to sail." He held the instruments toward the sky, then with his hand made a ship sailing through the sky toward the stars.

"Would you teach me to navigate?

"Sure."

Captain Roberts strolled forward and stopped near them. He cleared his throat gruffly.

"Mister Costain, see to the watch, please. I make it three bells," he said, looking at his pocket watch.

"Aye, aye, three bells it is, sir," Mark said. He walked aft to the bell near the wheel and picked up a leather-covered clapper. He struck the small brass bell three times.

A large, red-bearded man came up on deck and began to erect a whipping-post.

"Who are you?" Mark asked.

The man looked at him through narrowed eyes. "The name's Bell, sir," he said. "I'm master o' the cat."

"Master of the cat? You mean the cat-o'-nine?"

"Aye."

"And that's your sole duty?"

"Aye."

"I've never heard of a crew with a fulltime flogger."

The red-haired man smiled. "Well, now you have, sir. The Cap'n 'n' Pigg like to run a tight ship. Oh, beggin' your pardon, sir, there ain't no more Pigg, bein' as how you done killed him. That'll take some gettin' used ter. Me 'n' ole Pigg, we pissed over a lot of rails together. He was my frien' 'n' gonna miss him."

"I'm sorry about your friend," Mark said. "I really didn't have a choice."

Bell laughed. "Pigg was like that. All us a'hollerin' 'n' carryin' on. I told him lak as not someone was goin' ter carve his stomach open one o' these days, and damn if that wasn't exactly

what happened. I guess I got 'em on that one,
I did."

All the time the master o' the cat was talking, he continued to work on the whipping-
post he was putting up.

"What are you doing?" Mark asked.

"Why, I'm riggin' up the tee for the whippin'
o' that nigger," he answered. "You heard the
cap'n assign the whippin'."

"I heard it," Mark said. "He's but a boy, Bell,
remember that."

"Mr. Costain, I knows but one way ter perform my duty, 'n' thet's the best I kin. Boy or
no, he's been assigned five lashes by the cap'n. I
aim ter see that them five lashes is well laid
on."

He produced his whip and began to straight-
en the lashes out on the deck with great care.

Mark's eyes flashed angrily, and he stepped
over to the rail to let the sea-spray cool him.

"Mister Costain, sir, don't feel bad," Tinker
said, stepping to his side.

Mark started to say something, but he knew
that in his present mood he would find it hard
to suppress his feelings about the captain's action, and for a second-in-command to speak
out against the captain was unpardonable.

The crew began to gather aft in quiet groups,
awaiting the flogging. There was a perverse
pleasure in watching another man flogged:
everyone was relieved not to be in Tinker's
place.

Shortly before six, Bell ordered Tinker to remove his cloak and shirt, and, stripped to the waist, step up to the whipping-post.

"Now put your arms up here, boy, so's I kin lash you down. Thas' ter keep you from squirmin' too much when the ole cat begins ter claw inter your back," Bell said with an evil chuckle.

Captain Roberts stepped up from his cabin then and pronounced the sentence. "Entered into the log of the *Mary Luck* on March 15, in the Year of our Lord, eighteen hunnert 'n' forty-three. This day the surgeon's slave boy, Tinker, was disciplined by the application of five lashes, well laid on. Said punishment as penalty for striking an officer. The unusually light sentence for striking an officer is because in so striking the officer, Tinker saved his life, it being in jeopardy at the time by a falling block and tackle. The author of this entry is Captain Jason Roberts."

Captain Roberts slammed the book shut and looked up. Mark stared into his eyes—he was enjoying it—and then he looked into the eyes of the others. Tinker's eyes, he noticed, were lit with terror, the surgeon's eyes with anger. Kanole's eyes reflected both anger and confusion; it was obvious he couldn't understand such senseless brutality.

But neither could Mark.

"Mr. Costain, kindly strike the bell for the watch, then toll the lashes," Captain Roberts ordered.

"I'm to toll the lashes, sir?"

"Yes," Captain Roberts replied.

Mark clanged the bell four times, then steeled himself to watch the flogging.

"Lay them on," he commanded. The ship's crew held their breaths as one man, and the cat whistled through the air and slashed across Tinker's back.

"One."

Tinker twisted violently in his harness, and let a cry escape from his lips. The severity of the blow surprised Mark, and his fist clenched by his side as he longed to step in and stop it.

Bell chuckled slightly, and brought the whip singing around for another slash, crisscrossing the welts which had already appeared on the youth's smooth back.

"Two."

A low murmur passed through the crew. They, too, were a little surprised by the severity of the flogging, and what had been almost a feeling of eager anticipation earlier was now replaced by a general embarrassment and a twinge of sympathy.

As the whip lashed across Tinker's body again, there was an exclamation, almost of pain, from the crew.

"Three."

After the third blow, Tinker's back was completely covered with welts. Because the whip's handle had nine knotted lashes, Tinker had received a total of twenty-seven lash marks on his back.

"Four."

As the whip fell across his back this time, many of the welts, which were badly puffed, split open and blood began to run down Tinker's back.

"Five. Cut him down," Mark ordered quickly, as Bell lashed Tinker harder than ever, opening up still more of his back.

Bell brought the whip back as if to swing it again, but Mark stepped in quickly and jerked it away from him.

"You son-of-a-bitch!" he yelled. "Didn't you hear me toll five?"

"I'm sorry," Bell said smoothly. "I lost count and didn't hear you."

Mark stood glowering at him, hoping that Bell would take offense and swing at him. But the burly man played it smart and just smiled.

"May I have the cat, Mister Costain?" he asked.

"Mr. Costain, sir," one of the seaman who had cut Tinker down said, "the boy's back is cut up pretty bad. What do you want done with him?"

Mark continued to glare at Bell, tempted to throw the whip overboard. Finally, he threw it at Bell's feet in disgust.

"Take the boy to my cabin," Mark ordered. "Surgeon, prepare the salve."

"That won't be necessary, Surgeon," Captain Roberts interrupted. "Bathe his back in saltwater. That is prescribed."

Captain Roberts then turned his back on them all and strolled about the deck, checking various fittings, as if he had completely put the incident out of his mind.

As several crew members picked Tinker up, he moaned with pain, and Mark ordered them to go easy with him. "Surgeon," he said as they were going down the ladderway and were out of hearing of the captain, "bring salt-water, but use your salve."

Doctor Quince pulled a small jar from his jacket pocket. "Aye, sir. I was goin' to."

Mark watched as the youth's back was treated.

"Tell me, Doctor Quince," Mark said quietly. "What sort of hell ship have I sailed with?"

Chapter Fifteen ─────────────

MARK SET THE midnight watch, then leaned over the quarterdeck rail to look at the night sea. It was his favorite time . . . a time when he could be alone with his thoughts.

The night air was clear and sharp, and the sea stretched to the horizon in gently rolling blue, textured by the foam which rose like a candle flame when a wave spilled over. In the water just below the ship hundreds of brilliant green streaks, phosphorescent fish, glowed like a city of lights.

During these late-night introspective moments, Mark would often trace the strange twists and turns his life had taken to lead him to this point in time. Here he was, on a tramp merchant ship, first officer to a diminutive but extraordinarily evil captain, sailing in the Pacific Ocean several thousand miles away from where he was born.

Mark was born in Baltimore. His father had been a naval officer serving with Captain James Lawrence of the *Chesapeake* when the dying Captain Lawrence issued the famous command, "Don't give up the ship." Mark's father held Captain Lawrence's head in his lap as the captain died, then, moment later, Mark's father was killed himself.

Mark was but a year old then, but his mother kept the memory of her husband alive in her son, and that memory destined him to become a naval officer.

Then came the dishonor.

He had one consolation. His mother had died six months before he was cashiered from the Navy, and thus didn't have to live with his shame.

He had drifted since then, taking little interest in anything, and believing in nothing. He had no ambition, no hopes or dreams. He felt like a wave, rolling relentlessly to shore, only to burst and be wasted and uncounted at the end of the journey.

But now his indifference had been shaken. Since the aborted revolution, there had been a haunting presence in his mind, an unbidden memory which plagued him and disrupted the uneasy peace he had attained.

It was the memory of a woman.

Although life had lost any meaning for him, his sexual appetite had not been dulled. He consumed women the way fire burns up dry timber. They were the means of achieving physical release. A temporary release, to be sure, because the last woman was never re-membered, and the next woman was not yet known.

Until the one called Leilani.

There was something extraordinary about her. Something which had taken root in his mind, and awakened feelings he had thought were impossible.

Leilani. Somehow, some way, he knew that he must see her again.

Mark looked out to where the rolling sea seemed to meet the sky. He could almost see her face just over the horizon, waiting for him.

Chapter Sixteen

LEILANI SAT ON a stone atop the tallest mountain of her island and looked at the stars. Her days here had been a time of solitude and meditation. She had heard no human voice except her own.

It had been a time in which Leilani managed to still the aching in her heart and the doubts in her mind about who and what she was. In that quiet contemplation, a measure of contentment came to her.

There was much beauty to enjoy on the island, and Leilani, whose training as an Alii-Nui had taught her to use all her senses, appreciated all that was around her.

Though the bright colors of the flowers were now muted by the darkness, the diamond brilliance of the stars, the shimmering iridescence of the sea, the moon-silvered highlights of the rocky hills and the beach set her eyes dancing

161

with colors. She was serenaded by a symphony
—the wind blowing through the reed grass,
the pulsing rhythm of the surf, the delicate song
of the nightbirds. And all about her floated
the fragrance of the flowers' perfume as silken,
softly blowing breezes caressed her skin. As
she drank the sweet nectar of one of the island's
fruits from a cup she had fashioned, she sat in
majesty over the world which was hers to enjoy.

There was a spiritual and physical contentment which was complete and soul-satisfying.

But something was missing. Far down, in the
most secret recesses of her heart, there was a
longing, an unfulfilled need, which tugged at
the edge of her being and increasingly called
to her.

So Leilani meditated. She turned her powers
of concentration inward, examining all that was
her, to find the seed of discontent which was
growing from within.

What was it she wanted? What more could
she possibly need in this paradise?

And the answer came to her. At first it was
small and quiet, no more than a timid cry from
somewhere deep inside her.

Love.

When the word first surfaced, she discarded
it the way a person, while looking through a
drawer for a pair of gloves, will sometimes dis-
card an unneeded scarf.

But again, love.

Still, it made no impact on Leilani. Love was
something which thus far had held only phys-

ical connotations. Making love meant the art of sex, or sexual fulfillment and physical gratification. But she had not even known that to its fullest, until she had been taken by the passionate ship's captain.

She remembered that experience in vivid detail and even the memory of it sent a tremble of ecstacy through her body.

Love.

Love?

Not sex, love. The love one person feels for another. The love a woman can know for a man when thought and reason are set aside and pure, unrestrained truth can surface. Love is the knowledge that a man isn't enjoyed because of the sex, but sex is enjoyed because of the man.

No—she couldn't be in love with him. Hadn't he taken her by force? Wasn't he responsible for the revolution? But despite Leilani's carefully reasoned arguments to herself, the one recurring thought moving to the surface was still —love.

And once Leilani accepted it, quit trying to force it back, her heart began to spill the information as if it had been bottled up for too long. The man she loved, the person to whom her heart wished to give itself, was the *haole* Mark Costain.

"I love Mark Costain," she said. Her words, though the only human sounds on the island, blended with the harmony of the island's sounds. The music of her voice was part of the nature of things.

Leilani thought again of Mark Costain. She pictured him as he came to the orlop deck to make his choice among the girls there, still flushed with his victory in battle. He was a man who was confident of his abilities, and aware of his masculine appeal.

Perhaps he had been a bit too sure of himself, she thought. But he had some justification for his self-assurance, for even as she fought against him, she had been betrayed by her own passions, passions which had been unlocked by Mark as he played on the erotic chords of her body with the skill of a master. Despite her resistance she had responded to his sure touch, had given under his insistent persuasion, his powerful magnetism. And even though she had won the battle of wills when he came to her the second time, Leilani knew that she had succumbed to her own passionate awakening as well.

Later, as she had stood near the powder locker ready to destroy his ship, she felt the same strong attraction to him. While the others on board had cringed in fear or shouted in anger, only he had maintained a cool sense with an easy acceptance of the things which he could not change. She saw the expression on his face just before she set off the explosion and read in it curiosity more than fear, admiration more than anger.

For one fleeting instant, she had felt a powerful tugging at her heart which almost caused her to abandon her plan to destroy the ship. But she had fought against it with more success than she had fought against him while they were making love, and with a painful effort of will, she had thrown the burning brand into the powder locker.

She remembered how he had appeared in her hallucinations as she nearly drowned in the sea. He had made a profound impression upon her, and had burned himself indelibly into her memory.

Now, it appeared, he had burned himself into her heart as well.

Chapter Seventeen─────────────────

THE SAILORS WHO came to Lahaina and wanted the services of a girl visited the Customs House. There, in addition to the official business being carried on for the government of King Kamahamaha III, unofficial and much more profitable business was being carried on by the crooked servants of Governor Kekuanna.

Calvin was too frightened to go in through the front door so he went around the back, and waited in the store room. An old woman saw him and asked him what he wanted. He asked to speak with one of the customs officials.

"What do you want, *haole*, that you cannot come through the front as does everyone else?" the customs official asked.

Calvin cleared his throat. "I—I would like a girl," he said. His cheeks flamed red with embarrassment, and his heart beat madly.

The official, a big Hawaiian laughed. "You

don't have to come through the back door for that. The governor knows what we do."

"But I don't want anyone to know I am here," Calvin explained.

The Hawaiian smiled and rubbed his chin with his hand. "Who are you? Do I know you?"

"No," Calvin said quickly. He certainly didn't want it known that he was the son of the missionary. "I'm a sailor from one of the ships," he said. "But I don't want my captain to know I'm here."

"Special service will cost you extra."

"I will pay."

"And you must take the girl I choose."

"That will be fine."

"You have money now?"

"Yes."

The big Hawaiian took Calvin's money and disappeared up front. After a short time, during which Calvin paced around nervously, the tapa curtain was pulled to one side and a woman came through.

"Are you the one who wishes to make love?" the woman asked.

Calvin was a little startled. He had expected a young girl, like the young, lithe animals of the village who paraded their nude bodies before him shamelessly. But the woman standing here was old, nearly as old as his mother.

"I, uh, thought I would get a girl," he said.

The woman laughed. "What do you think I am, a man?"

"No, but . . ."

The woman interrupted him. "Come with me, young one. You will enjoy what I will do for you. A young one like you, you need an older woman to guide you in the art of making love."

Calvin followed the woman out the back door and through a narrow, twisting street which led out of Lahaina. The street turned into a path which climbed halfway up a mountain, then ended at a small clearing where there was a lone grass house. There were no other people around.

"Kahaula said you did not want to be seen," the woman said. "Here there is no one."

The woman slipped out of her muumuu, and Calvin watched. Her body was not trim and athletic like the young girls, but it was fuller and more sensual, and Calvin felt the first stirrings of lust beginning to grow inside him.

The woman undressed Calvin, then pulled him gently but firmly to her.

"You will like," she said again. "You will see. I will make you like."

She led Calvin to a sleeping mat, then lay back and pulled him down over her. By now Calvin's need was great, and he forgot about her age. He attacked her savagely, responding to the terrible hunger which had nearly driven him out of his mind.

The woman, who was accustomed to sailors releasing several months of pent-up sexual energy with her, responded eagerly. She raised her legs and welcomed Calvin's savage thrusts. Their bodies rocked against each other, and their breath came in labored gasps.

A climax finally arrived for Calvin, but even as he felt the terrible sexual pressure spurting from him, the spiritual pressure remained, and Calvin knew that atonement for his sin would be necessary before he could experience total relief.

When Calvin was sexually satisfied he lay quietly for a moment or two, praying for guidance in bringing this lost soul to the Lord. Finally he got up and turned his back to dress. He gave the woman what he considered a reasonable length of time to cover herself, then he turned around.

She was still nude.

"Why do you allow me to gaze on your nakedness?" Calvin asked. "Don't you realize that in so doing you are an abomination before the Lord?"

"What?" the woman asked, surprised by the sudden change in the strange young *haole*.

"You have sinned," Calvin said. "And you will burn in the fires of eternal hell." He pointed an accusing finger at her.

"*Haole*, you are *pupule*," the woman said. "How do you say *pupule*? Yes, crazy. You are a crazy one. I do not like to be near crazy people."

"Kneel before me," Calvin said, paying no attention to her remarks. "Get down on your knees, you miserable sinner, and confess your sins before Almighty God. Beg Him for His forgiveness. If you do this, I will grant you salvation."

"You go away now," the woman said. "I don't like it when you talk like that. You leave me now." She was angry.

"No, wait," Calvin said. "We will pray together. We will ask the Lord to forgive you for your sins. He will listen to me. I am His chosen messenger."

"You go now!" she said angrily. She picked up a stick and held it menacingly.

Calvin was confused. This wasn't going as he had planned. The woman should have fallen to her knees before him and begged for forgiveness. He couldn't send her to the Lord as a sinner. His job was to save souls for the Lord, not condemn them to hell. If he killed this woman now, she would die an unsaved sinner.

"But you don't understand," Calvin said, almost desperately. "You have to ask for forgiveness, don't you see? You must repent before I can save you." He wrung his hands helplessly.

The woman swung the stick at him, making a swishing sound just over his head. "Get out," she said angrily. "Get out before I break your head."

"I'm going, I'm going," Calvin said, backing fearfully across the dirt floor toward the doorway. He tried once more before leaving.

"Please," he begged. "Please, let me save your soul."

"Get out of here!" she shouted, throwing the stick. It hit the wall just beside him, peppering his face with sand and splinters.

He turned and ran from the house. His mind was in a turmoil. He was confused and didn't know what to do next. He had sinned! He had fornicated with a whore, but failed to win her soul. That left him uncleansed of the act, for only if he had won a soul and sent her to heaven could his fornication be considered sanctified. Without that, fornication was certainly a sin.

Calvin wandered through the streets of Lahaina and down to the waterfront. He walked aimlessly by the docks, along the row of warehouses. He was in terrible despair over his own salvation. He could not atone for his sin without sending the woman to the Lord. And he could not send her to the Lord if she would not ask forgiveness.

" 'Scuse me, mate, but you look like a fine, Christian lad. Could you spare an old sailor a mite for somethin' ter drink? Jes' ter ward away the chills you un'nerstan'. I've no wish fer it fer the drunkenness of it."

The speaker was an old wreck of a man. He had stepped out of the shadows of a warehouse and now tugged at Calvin's sleeve. His clothes were rags, and his face and hands were marked with the disease the Hawaiians called the Sailor's Pox.

"What do you want?" Calvin asked.

"Bless you kindly, lad," the old man said. "I'm

an old seafarin' man, but I've grown sick and can no longer get a berth. I can't even work my passage home to where my lovin' family could care for me. I'm to die in this place. 'N I was askin' you out of the kindness of yer heart, to take pity on an old sailor."

Calvin looked around. The hour was growing late and he was in a quiet part of town, near the most remote area of the warehouses. He smiled at the old man.

"Perhaps I can help," he said.

"Bless you lad!" the old sailor exclaimed happily.

"But you must do something for me."

"What is it you wish, lad? I'll do anythin' you ask."

"You must get on your knees and pray for forgiveness for your many sins."

"I'll do that for you, lad. In a jiffy I will." The sailor started to kneel.

"No," Calvin said. "Over here, in this alley. This is something which requires only you, me, and the Lord."

"Right you are," the old sailor said, limping quickly, happily, into the alley. He knelt beside a stack of boxes. "How's this, lad?"

"Fine, fine," Calvin said.

Calvin saw a small crow bar on one of the boxes. It was used for prying open the lids of crates and probably had been left there by the dock workers at the close of the day. Calvin picked it up and held it behind his back.

"I'm on my knees now, lad," the old sailor said, looking up.

"Now," Calvin said, "Close your eyes and pray with me." Calvin put his left hand on the sailor's head. His right he held behind him with his fingers wrapped securely around the crowbar.

"Oh, Lord, as your messenger, I have found another soul for you. It was not the person I expected, but then you work in mysterious ways, your wonders to perform." Calvin looked down at the sailor. "Do you ask for forgiveness for your sins?"

"Oh, I do, lad," the old sailor said.

"And do you want to be saved from the burning fires of hell?"

"Oh, I do, I do."

"Then I shall send you to heaven," Calvin said.

The sailor looked up in question just as Calvin came smashing down with the cow bar. The old man's eyes showed only an instant's fear before the blow took his life.

Calvin placed the crowbar carefully back on the crates, then brushed his hands together to rid himself of the sailor's sinful contamination, and walked back to his quarters.

He felt relieved. Although he had committed the sin of fornication and not paid for that sin with the soul of the fornicator, he had balanced the scales by sending to the Lord the soul of another sinner. It all evened out, he was certain. Fornication had to be paid for with a soul, but it didn't really matter whose soul it was. As long as it was the soul of a sinner he had saved.

Chapter Eighteen

By THE TIME the *Mary Luck* had been at sea a week, seven men had gone to the whipping post. In fact, the whippings were ordered with such regularity that the post was left in place, both to save the time of erecting it, and to serve as a reminder to the crew that the cat-o'-nine was always available. This, Captain Roberts believed, would ensure the strictest discipline.

It was not a fact of which he was particularly proud, but Mark Costain had been indirectly responsible for two whippings. The first was the youth, Tinker. The second was a seaman named Lacey.

Mark had asked Lacey to move a coil of rope. A few minutes later, with the coil of rope still not moved, Mark asked Lacey again, reminding him that this was his second request.

Captain Roberts had overheard Mark's reminder and had had Lacey whipped for failure to obey an officer. Mark protested in vain, then stood at the ship's rail in shame as the whipping was administered.

Mark realized that he and Captain Roberts were on a collision course. It was just a matter of time until the showdown came, and then Mark had no idea what would happen.

He soon found out.

Bell, the master of the cat-o'-nine, saw Tinker practising navigation with the ship's sextant. Though Mark had given Tinker permission to use the instrument, Bell began yelling at Tinker and hitting the youth with his whip. Kanole, who was nearby, stepped in and decked Bell with one well placed punch.

Bell was technically a ship's officer, so Captain Roberts ordered Kanole to be given six dozen lashes immediately.

"No, sir, I will not carry out that order," Mark said, realizing, even as he spoke, that he had just crossed the line.

"You refuse me, Mister?" Captain Roberts asked in surprise.

"Yes," Mark said. "Kanole was correct in preventing abuse of the boy."

"You two men," Captain Roberts said, pointing to a couple of seamen who stood watching fearfully, "tie Mr. Costain up. He is relieved of duty."

The two men hesitated for an instant.

"Is this mutiny?" Captain Roberts asked.

"We're not mutineers, sir," said Lacey, who

was one of the two men. "But we just don't think we should do what you say."

Captain Roberts pulled a double-barreled pistol from his belt. There was an explosion, an orange flash, and a puff of smoke. Lacey reeled over backward with a pistol ball in his brain, and blood streaming from a gruesome black hole in his forehead.

"I have another barrel," Captain Roberts said. "Who else thinks not to obey me?"

For just a moment, Mark entertained hopes of a rebellion . . . a full-scale mutiny which would overthrow this tyrant.

"I'm with you, Cap'n," a big seaman said. The seaman was a friend of Bell's, and, Mark knew, of Pigg's as well.

"Me, too," another said. This was the sailor from whom Kanole had taken the knife when Mark fought Pigg.

"Good," Captain Roberts said. "You two men are promoted to petty officer rank. Now, tie this mutineer to the mast. I want him to witness his friend's punishment."

The support of the two sailors overcame all indecision, and Mark realized that any possibility of a rebellion was over. Captain Roberts was as firmly in control as ever.

Bell administered the whipping with particular relish, but, through it all, Kanole managed to maintain a strength and dignity, even though his back was bleeding when the final blows fell. Mark felt very proud of his friend.

Kanole had won the battle of will, and it was thrilling to see the big Hawaiian walk away from the whipping under his own power, while Bell, exhausted after administering the seventy-two lashes, could only lean against the rail and wheeze for breath.

The brig in the forward hold was dark and damp, and it smelled of foul bilgewater. Once, during the night, Mark felt something moving on his legs, and he raised up quickly to see a rat scurrying across the deck and into the 'tween spaces of the bulkhead. The sight caused his flesh to crawl, and he shivered involuntarily.

"Alii-Nui, Alii-Nui, Alii-Nui," Kanole said, leaning forward to put his forehead to the deck.

"What do you mean—Alii-Nui?" Mark asked.

"The spirit of the Alii-Nui was in that rat," Kanole said. "I know this. She has returned from the grave to punish me."

"Nonsense."

"It is true."

"Kanole, you don't really believe that," Mark said. "You can't believe that."

"I do believe that."

"How did she get here?"

"She came as a dolphin," Kanole said. "Most often she takes the form of a dolphin. Sometimes she takes other forms. Such as the girl who destroyed your ship."

"You mean the girl who destroyed the ship wasn't a real girl?" Mark asked.

"She was the Alii-Nui. She was the spirit of the Alii-Nui. She wasn't real."

"Kanoli, that was a real girl," Mark said. "Believe me, she was more real than aynone I have ever known."

"You say this because you made love with her?" Kanole asked.

"Well, yes," Mark agreed.

"The Alii-Nui are very skilled with sex. As a spirit, she would still have the same skill."

"I don't believe that," Mark said. "I'm not exactly inexperienced in these things. I've known many other women. But never have I known a woman like Leilani."

"It is because she is not a woman," Kanole insisted. "It was the spirit of Leilani in a woman's body. Just as she is sometimes in a dolphin's body, and now is in that rat."

Mark laughed bitterly. "Well, if she can come to the ship in any form as you say she can, I'd a hell of a lot rather see her as she was before than as a rat."

"Mr. Costain," a voice suddenly hissed from outside the brig.

"Yes?" Mark answered. "Who is it?"

"It's me, Tinker. I have the keys to the brig."

"Tinker, you shouldn't have taken a chance like that," Mark hissed. "If you are discovered, they'll hang you."

"They won't discover me, Mr. Costain. I'm leaving with you."

"Leaving?"

There was a rattling noise as the door swung

open. "Yes, sir," Tinker said. "We're goin' over the side in a boat. The four of us. You, Kanole, the surgeon and me."

"Good lad," Mark said. "Kanole, how do you feel? Can you make it?"

"Yes," Kanole said.

"The surgeon has loaded the launch," Tinker said. "He has ten pounds of bread, twenty gallons of water, and a half gallon of rum. I have hooks and line for fishing."

"Good, good," Mark said. "Does the surgeon have a watch?"

"No," Tinker said.

"We need a watch."

"Why?"

"If we can set the watch to the ship's clock, then we can find our longitude no matter where we are. It is not difficult to make a cross-staff, and with that I can find our latitude. We'll need that in order to navigate across the open water."

"The captain is the only one on board who has a watch," Tinker said. "It stays on his desk in the great cabin when he's sleeping. I've seen it there when I've gone to awaken him. I'll get it."

"No, I won't let you risk that," Mark said. "I'll do it. That way I can set it to the ship's clock and take a look at the chart at the same time. I need to fix the positions of the nearest islands in my mind."

"What can I do?" Tinker asked.

"You and Kanole get topside to the launch. Stay with the surgeon. If anyone sees that the launch has been loaded, they'll know our plans. I'll meet you there."

"Aye, sir," Tinker said.

"Oh, and Kanole, you'll have to take care of the deck watch before we put the launch over. It's so heavy that we'll have to lower it with the windlass, and if any of them come near the aft davits, they are likely to see what's going on."

"The deck watch will not see us," Kanole promised.

"How blows the wind?" Mark asked.

"Sou' so'east," Tinker said.

"Then we'll launch to the starboard. That way if we're seen, the ship'll not answer the helm as quickly. Now, get to it."

Tinker and Kanole climbed the ladderway, and Mark slipped into the captain's cabin. He eased the door open and stepped quietly inside, scarcely daring to breathe.

The lantern hanging overhead was unlit, but since Roberts had left all the hatches open to take advantage of the breeze, inside the cabin was quite bright with moonlight.

Roberts was snoring loudly, but it was reassuring to Mark, because if the snoring stopped suddenly, it could serve as a warning to him. Mark rummaged around the desk until he found the captain's timepiece. He held it to his ear and heard the satisfying sound of ticking, then adjusted it to the ship's clock and dropped it in his pocket. After that he looked at the chart, fixing the position of all the islands in his mind, searching for the closest landfall.

As he leaned across the table, he knocked over Roberts' mug, and it fell to the floor with a loud clang.

"What's that?" Roberts called out. "Who's there?"

Mark's heart leaped, and he slid under the table as quickly as he could, trying to stay motionless.

Roberts sat up, looked around his cabin, then stretched to look out the porthole, which was open over his bunk.

"Must be the swell," he mumbled, then lay down on his bunk again.

Mark stayed in the same position for several anxious moments, until he heard Roberts resume his snoring. He then slipped out from under the table and hurried up the ladder to the deck.

"Any trouble?" the surgeon asked.

"No, not really," Mark answered. He looked around. "Where's the deck watch?"

"They sleep," Kanole said, smiling broadly. "And the helm is lashed."

"Then let's get this thing swung over," Mark said as he began to loosen the latches on the windlass.

With one or two revolutions of the windlass, they knew they were going to have some trouble. The ratchet snapped against the beveled gear every time a tooth passed, and the noise was frighteningly loud.

"They will hear us below decks," the surgeon whispered.

"I can hold the ratchet off," Mark said. "But you'll have the entire weight of the launch on you then. Do you think you can lower it slowly enough?"

"I think we can," the surgeon said.

Kanole flexed his muscles, then grabbed hold of the windlass. He looked at Mark and nodded his head.

Mark held back on the ratchet. The mechanical advantage of the gear was gone, and the entire weight fell against Kanole, the surgeon, and Tinker. The surgeon and Tinker didn't realize how heavy the boat actually was, and they lost their grip. That threw additional weight on Kanole, and the windlass jumped out of his hand, spinning wildly. The rope went singing down as the boat fell toward the water.

Mark almost yelled when he saw the windlass start to spool. But Kanole grabbed the rope with his bare hands. The rope slid through the big man's fingers for a couple of feet, then his hands closed like a vice and the boat stopped falling, just inches away from the water. Kanole lowered it the rest of the way, and it kissed the surface so quietly that Mark couldn't hear the splash.

"Good job, Kanole," Mark said. "Now, get the touch holes on this side, and I'll get them on the larboard."

The touch holes were the holes in the breaches of the cannons by which they were fired. Jamming a piece of wood into each one would leave the guns useless until the wood was cleared out, and by that time Mark hoped they would be out of range. There were only eight guns, four on each side, and Mark and Kanole soon had them taken care of.

"Now," Mark said, "into the boat."

He waited until the other three had climbed down, then he started to go over the rail. At that moment, someone put a hand on his shoulder.

"What are you doing up here?" Bell asked.

The sudden appearance of Bell startled him, but he was able to throw a quick jab into Bell's stomach before the new first officer could react. The punch knocked the breath out of Bell and gave Mark time to dive over the rail.

"Pull away!" Mark yelled, just as he went over the side.

When he surfaced, he saw the boat drifting toward the stern of the *Mary Luck*, and he heard shouting and commotion from the *Mary Luck*'s deck.

"Mr. Costain, swim this way!" Tinker shouted.

Mark started toward the boat, and he saw Kanole standing up by the *Mary Luck*'s rudder post. Kanole swung an axe, and in two heavy blows, cut the rudder post. Now the ship would be unable to maneuver until lengthy repairs were made.

Rifle fire erupted from the deck above and Mark saw the surgeon pitch out of the boat. Tinker yelled and stood up, and he, too, was cut down, falling into the sea with a splash. Mark made it to the edge of the boat, and Kanole reached down and pulled him up as easily as if he had been a child. At that moment, Mark heard the angry buzz of a rifle ball as it snapped passed his ear, and the hollow thump as it dug into Kanole's chest.

"We must go now," Kanole said, as if nothing had happened.

"Kanole, were you hit?"

"It is nothing," Kanole said.

"What about the others?"

Mark looked into the water. Tinker was floating away, head down, arms and legs extended. There was a flurry of white water near the surgeon's body, then a spreading pool of blood. Mark looked away quickly as he realized that sharks had hit Doctor Quince.

"Thank God, they're both dead already," Mark said.

"We must go now," Kanole said. They both began to work the boat, and between the two of them, they were quickly able to widen the distance between them and the *Mary Luck.*

Thanks to the severed rudder post, the ship could not come about. And her set sail, even trimmed, helped to make the distance between the two vessels even wider. Within a very short time, they were out of range of the sailors' rifle fire. And within an hour, darkness had completely swallowed up the ship.

"We made it," Mark said happily. He suddenly sobered as he thought of the surgeon and Tinker. "At least two of us made it."

"No," Kanole said. "One made it."

"What?"

"I will die soon."

"Die? No, you aren't going to die. You can't die."

"The bullet has gone too deep," Kanole said. "I cannot fight off death."

"Yes, you can," Mark said. "Hang on, friend. We'll both make it. We'll fight it together."

"I will try, but I do not think I can win," Kanole said. He began coughing, and as he coughed, Mark could see the wound in his chest was sucking air, making bubbles in the blood. "I will try and sleep now," Kanole said.

"Yes," Mark agreed. "Sleep. It will be good for you."

Mark looked at the big Hawaiian for a few moments, until the rasping, but regular breathing told him that Kanole was asleep. He wished that Tinker and the surgeon had made it with them. Not only for their sakes, but because the surgeon might have been able to help Kanole.

Mark raised the lugsail and looked at the sky. He took up a course of north, north-west by the stars, and started back for the Hawaiian Islands. That was the closest land according to the charts. So whether he wanted to go there or not, he really had no choice.

"Leilani," he said softly. "I am coming back to the islands, and I am going to find you. And when I do, I'm going to see what there is about you which haunts me so."

Chapter Nineteen ————————

THE TINY BOAT carrying Mark and Kanole moved through the night and into the next morning propelled by the lugsail. The sunrise was magnificent and spilled colors from the sky in every conceivable shade. When the sun was high, the sea was calm, and it was as if they were but a small dot on the surface of a great, polished, silver mirror.

Mark tried to calculate their position when the sun rose, but to his dismay, he found that the watch which he had obtained at such risk was now worthless. It had been ruined when he dived into the water. Other than dead reckoning from the direction of the stars he followed the night before, helped by his knowledge of where they were when they left the ship, Mark had no way of determining where they were now.

Being adrift without navigating means wasn't Mark's only problem. During the night, he had felt the first faint symptoms of a malaria attack. His skin had become tingly and the joints in his arms and legs ached. He also felt light-headed. Generally these were sure signs that a malaria attack was imminent. These sensations would be followed some hours later by chills. The chills would last for up to twenty-four hours, coming in waves, then a few hours later the fever would come. The fever was by far the worst part of the attack, because during it, he frequently lost all awareness, becoming delirious with the high temperature.

Of course, it might not be a malaria attack coming on at all. It could just be soreness and exhaustion from the efforts of the night before. At least, that was what Mark hoped.

Kanole groaned and Mark lashed the tiller, then moved over to see to him.

"How do you feel?" Mark asked.

"I feel pain," Kanole answered.

"Here," Mark offered, handing the jug of rum to him. "Drink some of the rum. It may help to dull the pain a little."

"Thank you," Kanole said. He turned the jug up and took several long, bobbing swallows, then set the jug back down and wiped his mouth with the back of his hand. He looked around, holding his hand over his eyes to shield them from the glare of the sea.

"Here," Mark said. "Have some breakfast."

He offered Kanole a piece of bread, but Kanole refused it. Mark looked at the bread. He knew that he should eat, but he felt no hunger. That was another sign of a malaria attack, he knew. So, in order to lie to himself, to try and convince himself that the malaria attack wasn't coming, he forced himself to eat the unappetising piece of bread.

He leaned back in the boat and put his hand on the tiller. He had no real way of navigating, other than estimating the time by the sun's position. He put a stake on the bow, used the shadow to estimate the cardinal points, and, as near as possible, held a west, northwest heading.

Kanole slept through most of the rest of that day, and that night. By the next day, he seemed a little better. Still, Mark knew that the bullet would have to come out if Kanole were to have any chance.

"Do you want to eat today?" Mark asked.

"No," Kanole said.

"You must eat."

"No. I will soon die. I should not waste the food you can use."

"Don't give up yet," Mark said. He had made several scratch marks on the board beside him, and he looked down at them. "According to my best guess, we're about a thousand miles from the Hawaiian Islands. And we're making about three knots. If we can hold this, we should reach Hawaii in about twelve or thirteen days."

"There is an island there," Kanole said, pointing just over the larboard bow. "It is only twenty miles from here. We will see it today."

"What?"

"We are close to an island," Kanole repeated. "No more than twenty miles."

"An island twenty miles from here? No, you are mistaken, Kanole. There are no islands charted near here."

"I can see this island in the sea," Kanole insisted. He looked at the water. "It is small. We must land there, my friend. You should not be at sea when the fevers come."

Mark had not mentioned the chills to Kanole, and he was surprised that Kanole knew the attack was coming.

"You know about the fever?"

"Yes," Kanole said. "So you see, you must land at the island."

"Kanole, I'm very sorry," Mark explained patiently. "But there are no islands near here. I examined the charts very carefully."

"We must land there," Kanole said again, as if he didn't hear Mark. "I will sleep now. When I wake, the island will be in sight."

Kanole lay back and, within a few moments he was asleep. Mark realized sadly that Kanole would not survive the voyage. He was very sorry about that, because he had come to admire Kanole more than any man he had ever known.

In fact, as Mark thought about it, he realized that his own survival was uncertain. Although the fever had not yet begun, the first shivers of a chill were already upon him. Within twenty-four hours, he would be burning up with a temperature so high that he would be com-

pletely out of his head. During that time, he
realized, the boat could drift anywhere. As long
as he could remain clear-headed, he could
estimate their positioning by dead reckoning.
But a prolonged bout of unconsciousness could
have fatal consequences. When he came to, if
he came to, he would have no idea where he
was. If that happened to him, he hoped he
would have enough courage to roll over into
the sea.

At about two o'clock that afternoon, Mark
saw it. It was a pale, purple line on the horizon,
shimmering and wavering under the sunlight.
At first he thought it was a mirage, brought on
by the light-headedness which accompanied the
chill of his malaria attack. But the dizziness was
coming and going, and as he shook his head
clear, he saw the island sharply, and knew that
it wasn't merely an apparition. It was really
there!

"I'll be damned," he said aloud. "That's impossible."

"You've seen the island?" Kanole asked from
the bottom of the boat. He neither raised up nor
opened his eyes.

"Yes," Mark said. "But how can this be? There
is no island charted here. I know that for a fact,
Kanole."

"The *haole* charts are wrong," Kanole said.

"You mean the Hawaiians have it charted?"
Mark asked.

"Yes," Kanole said. "In the sea."

"I don't know what you mean."

Kanole pulled himself up and pointed to the surface of the ocean. "Can you not see the picture of this island in the sea?"

Mark looked at Kanole as if he had lost his mind. He laughed uncertainly, then shook his head. "No," he said. "No, I'm afraid not."

"Look at the waves," Kanole said. "As they flow back from the island, they ripple in the shape of the island."

"I'm sorry, I see nothing," Mark said. "But tell me, does this island of yours have water?"

"This I do not know," Kanole said.

"Have you ever been to it?"

"No."

"Ah, I see. But you know someone who has?"

"No."

"Then how did you know it was there?"

Kanole started to explain the picture in the sea again, then he gave a rather exasperated sigh and lay back down in the boat. "Mark Costain, how did the *haole* ever invent such magnificent things as cannon and writing when they understand nothing?"

Mark laughed. "I don't know, Kanole. Perhaps I understand less than others."

"No," Kanole said. "All *haole* understand nothing."

Kanole slept again as Mark steered the launch for the island. As he approached it he saw that Kanole was right in describing the size of it. It was small, with a low-lying ride of mountains, and two prominent hills at one end. And he noticed with gratitude, there didn't seem to be any reefs with which to contend.

He wondered if anyone lived there. It was unlikely, for it was as remote as the moon.

Chapter Twenty

LEILANI WATCHED THE strange boat approach her island. Who was it? It certainly wasn't a craft from her people, it was much too large, and it didn't use the same sail rigging. But it was too small for a *haole* craft. *Haoles*, Leilani knew, went to sea in large ships. None would dare venture this far in such a small boat. Unless, of course, they were the survivors of a shipwreck.

She decided to play safe. Until she found out more about the people coming ashore, she wouldn't let them know she was here. She hurried, running to the site of each fire she had built since coming to the island, and erased all their traces. She had not constructed an elaborate shelter for herself, but she took down what she had built and swept the area clean. She would leave no sign of her presence for the people on the boat to find.

When she was satisfied, she returned to watch

the boat. It was being expertly handled through the breakers—not with the surf-boarding finesse of an island outrigger, but rather with the dogged determination of a skilled seaman. It plugged solidly through the remaining waves, then coasted into shallow water. A man leaped out and pulled it ashore.

Leilani suddenly felt a surge of joy when she saw who it was. The *haole* Mark Costain!

He has come for me, she thought impulsively, and she was tempted to run down to the beach to greet him.

Then caution returned. How could he have come for her? He had no idea where she was. And he couldn't possibly know of her love for him. Her own realization of it was the result of many days of meditation, the essence of the mixed feelings which coursed through her during her time alone. Mark Costain would not yet be aware of this so why would he come for her?

She watched him lean over the boat and help someone out. She recognized Kanole. He was a distant cousin whom she knew slightly. He had also participated in the revolution, and perhaps in the raid on her village. Though she knew that Kanole must be at least partially responsible for her mother's death, she had no wish to seek revenge. Besides, revenge wasn't necessary. Kanole was dying, Leilani realized. She sensed that he would not survive the night.

Leilani watched for several moments, then stood and walked down to them, her heart pounding wildly the closer she came.

Kanole was dozing and Mark had his back to her. She stood within a few feet of them for a few moments, just watching. Finally she spoke.

"I am glad you have come."

"My God!" Mark said with an astonished look. "Where . . . where did you come from?"

"I came from the sea," Leilani answered. She wasn't trying to be mysterious, she was just stating a fact.

Kanole opened his eyes and smiled. He showed no surprise at seeing her there.

"Have you come to forgive me, Alii-Nui?" he asked.

"You have done a cruel thing," Leilani said. "Innocent people died because of you."

"I did not make the raid on your village," Kanole said. "But of course, you are a spirit now, and you already know this."

Leilani hesitated for an instant, sensing that, for the time being, she should maintain whatever advantage her mystery gave her. She would say nothing, for a while, to change Kanole's idea that she was a spirit.

"You did not make the raid, but you made the revolution," she said after a moment.

"I am mightily sorry," Kanole said. "You may have my life."

"I do not want your life," she said. "There is very little of it left. You may keep what you have. I forgive you."

"Thank you, Alii-Nui," Kanole said. He smiled a contented smile, and closed his eyes.

Leilani looked at Mark. He was shivering and

his face was ashen. There was a strange look in his eyes.

"You suffer from the chills."

"Are you real?" He looked up at her, squinting his eyes. "Or am I having hallucinations from the malaria fever?"

"What do you think?" Leilani asked, holding back the longing that clutched at her.

"I . . . I'm not sure. God help me, I don't know what to think," Mark said. "What are you doing here? Where did you come from? Why do you haunt me so? Why can't I forget you?"

He suddenly started shaking violently. Her heart constricted for him, and she dropped to the sand at his side. She reached out to him, nearly trembling with love.

"You will not be cold long," she said softly. "I will warm you."

She put her hand on his shoulder in that special place she had discovered on board the *Sea Eagle* and applied a very gentle pressure. As before, Mark was immediately aroused, and the heat of his desire warmed the cold of his chill.

"Is this not better?" she asked, leaning against him and kissing him. His lips were hot against hers, but she felt him struggle against the kiss and lost her balance as he pushed her away. "No, leave me be," he said. "Who are you? What are you doing to me?"

Smiling to herself at his *haole* fear, Leilani rubbed her hand across his cheek, through the stubble of a week-old beard, and along the white, raised ridge of the saber slash. She spoke softly to him, and, as in the cabin of his ship, her bell-like voice aroused him even more.

Once, years before, Mark had read the story of Odysseus, and he remembered the part where Odysseus had to tie himself to the ship's mast so as not to succumb to the song of the sirens. He thought of that now and clapped his hands over his ears. "Be still, siren," he said. "I won't listen to your sweet song!"

His strange words startled her. She knew they came from the sickness he fought. Expertly, she pressed against him, feeling the heat spread through her like liquid fire and move into his body to warm him. She tasted the salt on his lips and felt the muscles on his chest and in his arms.

"No!" He was pleading. "Go away! Don't haunt me. You aren't real. Don't you think I know that you aren't real?"

"I am real," Leilani said, fearful now that she had allowed him to believe otherwise.

"No," Mark replied. He put his hand to his forehead. "I'm hallucinating from malaria. You're like the sirens in *The Odyssey*. You're in my mind."

"Feel my body, Mark," she said, summoning her most powerful voice. "Is this not the body of a woman?"

She took his hands and led them over her skin, moving his fingers up the smooth curve of her hips and then across her swelling breasts. She rubbed the palm of his hand on her nipples, so small and hard after the soft, firm feel of her breasts, and then she guided his fingers over the slope of her shoulders into the softness of her hair.

"Can you not smell the sun and the sea? The flowers? My own musk?" she asked. "Are these things not real?"

"I don't know," Mark said. "I'm not sure."

Her soul ached for him. The trip in the open boat and the coming fever . . . her beloved Mark had become unable to cope with what was happening.

"Don't talk," she whispered. "Just make love to me."

The sand of the beach was as fine as the most delicate powder, and when Leilani pulled him down to her and lay back in it, there was no grittiness nor roughness beneath them. The beach was as soft as a bed.

They had made love twice before. The first time Leilani had tried unsuccessfully to fight against the passionate desires of her body. The second time it had been a battle of wills—and sexual skill. But this time it was as it should be —pure lovemaking—and for Leilani, Mark was all men and she was all women, the more so because they were on an isolated beach on a deserted island in the middle of the ocean, a thousand miles from the nearest civilization.

The surf thundered behind them, pulsing in the same rhythms of their intimate ballet. A gentle sea-spray fell on them. And they were truly children of the sun.

Leilani lay beside Mark for a while after they were finished, allowing the heat of her passion to drain away slowly, enjoying the last, subtle vibrations which passed through her body. She felt his arm around her, and his hand affectionately squeezing her shoulder.

"Leilani," he said. "Leilani. I've been unable to get you out of my mind. You've haunted me as surely as any ghost. I've known no peace since that night."

"I know," she replied. "I have felt the same thing."

He raised up on one elbow. "It is hard to believe you are real."

Leilani laughed. Such a strange *haole*. What sort of proof did he need? "Do I not look real? Did I not feel real as we made love?"

Mark returned the laugh. "Yes," he said. "But there have been some strange things happening. I don't even know how you got here."

"It doesn't matter," Leilani said. "It is only important that I am here. That we are here."

She searched his eyes for a moment. It was enough that they were here together but she saw his *haole* desire to express it all in words. "I thought I didn't believe in love," he said. "But I know for sure that I am in love with you." He kissed her. The need and hunger were gone, but the gentleness and love remained. Mark broke off the kiss and looked at her, then laughed. "I do love you," he said. "I don't care who you are, or what you are, or how you came to this place. I know only that I've known no peace since I met you. You have taken over my body, mind, and soul, and I love you."

"I love you, Mark," she said, when he had finished. She touched his face, tracing a finger across the scar. "I love you with all that I am, and all that I will be."

They kissed again, then Mark lay down and closed his eyes. They were quiet for several moments before he spoke. "I am very sleepy. Promise me, when I wake, that you will still be here. You will still love me. Promise me that you are not a dream."

"I will still be here," Leilani said. "I will still love you. I am not a dream." She looked down at his face, peaceful now.

He was asleep almost immediately. It was a deep sleep, brought on by exhaustion, malaria, and the total relaxation he enjoyed after making love with Leilani. She lay beside him, rejoicing in the love they shared.

"You do love him, don't you?"

Leilani started. She had forgotten all about Kanole's presence. She suddenly realized with some embarrassment that he had watched them make love.

"Yes, I do love him."

"I am happy, for he is a good man," Kanole said. He held his hand across his chest, and Leilani could see the blood spilling between his fingers.

"Kanole, is there anything I can do for you?" she asked, hurrying over to him.

Kanole smiled. "Yes. I would have that you

think no evil thoughts of me. Allow my spirit to
rest."

"I will think no evil of you."

"You are not a spirit, are you?"

"Which do you want me to me?"

"I want you to be a real woman."

"I am a real woman."

"I want you to make Mark Costain happy."

Leilani looked back at Mark's sleeping body.
"I will try, but he is not a man at rest."

"He suffers from malaria and this troubles
his mind. Also, he has seen many evil things
happen. But he is a good man, and your love
will make him well again."

"I will give him that love," Leilani promised.
To Kanole and to herself.

"There is something else you can do for me,"
Kanole said.

"What?"

"Go to the highest mountain on this island.
Pray to all our old gods for me, as in the days
of old."

"But I am a Christian now," Leilani said.
"And you are, too."

"I will pray to the new Christian God," Kanole
said. "But I do not want the old gods to be
angry. Will you do this for me?"

"Yes, Kanole, I will do this," Leilani promised.

"Thank you," Kanole said. "Now, you must
erase all your signs. The old gods must not see
that you have been here, or they will not listen.
Leave no footprints."

"I know what to do," Leilani said.

He smiled contentedly. "Of course. I almost forgot that you are an Alii-Nui."

"Do you want food or water before I go?"

"No," Kanole said. "But you must hurry, for I will die soon. You must be on the mountain top praying to the old gods to keep them busy, or they will steal my soul from the Christian God."

"Do not worry," Leilani said. "I will take care of everything."

She stood then, put her hands beneath her chin as if praying, and dipped her head in a slight bow. Then she took a palm frond and erased all her tracks, and left the beach by stepping from rock to rock. By the time she disappeared, there was no sign that she had ever been there.

Chapter Twenty-One

WHEN MARK AWOKE much later, the sun was just coming up. He sat up quickly, as if suddenly aware of where he was. Behind him a bird called, and trees whispered in the wind. The chills were over, but he knew the fever was beginning, because the temperature of his body was slowly rising.

"Kanole?"

Kanole was lying in the sand nearby, and Mark walked over to him. "Kanole, how do you feel?" he asked, kneeling down beside him.

Kanole didn't answer, and when Mark touched him, he discovered that the Hawaiian was cold. Kanole was dead.

"Kanole, damn, I'm sorry," Mark said. He took the big man's hand in his own and noticed with surprise that the palm was raw. At first, he was puzzled, then he remembered how Kanole lowered the launch on his own. When he grabbed

the rope, he must have burned both hands
badly, though he kept silent and later never
complained about it.

Mark walked over to the boat and took out
one of the oars. He carried it up the beach and
used it to scoop out a hole big enough to bury
Kanole.

It wasn't until he had finished that he remembered Leilani. She had appeared yesterday
afternoon as if out of nowhere. They had made
love, then afterward, exhausted from the voyage and weakened by the malaria, he had fallen
asleep and had slept the rest of the day and
through the night. During the night Kanole had
died, and Leilani had slipped away as if she had
been a dream. But he knew she was real. His
body told him so.

"Leilani!" he called. "Leilani, where are you?"

His voice raised a flight of white birds, and
they flew over the island with their flapping
wings catching the sun, like a living cloud.
Their calls of surprise and anger echoed through
the hills, but there was no other sound.

"Leilani!" Mark called again. He rubbed his
hand against his scar, and felt the heat of his
skin. The temperature was shooting up rapidly
now, and he realized he was slowly losing control of his body.

Why did Leilani leave? Well, no matter. It
should be easy enough to track her. Every foot-
print was still in the sand. The mark the boat
made as it was dragged across the shore was
plainly visible, as were the footprints of Mark

and Kanole where they left the boat. He could also see his tracks leading back to the boat when he had gone to get the oar, tracks leading to the mound of dirt where Kanole lay buried, and back to where he now stood.

But there were no tracks to show that Leilani had been there.

Impossible!

She *had* been here. She was here yesterday afternoon. Mark knew he hadn't imagined that. She had been here and they had made love!

"My God, Leilani, are you real?" Mark shouted. "Answer me! Are you a woman, or some devil come to torment me?"

"Leilani . . . LEI . . . LAN . . . IIIII !"

"EEEEEEE," came back the ghostly echo of his own voice.

And the crashing boom of the surf.

And the whisper of the wind.

But nothing more.

He felt himself becoming very light-headed. It was the fever; and he was going to have a bad dose this time.

But no! No, he would fight it! He would not succumb to the fear and fever on some desert island, haunted by a she-devil. He would escape from here and sail back to Hawaii. He was a sailor, not a superstitious native frightened by some damned legend.

He staggered back to the boat and began pushing it into the surf with what strength he had left. If he could just get back into open water, he'd point the bow in the right direction, set sail, and lash the tiller. He'd make it back. He was determined he would make it back.

His head was pounding and his temperature was dangerously high. His face was so flushed that his scar now looked like a jagged white streak of lightning against a red sky. His skin burned and his ears hummed. Everything was a blur to him.

He slowly climbed into the boat, obsessed now with leaving the island. If he had reasoned things out, he would have realized that he should stay on the island until the fever passed. Then he would at least have a point of reference from which to continue his dead reckoning navigation. But reason was not with him. Only the terrible burning fever, the spinning dizziness, and the haunting memory of a woman.

Or a devil.

A dolphin appeared in front of the boat and emitted a high-pitched, shrill laugh, as if mocking him.

"No," he shouted wildly. He threw one of his oars at the dolphin.

"No, leave me alone, you devil you!"

When Leilani returned from the mountain where she had been praying for Kanole, she saw Mark launching the boat.

"No!" she cried, suddenly frightened that in his sickness he might leave. "Mark, no!"

He didn't hear her, or, if he did, he ignored

her. He continued to work, furiously pushing the boat into the surf.

Leilani was panic stricken. He was too ill to leave alone, and terror filled her at the thought of losing him. What manner of devils possessed her *haole* captain? She felt a cry rising in her throat as her mind raced for a way to stop him. Even running, she would never reach him in time, for already the boat was in the water. If he didn't die from his exertion with the boat, he would surely die alone at sea.

It came to her suddenly as a rising wind—the dolphins. "Mahimahi," she called, her voice carried by the wind, "mahimahi, stop him!"

A dolphin surfaced smartly in front of the launch. As she ran down the slope she saw Mark struggle into the boat, waving and shouting at the dolphin. Then he raised an oar, and with an oath, threw the paddle at the mahimahi. The dolphin dived into a wave, and Mark sank down into the boat. Leilani couldn't see him anymore, and murmured a prayer to all the gods that he still lived.

Without oars, even if Mark had been able, the boat couldn't travel fast. By the time Leilani reached the surf, it had been carried only a few hundred feet from shore. She dived into the sea, and with a few powerful strokes, soon drew level and pulled herself over the gunwales into the boat.

Mark's eyes flashed wildly, and he shouted at her like a man gone mad as she appeared over the side of the boat. Then he passed out.

PART TWO_____

Chapter Twenty-Two ─────────

MILAM BEEKER HAD been at sea for more than thirty years. He'd sailed out of Boston as a twelve-year-old cabin boy and had never stayed more than three months in a row on dry land since then. Now, at the age of forty-two, he was about to realize a life-long ambition. He was retiring to live in the Hawaiian Islands.

Milam took all his savings out of the bank, bought the brig *Distant Star*, and placed the following ad in the *Boston Evening Transcript*:

> *Leaving soon for Hawaii, the Brig Distant Star, under the able command of Captain Milam Beeker, Esq. Anyone who has cargo, mail, or other such dunnage as would require transport to Hawaii, may make arrangements with Captain*

*Milam Beeker for their safe and
swift transport.*

Captain Beeker had already sold the ship
for a profit to Dr. Angus Pugh in Lahaina, and
Dr. Pugh had agreed to let him keep any money
made during the voyage out to deliver the ship.
It was Beeker's intention to open a bar in
Hawaii with his profits.

The ad was answered by a very beautiful
woman of about thirty, who introduced herself
as Mrs. Rose McPheeters. She made a generous
offer to rent the whole ship for her cargo.

"What, may I ask, is to be the cargo?" Beeker
asked, very pleased with her offer.

"Girls," Mrs. McPheeters answered. She
touched her blazing red hair and smiled broadly.

"Girls?" Beeker asked, puzzled. "What sort of
girls?"

"Beautiful ones," Mrs. McPheeters said.

"Mrs. McPheeters, I don't understand."

"Please call me Rose. And I'm certain that
you do understand, a man who is as worldly as
you."

"My God, woman, do you mean whores?"
Beeker asked, suddenly catching on.

"Yes," Mrs. McPheeters answered, completely
unperturbed. "I think my girls would be quite
a profitable operation in Hawaii, don't you?"

"Well, I . . . madam, I . . . I'm at a loss for
words," Milam sputtered.

"The only words I need, Captain, are words

saying you will do it. Will you? Or do you have strong feelings against whores and the men who visit them?"

"No, of course not. I've been in a few whore houses myself," Beeker said. "But I've never carried a troop of them on my ship before."

"I'll keep them out of trouble, I promise you," Mrs. McPheeters said.

"It's the sailors I'm thinkin' of," Milam told her. "They're apt to be quite randy after a long time at sea. I'm not at all sure I can keep them separated from your girls."

"Why try, Captain?" Rose asked mischievously. "Surely it would make the passage more pleasant."

Beeker looked at her in surprise, then threw back his head and laughed. "Aye, 'n' you've a point there, I'll confess," he said. "Very well, Mrs. McPheeters . . ."

"Please call me Rose."

"All right, Rose it is. Rose, have your girls on board at nine on the morrow, and we'll get underway."

"Thank you, Milam," Rose said, smiling prettily.

Now, eight weeks later, and nearing the end of the voyage, Milam stood on the quarterdeck smoking a cheeroot and thinking of how easy it had all been. Though he had expected fights to break out over the girls, there had been no trouble. The sexual encounters had never once interfered with the running of the ship.

"Cap'n, there's a ship, mast up, off the star-board bow," the lookout suddenly shouted down.

"What type ship she be?"

"I think she be a sloop, Cap'n. But there're no sails showing."

"No sails?"

"No sails, sir."

That was odd. There was a fair breeze, and the sea was calm. Why then would she not be showing sails?

"She 'pears to be dead in the water, Cap'n," the lookout shouted.

Rose heard the shouting, and she came up on deck to see what was going on.

"Rose, best you and the girls stay below 'til we figure out what this is all about," Beeker said.

"Why?"

"I've no wish to let another ship see that we're carryin' a cargo of . . . of . . . I just don't want them to know about you, that's all."

"On the contrary, Milam," Rose said easily. "Their money's as good at sea as it is ashore. I'd like to invite them over."

"No, madam," Beeker said sternly. "They'll not be visiting this ship for such purposes."

"Then perhaps we can visit them?"

"Cap'n, she's showin' signals," the lookout shouted.

"What do they say?" Milam asked, thankful for the opportunity to interrupt the interchange with Rose.

"She's dead in the water effecting a repair. Her rudder post's been cut."

"That's a damned unusual place to have an accident," Beeker said, rubbing his chin apprehensively. "Mr. Parker, stand by the starboard guns."

"Aye, sir," Parker replied. "You want them loaded and run out?"

"Load them. Don't run them out yet."

"Gun crews, shot and ball," Parker yelled.

As the *Distant Star* approached the other vessel, the lookout was able to fix his spyglass on the ship, motionless in the water.

"She be the *Mary Luck,* sir," he called down.

Beeker held a big red book with gold lettering in his hand, *American Lloyds' Universal Standard of Shipping*. He looked through it until he found the *Mary Luck*.

"Out of Norfolk," he said. "A hundred eighty tons. Armed with eight cannon. Captain Jason Roberts commanding. Mr. Parker, note our position and make an entry . . . *Mary Luck* spoken this time and day."

"Aye, aye, Cap'n," Parker answered.

"Cap'n, she's requesting to send a boarding party."

"Damn," Milam said, "there's no way they won't see the girls now."

"Then I'll get them dressed for the occasion," Rose said, smiling triumphantly and hurrying below.

Beeker retired to his cabin to put on his best

uniform. Although he intended to quit the sea as soon as his ship reached Lahaina, he meant to make as good an impression as possible on Captain Roberts. By the time he returned to the deck, the gig from the *Mary Luck* was nearly alongside.

"Pipe the captain aboard, boatswain," Beeker ordered.

"Aye, aye, sir," the boatswain answered. His shrill whistle rose, then faded, and sideboys saluted the visiting captain aboard. Beeker was amazed how small he was and how unpleasant his face looked. He was trying to smile as he held out his hand, but even then there was something about the set of his mouth and the glint of his eyes which caused Milam Beeker to feel an instant dislike for him.

"Thank you for allowing me to board your ship, Cap'n," Roberts said.

"I'm glad I could be of service, Captain Roberts," Beeker said.

"Do you know me, sir?"

"I looked it up in the book."

"Forgive me, sir, for not extending you the same courtesy."

"'Twould have done you no good. I've just purchased this ship for resale, and it wouldn't be properly listed. My name is Milam Beeker. Are you in need of material for repairs?"

"No, sir," Roberts answered. "We've nearly finished with the repair. We will be putting about and returning to Hawaii shortly."

"If you've no need of assistance, why were we hailed?"

"I am looking for two men," Roberts said. "One is an American named Mark Costain, and the other a big Hawaiian named Kanole. They, and two other members of my crew, mutinied a few days ago. We managed to kill the other two, but Costain and Kanole stole the launch and got away. I intend to find them and see them hang."

"I understand," Beeker said. "Mutiny is a terrible thing. I can well understand your desire to see justice done. You said you are returning to Hawaii. Are you in ballast?"

"No. I have a load of sandalwood which I will consign to another ship."

"You'll be giving up a payload?" Beeker asked incredulously.

"I will, sir. Absolutely nothing takes precedence over finding the mutineers," Roberts answered resolutely.

"How do you expect me to help you, Captain?"

"Have you come across a launch with two men?"

"No, sir, we have not."

"May I look through your ship, sir?"

"I beg your pardon?"

"I would like to look through your ship to satisfy myself that they are not on board."

"Captain Roberts, are you disputing my word, sir?"

"Not at all," the little captain said easily. "'Tis no more than a courtesy I'm aking. It should be no trouble if you've nothing to hide."

But Beeker did have something to hide. He didn't want Roberts to see the girls he carried. But suddenly there were loud giggles behind him. He looked around and saw Rose and her girls standing in the open for everyone to see.

"Thunderation, woman, didn't I tell you to stay below?" Beeker exploded angrily.

"I chartered this ship, Captain," Rose answered easily. "And where I respect your authority in matters which may represent a danger to us, I withhold the right to dictate my own affairs otherwise. Captain Roberts, your crew is composed of men, I presume?"

"Yes, madam, of course," Roberts answered.

"Then perhaps you would allow your men to entertain my girls?"

"What?"

"They're all doxies, Captain," Beeker said, "'Twould cost your men."

Roberts smiled slyly. "That might be just what I need. The men are on edge since the mutiny. This would calm them down again. 'Twas always the best thing about running slaves. The black wenches helped keep down trouble with the crew. Yes, I'd like to have your girls visit us."

"Madam, we've no time for this," Beeker spluttered.

"Then find the time, Milam," Rose said easily.

Beeker let out a disgusted sigh. "Captain Roberts, you may feel free to search my ship for your deserters," he said.

"That won't be necessary, Captain," Roberts replied. He looked at the girls and smiled again. "I can see now why you weren't anxious to allow any snooping around. I can't say that I blame you. But, if you'll stand to overnight, I'll have them back first thing in the morning."

Rose didn't go over to the other ship. She stayed back and tried to talk to Beeker, but he was so angry he ignored her. He sat morosely on the captain, long after the sun had set, and smoked his cigar and looked at the golden winks of light from the dark shadow of the *Mary Luck*.

Beeker was awakened by a knock on his cabin door early the next morning.

"Cap'n, the girls are back," Parker called.

Beeker sat up and ran his hand through his hair. There was an ache of rheumatism in his joints, and he longed for the voyage to end. Though he could have sailed for twenty more years, he knew he would not miss the sea. He had looked forward to retiring to Hawaii ever since his first visit to the islands.

He was very young the first time he saw Hawaii, but even then he had been much impressed by the land's beauty and climate, and by the attractive and friendly people. For nearly thirty years he had had the dream of leaving the sea to live in the island paradise. Perhaps he should have savored this last voyage, but he merely looked forward to its end—and the start of living his dream.

"Very well, Mr. Parker, let's get underway," he said. "Let's hang all the sail we can carry. We've lost time to make up."

"Aye, aye, sir," Parker replied.

It wasn't until some four hours later that the ship's surgeon came to speak with Beeker. He had a glum expression on his face.

"What is it, Jim?" Beeker asked.

"It's the girl Darcey, Captain. She's in a bad way."

"A bad way? What do you mean? What's wrong with her? She was just fine yesterday."

"It was the visit to the other ship, Captain," the surgeon said. "It was Captain Roberts. He . . . he . . . hurt her."

"Hurt her?"

"He was very hard on her, sir. He abused the girl terribly. He did some serious damage. She's starting to hemorrhage."

"My God, why wasn't I told this immediately?"

"The girl didn't tell anyone about it at first," the surgeon said. "She was too ashamed. It wasn't until she started hemorrhaging that she grew frightened. Then she spoke of it."

Beeker felt as if he was going to be sick. He poured himself a strong drink before he spoke again.

"Very well, Jim. Do what you can for her. How about Rose? Has she been told?"

"Aye, sir. She's feeling pretty bad about it. She's with Darcey now."

"She should feel bad," Beeker said angrily.

Chapter Twenty-Three————————

LEILANI NURSED MARK through his malaria attack as well as she could. During his fever she bathed him in sea water and put fresh water from the scuttlebutt on his lips and tongue. To overcome his chills, she warmed his body with hers.

He had very few lucid moments, and even when he seemed otherwise all right, he didn't recognize Leilani. In fact, he spoke to her sometimes as if she were Kanole.

In his few lucid moments, Mark was able to instruct Leilani in how to handle the boat, although it was hardly necessary because of her own knowledge of the sea. When he was clearheaded, Mark worried over their navigation, working almost automatically, and when the actual business was taken care of, he would drift back into a delirium again, fighting the personal devils of his private hell.

On the third day, Leilani spotted a ship. She stood up and shouted excitedly.

"Kanole, why are you yelling?" Mark asked.

"A ship, there is a ship!" Leilani said.

Mark raised himself up and shielded his eyes against the glare of the water. "He won't see us," he said. "We're too low, and the glare from the water is too great."

"But he must see us," Leilani said.

Mark lay back down. "He won't see us," he said again. "Perhaps it is an illusion, like your island. Perhaps the ship isn't there, just as your island wasn't there."

"Get up. Get up and set the sail," Leilani commanded. "Please, Mark, set the sail so that we might catch the ship."

Mark steeled himself and made a great effort to adjust the sail. The boom swung back across the boat, and Leilani dodged it only just in time. The little boat heeled over and started cutting through the water toward the ship. Leilani watched anxiously as they drew closer. Suddenly she saw the ship's great sails spilling air as it backed down.

"Mark, they've seen us!" she shouted excitedly. "They've seen us and they're stopping!" She fell quiet suddenly as she turned to him. He was draped across the tiller, unconscious.

Chapter Twenty-Four ——————————

"Oh, you poor, poor thing," Rose said. "What an ordeal you've been through! Here, you must take some more soup."

Leilani was in Rose's cabin, wearing one of her nightgowns and sitting up in Rose's bed. The older woman was holding a bowl of soup out to her.

"Thank you," Leilani said. "How is Mark?"

"He is sleeping," Rose said. "The ship's surgeon has given him quinine. It will probably take hold during the night."

"He has been out of his head for three days," Leilani said as she sipped the soup.

There was a knock at the door.

"Do come in," Rose called.

Milam Beeker stepped in and crossed over to look down at Leilani. He looked worried, and Leilani sensed his concern. She liked him almost immediately.

"How did you two get here?" he asked.

"From an island near here."

"There are no islands near here," Beeker replied. "The closest islands are the Hawaiian Islands."

"There is an island even closer," she insisted calmly. "We sailed from it three days ago."

"Perhaps I am wrong," Beeker said. He patted Leilani gently on her shoulder. "You must try and rest now."

As Beeker left, he motioned for Rose to follow him. Once outside, he whispered to her, "Has she shown signs of lunacy?"

"No. Why do you ask?"

"There are no islands anywhere near. Yet she insists they sailed from one three days ago. That is not the talk of a person with complete control of her faculties."

"It's obvious why she's saying that, isn't it?" Rose said. "The man with her is Mark Costain. He is the man Captain Roberts was looking for. I think she is just trying to protect him."

"Yes," Beeker said thoughtfully, "You are probably correct. But she need have no fear that I am going to turn Costain or anyone else over to Roberts. He's an animal, and if justice were done, he would pay for killing poor Darcey."

At the mention of the girl they had just buried at sea, both of them grew solemn for a moment. Finally Rose said, "I'll tell the girl that you've no intention of turning Costain over to Roberts. Perhaps that'll ease her mind somewhat."

"Perhaps it will," Beeker agreed. He left to get back to the ship's business and was on deck before the question hit him.

Where did the girl come from? Roberts had mentioned no girl in regard to the mutiny.

Leilani recovered her strength quickly and was soon up on deck, as curious as ever about life on the sea. She had watched great ships like this one from afar for a long time. But the only time she had ever been on one was the time she was taken out to the *Sea Eagle*, and she had had very little chance then to look around.

"May I hold the wheel which steers the ship?" she asked the helmsman.

"I'm sorry, Miss, but the cap'n wouldn't allow that," the helmsman answered. He was having a difficult time attending to his business, because Leilani still wore the lightweight nightgown, and she was sitting on the deck in such a way that the gown slipped forward, giving a fine view of her bare golden breasts. The helmsman, like all the other sailors, had had ample sex during the whole voyage. But Leilani's natural sensuality was much more attractive than the professional and hard-boiled sexuality of the *Distant Star's* cargo.

Leilani rose and walked around the rest of the ship. She stood quietly as the sailors worked with ropes, and watched as they holystoned the deck. She even climbed the rigging, startling the lookout so badly that he nearly pitched out of the crow's nest.

"Here, Miss," he said gruffly, "What are you doing up here?"

"I came up to have a look around," Leilani said simply. "My, you can see everything from up here."

"Aloft there!" a voice suddenly called up from the deck.

Leilani looked down and saw the figure of Captain Beeker far below.

"I didn't invite 'er up, Cap'n. She just clumb up," the lookout shouted down. "You're gettin' me in big trouble, Miss," he said to her.

"It wasn't the sailor's fault," Leilani called down.

"You come back down here at once!" Beeker called back.

Leilani looked at the sailor in the crow's nest and smiled, then feeling devilishly mischievous pitched over backward into space. She heard the lookout cry out in alarm from above and the captain bellow fearfully from below. She somersaulted once in the air and came out of the somersault just where she knew she would. She reached out and grabbed a line, swung from it to a shroud, then slid gracefully down the shroud until she was just above the rail. She jumped lightly onto the deck in front of the captain.

"Please don't be angry with the man up there," she said innocently.

Beeker just looked at her with his mouth

open, then, without saying a word, he turned and went to his cabin.

That evening, after sunset, the sailors who weren't on watch, or weren't visiting the girls, were on deck catching the soft, cooling breeze. Leilani was with them, and as some of the men had never been to Hawaii, she was telling them about her islands.

"Are there cannibals there, Miss?" one of the sailors asked.

"No," Leilani answered, laughing. "And we don't take the scalps of our enemies, the way they do in America."

"'Tis only Indians do that, Miss, not the white man."

Leilani shook her head at the *haole* prejudice in his words. Such odd beliefs these white men carried about other people. But it was not her way to argue and she quickly returned to the conversation.

"I have seen many ships come to Hawaii," she said. "They come to catch the whale, they come to deliver goods, they come to take the sandalwood or copra, they even come to deliver the missionaries. But never have I seen a ship which carries only girls. Why is this?"

"They're whores," one of the sailors said easily.

"Has Kekuanna started doing business with white whores?" Leilani asked.

"Kekuanna?"

"Our governor. He supplies whores to the ships. Are these white whores to be his?"

"Oh, no, all the girls belong to Rose Mc-Pheeters," the sailor said.

"I will watch this with interest when we reach Lahaina," Leilani said. "I will see what Reverend Jebediah Grimsley will do. He does not like Hawaiian whores. Perhaps he will speak differently of these whores."

There followed a general discussion about whores and missionary teachings about fornication. Although Jebediah Grimsley was the prime example, Angus Pugh's name also came up, and that was how Leilani discovered where the ship was going. As they talked, some of the other men would drift in and sit down, and one or two of those who had already expressed their views would excuse themselves and go out.

"Where are they going?" Leilani asked.

"They are visiting with the whores, Miss," one of the sailors answered.

Leilani imagined the girls, lying on a bed somewhere in the bowels of the ship, entertaining one sailor after another. It was cold, clinical, and inhibited, with no love in it and none of the spontaneous sexuality of the islanders. No wonder the whites had so much difficulty with sex.

"Does Captain Beeker visit with the whores?" she asked.

"No. He is not a sportin' man," one of the sailors answered, and they all laughed.

Others came and went, and the little group talked far into the night, while below decks, the girls, tired and sore and with aching backs, wondered why the sexual appetite of the sailors had suddenly become once more as hearty as at the start of the voyage.

Chapter Twenty-Five————————

LEILANI WAS GIVEN Darcey's bunk to sleep in, and she spent a restful night on board the *Distant Star*. She was awake with the morning watch and soon on deck to talk with her new sailor friends. She smiled as the captain approached her.

"Your name is Leilani, isn't it?" the captain asked in a pleasant voice.

"Yes," Leilani answered.

"Well, Leilani, you're a spirited girl, and I've no wish to hold you back. But for the safety of all on board, I'd like to ask that you not go climbing through the rigging again."

"It isn't dangerous for me, Captain," she told him.

Beeker smiled at her. "Damn me if I don't believe you're right," he said. "But you're apt to cause injury among the crew. Someone 'll fear for your safety, or, more likely, some damn fool will not want to be shown up by a slip of a lass and he'll try and match you. How did you get such skill in climbing the rigging?"

"By climbing trees," Leilani answered.

"I suppose that could be," Beeker agreed. "But promise me, Leilani, you'll not scale every piece of timber on this ship?"

"I promise you."

"That's a good lass," Beeker said. "Now, do you have a taste for coffee? I've some in my cabin."

"Thank you, no," Leilani said. "Coffee is much too bitter. I don't see why people find it pleasurable."

" 'Tis a puzzle," Beeker agreed. He pulled out a cigar and walked over to the smoking lamp and lit it, then drew a few puffs. He held it up before her. "This, too, is a puzzle, I'd imagine. But I've acquired a taste for all the vices."

"All the vices, Captain?" Leilani asked. "I was told by the sailors that you don't visit with the whores you have on this ship. Are you one who does not enjoy fornicating?"

Beeker was shocked by the boldness of her question, and in surprise he drew in too much smoke, then erupted into a coughing fit.

"Damn me, girl, that's a frank question you've asked," he said as he recovered his breath. "What do you know of such things?"

"I know of whores," Leilani said. "Governor Kekuanna supplies them to the ships. And I know of fornicating, and that some whites say it is wrong, but many do it anyway."

Milam looked at Leilani. He was certain that he had never seen anyone as beautiful, or as innocent, despite her openness.

"I don't think fornicating is wrong, Leilani," Beeker said. "But I find it more enjoyable when I've some feeling for the woman."

"Yes," Leilani agreed. "I, too, have discovered that it is more enjoyable if I've feeling for the man."

Leilani was drawn to Milam Beeker from the first. He was a very pleasant man, and now they had shared some personal thoughts. It moved her, and to a degree disturbed her. She should be talking this way to Mark Costain, not to Milam Beeker. This seemed to her, in a way, to be a betrayal of her love for Mark.

"Cap'n, the wind's getting ahead, sir," the helmsman called.

Beeker was annoyed at himself when he heard the sailor's reminder. He should have been paying closer attention and caught the wind shift himself. Instead he had been talking with Leilani, and was so captivated by her that he had neglected his duty.

"Trim the yards," Beeker ordered, allowing the anger with himself to show in his voice.

The sailors on watch jumped into action, and Leilani moved amidship in order to get a better view of their work.

Beeker watched her as she walked. He had

decided from the moment he agreed to transport the whores that he would not visit with
any of them. It was a difficult decision, because Beeker was a healthy male, with an enjoyment of sex. And Rose, who was the prettiest
of them all, and who did not entertain the
sailors, had offered to share her bed with him.
At first the offer was made out of a sense of
obligation. But there were many times as the
voyage progressed that the offer was repeated
because Rose was interested in him. That made
it even harder for Beeker to stick to his original
decision, but he steeled himself against dwelling
on such thoughts and took massive doses of salt-
peter to aid him.

Now, however, as he looked at the lithe
young body of Leilani and watched the way
she moved beneath the thin gown she wore,
he found himself aroused. There was a familiar rising pressure in the front of his pants,
and he turned to hide himself against the rail
until he could force the thoughts from his
mind and control himself.

The ship's surgeon came on deck and saw
Leilani.

"Good morning, miss," he said. "How do you
feel today?"

"I feel fine," Leilani answered. "How is
Mark?"

"I'm happy to say that the fever broke during the night. He is taking breakfast now in
Mrs. McPheeters' cabin."

"May I see him?"

"Certainly," the surgeon said. "A familiar face may do him a lot of good. There is one problem which seems to be bothering him now."

"What is wrong?"

"He suffers from confusion of thought," the surgeon said.

Leilani wasn't sure what the doctor meant, but she thanked him and hurried on to Mrs. McPheeters' cabin on bare golden feet which were quickened by thoughts of seeing him.

She knocked lightly on the door.

"Come in," Rose called.

Leilani opened the door and saw Mark sitting up in bed. As Rose had fed Leilani soup the day before, she was now spooning the hot liquid into Mark.

"Good morning, my dear," Rose said pleasantly. "You are looking very good today."

"I feel fine," Leilani said. She looked at Mark. "Mark, how do you feel?"

Mark looked puzzled.

"You called me by my name, girl," he said. "How is it you know me? I don't know you."

Leilani tried to hide her surprise. "I am Leilani," she said.

"Leilani?"

"Yes. Don't you remember me from the *Sea Eagle?*"

"Oh, yes," Mark said easily. "Of course, you must have been one of the governor's girls, sent to the *Sea Eagle.*"

As he said the name of his ship, Mark had a strange look on his face. He looked around the cabin. "What is this vessel?" he asked. "It isn't the *Sea Eagle*."

"This is the *Distant Star*," Rose said.

"*Distant Star?* I don't recall getting command of this ship."

"Mark, is it possible that you don't remember anything?" Leilani asked, her heart pounding with confusion and fear. Had this been what the surgeon meant?

Mark put his hand to his face and felt the saber-slash. "Yes," he said. "Yes, I remember now. I was cashiered from the Navy. I lost my command . . . and my honor."

"Don't you remember the island?" she asked. "Kanole? Surely you haven't forgotten your friend Kanole."

"Kanole?" Mark replied. He closed his eyes and an expression of pain crossed his face. "Yes," he said. "Yes, I remember Kanole. We escaped together. Kanole was killed."

"Yes," Leilani said. "And Leilani? Do you remember Leilani?" she asked with hope in her heart.

Mark suddenly touched his shoulder in the spot Leilani had discovered. For a moment, a fleeting instant, something like recognition leaped to his eyes, then, agonizingly, it slipped away.

"A girl," Mark said. "From the governor. A beautiful girl. We made love . . ." He touched his shoulder again. "Alii . . . Alii?"

"Alii-Nui!" Leilani said eagerly. "You do remember."

"No," Mark said after a moment. "I'm sorry, I don't remember."

Leilani could not hold the tears back. How could this be? Was it possible that the man she loved didn't even know of her existence? Was he being truthful with her?

"What is wrong?" Mark asked. "Why are you crying?"

Leilani whirled and ran from the cabin with tears stinging her eyes and a sob choking her throat.

"She is a very pretty girl," she heard Mark saying. "I'm sorry, but I seem to have upset her."

"Don't worry yourself about it," Rose said. "You just take some more soup. She'll be all right and I'll take good care of you."

Leilani ran to the rail and there, hanging to one of the shrouds, cried bitter tears of hurt and frustration.

"What is wrong, dear?" the surgeon asked. "Has he grown worse?"

"He doesn't remember me," Leilani said. "He doesn't even know who I am."

"I was afraid of that," the surgeon said. "Remember, I said he suffered confusion of thought? I hoped seeing you would bring him out of it."

"I don't know what that means," Leilani said.

"He suffers from loss of memory," the surgeon explained. "It's a little-understood malady. I believe it's called amnesia."

"Amnesia?"

"Very little is known of the disease," the surgeon said. "It occurs sometimes when a person suffers a blow to the head . . . or undergoes a great shock . . . or has a very high fever. Mr. Costain has suffered a very high fever, and has undergone a considerable shock as well."

"Can you give him his memory back?"

"No," the surgeon answered. "I'm afraid there is nothing I can do."

"Then he shall forever be this way?"

"Perhaps. Though often times the patients have a spontaneous recovery. That is to say, they get well on their own."

"Will Mark get well?"

"That I cannot say, miss," the surgeon said. "We'll just have to wait and see what happens."

After the surgeon left, Leilani thought on what he had said. If Mark was ill, then he couldn't help it that he didn't recognize Leilani. He wasn't to blame for that. Leilani would continue to love him, and wait for him to recover. Then everything would be all right.

She decided to return to Rose's cabin, to explain to Mark what was wrong with him. She would tell him that she understood, and that her love for him would still be there, waiting for him when he regained his memory.

She knocked on the cabin door, filled again with hope, but no one answered. She tried the handle and found it unlocked, so she pushed it open slightly.

"Mark," she called. "Mark, it's all right. The doctor told me what's wrong and I . . ."

"Honey, can't you see that we're busy?" Rose asked sharply.

Leilani gasped. There, on the bed, Rose and Mark, her beloved Mark, were making love.

Chapter Twenty-Six———————

LEILANI WAS TORN with confusion. She was willing to accept the surgeon's explanation for Mark's strange behavior. Amnesia could account for his forgetting the words of love he had spoken to her, and he would not feel inhibited in making love to another. But what strange malady had overcome her? Why was she so hurt by the simple fact of seeing Mark and Rose making love?

Sex for Leilani was a natural thing. Young women from her home often shared the same lovers, and never had there been hurt or jealousy among them. But now, seeing Mark with Rose, feelings were aroused in Leilani which she couldn't fathom, feelings of hurt and betrayal.

For the first time in her life, Leilani was beginning to understand why the whites felt as they did about sex. Without love, sex seemed a harmless diversion. But with love, it was a powerful thing. And it could cause feelings of pain as easily as it caused pleasure.

She leaned into the rigging and stared at the sea. It seemed unchanging, constant, eternal, as if mocking her. That didn't seem right. How could the sea continue to be the same?

She smelled the familiar aroma of Captain Beeker's cheroot, and she knew he was approaching her. She turned to look at him.

"Why so pensive, lass?" he asked.

"Pensive?"

"What are you thinking about that occupies your mind so?"

Leilani looked back at the rolling sea.

"Captain Beeker, when we spoke of sex, you said you enjoyed it more if you had feelings for the person."

"Aye. 'Tis the proper way of it."

"What if the person you have feelings for has sex with another? Does that upset you?"

"Of course it does."

Leilani leaned her head against the rope, and a tear slid down her face.

"Here, now, lass. What is the problem?"

"Has the surgeon told you of Mark's illness? That he remembers nothing?"

"Yes."

"He does not remember me," Leilani said.

"I'm sorry, girl," Beeker said gently. He put his hand on Leilani's shoulder and squeezed it affectionately. "He must really be ill if he can't remember someone as lovely as you. But not to worry. He'll soon be over that malady, I'm thinking, and it'll be as it was."

"It can never be as it was," Leilani said quietly.

"Why not, lass?"

"Because now, while he does not remember me, he has sex with Rose."

"Ah, now, that's a shame, Leilani. I can't imagine anyone being untrue to you. I know I could never be. But, then, I've no place for even thinking such ideas, being as I'm ugly, old, and foolish."

She was taken aback by his words. "You are not ugly or old, Captain," she protested. "And you aren't foolish."

"But I have not the attraction for women as does your handsome Mark Costain."

Something stirred inside her as they spoke. It may have been fired by the jealousy she felt over being wronged by Mark. It may have been an empathy with Milam Beeker for the intimate thoughts they had shared. Whatever set it off, it was, she knew, a totally new experience.

Leilani's sexual experience in the past, before Mark, had been purely physical. There had been only the young, handsome men who offered uninvolved sex. Such sex had usually been satisfying. But not until she met Mark had she known the heights to which her passions could take her.

With Mark, sex had been both physical and emotional, a combination which carried her to the summit of feeling. With Captain Beeker, she was experiencing an entirely new type of sexual interest. Milam Beeker was neither young nor handsome, but Leilani found herself strongly attracted to him emotionally. She was beginning to realize that just as sexual desire can be triggered by pure physical attraction, so it could also be triggered by the intellect and the emotions.

"Milam," she said softly. "You have much about you which attracts women."

She reached up to touch him, and she moved her fingers along his neck, feeling with the almost extrasensory perceptiveness of her fingertips for the spot which would activate Beeker's strongest sexual urge. Then she found it. A spot just below his left ear, no larger than a finger nail, but giving out a tremendous heat. She touched it and felt the tingling flow of his life energy, then applied a very gentle pressure. That energy stimulated him sexually, and without even knowing why, Beeker pulled Leilani to him and kissed her with the passion of a lover.

"Madam, I . . . forgive me, I . . . I don't know what came over me," he said breathlessly, breaking off the kiss when he realized what he was doing.

Leilani's hand was still on his neck, and her finger was still on the secret point. She held the light pressure. "Can't we go to your cabin, Captain?" she asked.

"Yes," Beeker replied. "God help me, yes."

When they reached his cabin, Leilani slipped her gown over her head easily, without fanfare or embarrassment. Beeker, who took pains to lock the cabin door, turned around to see her standing by the bed, as nude and as slender as a wood nymph.

"Oh, my dear child," he said softly, almost reverently. She saw the immediate reaction she had caused in him.

She lay on the bed, and the sun, splashing in through the slats on the hatch cover, painted bright bars of orange across her. The smooth lines of her body were almost catlike, and she reminded Beeker of a beautiful tigress he had once seen in India. She stretched, putting one arm over her head, and the swelling mound of flesh that was the breast beneath that arm nearly disappeared, marked only by the tiny, erect nipple which was highlighted by a bar of light.

Beeker's clothes were quickly removed, and he climbed into the bed beside her, and put one hand on her shoulder, then let it trail along her body.

Leilani felt the quickening of arousal as Milam moved his hands over her. It was not the white hot passion she had felt with Mark, but it was a pleasantness which began in her loins and flowed through her body, awakening her senses and heating her blood. In a way, it was as if she were responding to the sensations Beeker felt. As his hands caressed her, she could feel the barely controlled quivering in them, and the tremendous excitement he felt.

Beeker was shorter and thicker than Mark, but his shoulders were not as broad nor his arms as hard. Yet when he moved over her and then into her, the sexual and emotional feeling erased Mark from her for now. She gave all that she was to this man who was with her now, and at the moment of supreme pleasure, she felt not only her own sweet ecstacy, but his as well.

Afterward, as she lay with her head resting on his shoulder, she thought of the new aspects of sex she had discovered, and wondered if this knowledge had been omitted from her education through some error of her teachers.

But, as she reasoned it out, she decided it was not omitted through error. For this was something which could never be taught. It could only be experienced.

Chapter Twenty-Seven

WHEN THE *Distant Star* reached Lahaina, there was a gala celebration to mark the return of Leilani, the Alii-Nui and heroine of the revolution. Governor Kekuanna, who once claimed to have sneaked one of his own girls on board the vessel, now made a statement that he had known all along that Leilani was the real heroine. He invented the other story, he said, in order to prevent another attempt on Leilani's life.

Mark was thrown into jail, and Governor Kekuanna announced his intention of trying him for treason. When it was pointed out that Mark couldn't be tried for treason as he wasn't a citizen of Hawaii, Kekuanna granted him citizenship.

The trial was the final act of Kekuanna's personal whitewash, and in grand and glorious detail, he described the master plan for the revolu-

tion, and how he, personally, had thwarted it.
He acted as prosecuting attorney, as the prose-
cution's chief witness, and as friend of the
court. A verdict of guilty was a foregone con-
clusion, and as work had already begun on
building the gallows, a sentence of death by
hanging came as no surprise to anyone.

Of course Mark still had the right to have his
case reviewed, and in review either the verdict
or the sentence or both could be overturned.

Governor Kekuanna, who had been the
prosecuting attorney during the trial, now
served as the reviewing official. It was his decision that the verdict and the sentence would
stand, and Mark Costain was therefore scheduled to die by hanging at dawn on Friday
next.

Leilani called on Governor Kekuanna to ask
him to rescind the sentence, but he turned her
down. Invitations had already been sent out,
he said, and it would be a terrible breach of
etiquette to cancel the event now.

Chapter Twenty-Eight————————

"You CAN SEE him, Doctor, but only for a few minutes," the guard at the Lahaina fort said.

"Thank you," Pugh replied.

The heavy door was opened, and Pugh went inside the large cell block where Mark Costain was scheduled to spend his last night on earth. Mark had been sitting against the wall and he stood up to greet the doctor.

"Good evening," Mark said. He pointed to the floor. "Would you like a seat? I can offer you the whole floor."

"No, thank you," Pugh said. "I just came by to talk to you."

Mark walked over to the small window and looked out. He could see the beautiful waving palm trees, the colorful flowers, the magnificent ocean. But mostly he saw only the gallows.

"Are they really going to go through with it, Doc?" he asked.

"I'm afraid so," Pugh replied. He sighed. "Mark, is it true you don't remember anything, or was that a ruse for your trial?"

"I just remember bits and pieces," Mark said. "More of it is gradually coming back to me, but it's taking its time." He laughed hollowly. "And that's something I have very little of now."

"What do you remember?"

"I remember taking command of the *Sea Eagle*," he said. "I don't remember who gave me the command."

"You don't remember that it was Kekuanna himself who was the instigator of the revolution?"

"No," Mark said, "Though I wouldn't put it past the bastard."

"Do you remember what happened to your ship?"

"They say it was destroyed by the girl, Leilani," Mark said. He didn't realize it, but as he spoke, he put his hand to his shoulder, subconsciously rubbing that spot she had discovered on him. What was it? What was there, just on the other side of reality? "I don't know. . . . I can't remember."

"Do you remember the girl?"

"She . . . she was on the ship. One of the governor's whores."

"That's not possible," Pugh said.

"What?"

"She is the Alii-Nui. It is not possible that she was one of the governor's whores."

Mark rubbed the spot on his shoulder again. "But I seem to remember, there and on the island . . ."

"The island?" Pugh interrupted. His interest quickened. "What island?"

"I don't know what island," Mark said. "Kanole found it. He was shot as we escaped the *Sea Eagle*. The young black boy and the surgeon were killed. The sharks took the surgeon's body, but Kanole didn't die until we reached the island."

"What young black boy?" Pugh asked. "There were no Africans on the *Sea Eagle*."

Mark pinched the bridge of his nose and closed his eyes. "I . . . no . . . you're right. It wasn't the *Sea Eagle*. It was another ship, one that I can't remember." Mark rubbed the scar on his face. "I remember being cashiered from the Navy. The saber cut my face. My father . . . my father would have been very upset had he known. He was killed in the War of 1812. He would have been very upset with me for being cashiered."

Pugh suddenly realized that Mark was wandering, that his mind was still not clear.

"What about the island?" he asked again.

"Kanole found it by reading the wave patterns in the sea," Mark said. "It had a low ridge of hills, with two prominent hills at one end. It looked like a sleeping woman, and the two larger hills were breasts. It's funny, the island isn't on the charts. I looked before we escaped, and there was no island on the charts. I told

Kanole he was wrong, but it was there, right where he said it would be. He read it in the water. I buried him there, and Leilani was there and we . . ." Mark stopped and rubbed his shoulder. "Perhaps it was Rose. Yes, Rose McPheeters was there, on the island. She gave me soup and we made love. I had malaria, you see. I contracted the disease while I was in Cuba. And once while in the navy, we engaged a slaver ship. Gunner's Mate Peterson and his crew were killed during that engagement. They didn't swab the barrel, and when the bag of powder was placed in the tube, it exploded. I wrote to Mrs. Peterson and expressed my sorrow, but I couldn't go to visit her because I was dishonored."

Mark rubbed the scar on his face again.

"The island, man, tell me more about the island," Pugh demanded impatiently.

"How did Leilani get there?" Mark suddenly asked.

"I don't know," Pugh replied. "Was she there?"

"Why does she haunt me so? What is there about her?"

Mark walked over to the wall and slid down it to a sitting position. He lay his head on his knees and pressed his fingers against his temples. "I have a headache," he said. "I can't remember anything else. I'm sorry, Dr. Pugh."

"Mark," Pugh said. "Listen to me, because this is important. You keep trying to remember.

Try to remember everything. I'll get back to you. I'm going to get you out of here."

"There is one thing I remember," Mark said clearly.

"What is that?"

"I am going to be hanged tomorrow morning at dawn."

"No, you won't be hanged," Pugh said resolutely. "I'll see to that."

"You'd better hurry, doc. Time is running out," Mark said.

"Don't worry about it," Pugh said.

Mark laughed bitterly. "Less than twelve hours before I'm due to hang and you tell me not to worry about it. Do you really expect me not to worry?"

"I'll get you out," Pugh promised again.

Mark lay down on the floor and stretched out. "In that case, I'll be able to get a good night's sleep," he said.

Chapter Twenty-Nine —————————

ANGUS PUGH WAS very excited by his conversation with Mark. The island Mark mentioned had looked "like a woman sleeping," and wasn't on any of the charts. He was certain that it must be Drake's Sleeping Lady Island. And, with the Thorncrown Bird in his possession, it seemed to Pugh that the treasure was about to tumble into his lap.

Angus Pugh prevailed upon Reverend Jebediah Grimsley and Leilani to help him, and their combined appeal brought great pressure on Governor Kekuanna to release Mark. But they still might not have been successful if there not been a sensational and brutal murder of one of the new prostitutes recently arrived on the *Distant Star*.

The local newspaper had dubbed it the "pious murder" because the girl's body was found in the position of prayer, and a Bible was found in her hands. The girl's murder and the search for her killer had turned public attention away from Mark Costain, and Governor Kekuanna was able, in a magnanimous gesture, to grant Mark a pardon. The five hundred dollars Pugh paid Kekuanna had also helped.

Once Mark was released, he moved in with Dr. Pugh, and Angus began a systematic form of treatment, designed to help him regain all his memory. Mark was told to relax and not even to try to think about what had happened until Pugh questioned him. The nightly sessions were grueling, but effective, and within a few weeks, Mark had recalled practically all that had happened to him. He remembered the destruction of the *Sea Eagle*, the cruise of the *Mary Luck*, and the near mutiny when he and Kanole escaped.

He could also remember that there was an island, but he could remember nothing about it, nor could he remember how many days, or in which direction, he had sailed from the *Mary Luck* to reach it. And he remembered absolutely nothing about the voyage from the island until he was picked up by Milam Beeker.

"Leilani must have been on the island," Angus said.

"I suppose she was," Mark replied.

"She had to be. She was in the boat with you when you were picked up."

"How did she get there?" Mark wondered.

"Maybe she swam there after she destroyed your ship," Angus suggested.

"Impossible. We had covered more than a thousand miles with the *Mary Luck*, and the island couldn't have been more than two hundred miles from the point where Kanole and I quit the ship. He was badly wounded, remember, and would have died before we had covered a great distance. That would put the island at least eight hundred miles from here, and no one can swim eight hundred miles. So how did she get there?"

"Did she have a boat?"

"No."

"A raft, perhaps?"

"She could have fashioned a raft of sorts from the wreckage of the ship," Mark agreed.

"Eight hundred miles on a raft is not an unheard of accomplishment," Pugh suggested. "Especially for the Hawaiians. They are used to traveling great distances over the ocean in open boats."

"Have you asked Leilani?" Mark said. "What does she say about this?"

Pugh slowly filled his pipe. "Mark, did you tell the girl you were in love with her?"

"What?"

Pugh lit the pipe. "She is an Alii-Nui, you know."

"So I have been told."

"All Hawaiians are proud people, and Alii-Nuis are even more proud. They are of royal blood, you understand, and revered by their people above all but the king."

"I don't understand," Mark said. "What has all this to do with me?"

"Leilani has been badly hurt emotionally," Pugh said. "She won't speak to me about it. She won't talk about what happened on the island, or how she got there. But Milam Beeker tells me that she is in love with you. And she believed you were in love with her."

"Why would she think that?" Mark asked.

"You told her perhaps?" Pugh suggested.

"Oh, come, Dr. Pugh. I enjoy the ladies, and sometimes in moments of passion I may say words which I think they want to hear. But I don't feel I should be held responsible for those words."

"Beeker feels it was more than that."

"From what I have observed, Captain Beeker would like it more if it weren't true," Mark said. "I have been told that she frequently warms his bed."

"All the more reason to believe what he says," Pugh said.

Max rubbed the scar on his face, then felt the spot on his shoulder. He felt a slight dizziness. A shadowy image started floating up from his memory, then was lost again.

"No," he said finally. "I have said nothing to make her think I love her."

"That's too bad."

"Why?"

"I feel it would be to our advantage for her to think that you do love her," Pugh said.

"For what reason?"

"Perhaps she would guide us to the island."

"What makes you think she could find it?" Mark asked.

"Didn't you say Kanole found the island by reading the wave patterns?"

"Yes."

"Leilani knows the same skill. If you could navigate the ship to where the *Mary Luck* was when you and Kanole left her, I feel certain that Leilani would be able to follow the wave patterns to the island."

"Perhaps she will if you ask her," Mark suggested.

"I have asked her."

"And?"

"She will not." Pugh took a long, audible puff on his pipe and studied Mark for a moment. "But I feel certain she would if she believed that you loved her."

"No," Mark said. "I will not deceive her."

"Why not? She destroyed your ship, and she nearly destroyed you."

"I . . . I don't know. There is something about her . . . something which haunts me," Mark said. Again the wave of dizziness, and a fog-shrouded image passed Mark's mind, but he couldn't grasp it.

"If Leilani doesn't help us, we have no hope," Pugh said.

"Perhaps we can force her to help us," Mark suggested.

"How? You have already said that you won't deceive her."

"I won't lie to her by telling her I love her," Mark said. "But I would have no qualms about kidnapping her, and ransoming her freedom for her help."

"Are you serious?"

"Quite."

"I see no logic to you, sir. On the one hand you won't engage in a harmless deception, while on the other you would resort to kidnapping to force her cooperation."

"The deception you speak of is not harmless," Mark said. "There would be hurt which would take a long time to heal. A mere kidnapping will leave no such hurt."

"Perhaps you are correct," Pugh said. "But the question now is, how shall we kidnap her? She lives in the village as its leader, and there is no way we could sneak in for her. We would be killed if we tried."

"Mohammad need not go to the mountain," Mark said, "If the mountain comes to Mohammad."

"I don't understand."

"Leilani will come to see Milam Beeker. We merely wait for her, and grab her when she comes."

"Yes," Pugh said. "Yes, that is a good idea. But we should leave as soon as we get her. You'd best get the *Distant Star* ready to sail. You can use the same crew which brought her here."

"No. Leilani made too many friends among the crew. One might help her to escape. I'll get a new crew. Ben Hall and Mike Fitzpatrick are here from my crew on the *Sea Eagle*. I shall use them."

Pugh walked over to a shelf and unlocked a metal box. He removed the golden Thorn-crown Bird and looked at it lovingly. "Little bird, soon we'll have all your friends here, and I'll be rich."

"We'll be rich," Mark corrected. "For if I am to engage in this scheme with you, half will be mine."

"Agreed," Pugh said, smiling easily. There would be more than enough money for both of them, as well as generous shares for the crew.

Chapter Thirty

CALVIN LAY IN bed, spent and limp and unprotesting as the girl used a towel to clean him.

"I'll bet this is something the native girls don't do for their men," the girl, Sarah, said. "Rose says we have to provide a bit of extra service for our customers if we expect to compete with the Hawaiian girls. Of course, I'm thinkin' the sailors may have an occasional taste for white girls, too, and that should be an advantage."

When Calvin had begun his crusade, he was overcome with modesty at the end of each session, and offended by the nudity of the women who were with him. But he had grown used to that, almost jaded in fact, and it no longer bothered him to lay nude before them, or to see them nude before him. He reached down now to his clothes to make sure the small Bible was still in place.

The Bible had been a more recent addition to his crusade. He had bought an entire case of them, and intended to make a gift of them to each of the harlots whose souls he saved. It was a fitting gesture to the sacrament.

"Wasn't that just awful about poor Mary?" Sarah went on. "Do you know that's two of Rose's girls who've been murdered now? Of course, Darcey wasn't exactly murdered, but she's dead just the same, and that captain same as murdered her if you ask me. There now, are you all cleaned off, honey?" Sarah stood up and put the used towel on a table beside the bed. Her red hair, and the red triangle which crowned the junction of her legs, shone brilliantly in the afternoon sun. A spray of freckles decorated her nose and shoulders, but stopped before they reached her breasts, milk white and almost pearshaped.

"It is to be hoped that Mary found favor in God's eyes before she left this world," Calvin said.

"What? Oh, yes, I suppose so," Sarah replied, then added, "That's a strange thing to say."

"Why is it strange?" Calvin asked. "Is it not the hope of all to reach heaven?"

"Yes, but I mean to talk about it now . . . here," the girl said. As if moved by sudden modesty, she turned away from Calvin and began putting on her clothes.

He sat up and pulled on his pants and shirt. He finished dressing just as the girl did.

"Get on your knees with me and pray for forgiveness," Calvin said.

"No, I . . . I don't want to talk about this," Sarah said. "Please, go away."

Calvin was getting through to her. He knew it! He felt a spiritual excitement running through him as powerful as the lustful excitement he had felt earlier. He put his hand on her shoulder.

"But we must talk about it. Your soul is in jeopardy, for you have sinned before the Lord."

Tears welled up in Sarah's eyes. "Please," she said in a choked voice. "Please don't speak of this. My father is a minister, and I've disgraced him. It pains me to think of this. Please, do not do it to me."

Calvin was flushed with the scent of victory, and he continued his relentless assault on her soul. "It must be done," he said. He held up the small Bible he was going to give her. "For it sayeth in Ezekiel 23:48: *Thus will I cause lewdness to cease out of the land, that all women may be taught not to do after your lewdness.* As God's messenger, I must bring this about."

Sarah began crying. "I am a sinner," she said. "I am a terrible sinner and I am so afraid."

"Tell me, my child," Calvin said enthusiastically, "what do you fear?"

"As my father warned me," Sarah said. "I fear God's wrath."

"Oh, yes, oh, yes, oh, yes," Calvin said. His breath was growing more labored, and a bead of sweat appeared on his upper lip. His eyes were flashing with the fire of a zealot. "And what do you want?" he asked.

"I want salvation."

"That is good, that is good!" Calvin yelled excitedly. He handed the girl the Bible, then forced her to her knees. He put his hands on her head. "Before salvation, you must have absolution. You do want absolution, don't you?"

"Yes, yes," Sarah cried.

"Then pray for it, child. Ask your Heavenly Father to forgive you."

"Oh Lord," Sarah cried, "Please forgive me for the sinner I am."

"God, this is Calvin Grimsley, your messenger," Calvin said, looking toward heaven. "Through me, your spirit has moved into the body of this miserable harlot and sinner. Now, through the power You have given me, I cast the sin from this girl's body, and grant her your forgiveness, and Your salvation. And into Your hands, I commit her soul."

"Oh, yes, I feel the spirit, I feel the spirit," Sarah cried. She clutched the Bible Calvin had given her to her bosom.

"What a happy day this is for you, my child," Calvin said, "for on this day you will be with the Lord. I will send you there, just as I did the others, including Mary, our sister in Christ."

Calvin moved his hands down to Sarah's neck and began to squeeze. It was a moment before she realized what was happening, then with a strength born of a sudden fear, she grabbed his ankles and jerked, pulling him off his feet. He fell with a crash, losing his grip on her.

"You!" she cried, standing up and holding her throat. "You are the killer!"

She looked at the Bible, then threw it down. "Yes," she said. "They found a Bible in poor Mary's hands! My God! Help! Help me, somebody, here is the murderer!" she began screaming.

"No!" Calvin shouted. "No, please, you don't understand. It was so wonderful with us. You felt the spirit, didn't you? You said you did. Please, don't destroy that spirit."

"Help!" Sarah screamed again.

Calvin regained his feet and began backing away from her. He held both his hands out trying to quiet the girl's screams, but he was unsuccessful, and her shouts grew louder.

There was a sound of footsteps running down the hall toward the room. Someone began banging on the door.

"Sarah, what is it?"

"This man in here killed Mary," Sarah screamed. "And he's trying to kill me!"

"No," Calvin pleaded. "Don't tell them that. They won't understand. Only you can understand, because only you felt the spirit!"

There was more pounding on the door, then men's voices, and finally the door exploded into the room in a shower of splinters. Rose stood on the other side of the door, and with her were the two huge Hawaiians, her house bouncers. Rose pointed to Calvin. "Get him," she ordered.

Calvin felt pure terror welling up inside him, and he turned and ran to the window. He didn't hesitate but jumped through the glass, cutting his hand and tumbling onto the roof. He grabbed the edge to save himself from falling over, then swung down, landing easily on his feet.

"He's getting away!" someone shouted.

Calvin ran through the night, his legs pumping furiously, his heart beating so wildly that he could hear nothing behind him. He darted behind a building, then ran down an alley and cut in-between two more buildings before any of his pursuers could see where he went. After a wild run of nearly half a mile, he came pounding out onto the docks. A longboat, captained by a red-headed, freckle-faced man was just pulling away. The man's name, Calvin knew, was Fitzpatrick.

"Wait for me," he shouted.

"Hold it up, men," Fitzpatrick said. "Are you coming to join the crew, lad?" he called to Calvin.

"Yes," Calvin answered, panting hard.

"You made it just in time. We're weighing anchor right away."

Calvin got into the longboat and leaned against the gunwales, breathless, his chest aching. Looking back at the dark streets of Lahaina, he saw quick shadows searching for him, carrying torches now, looking up every alley and drive.

"Take a good look at the town, lad, for we'll be far at sea by sun-up," Fitzpatrick said.

"Good," Calvin replied. "I've need to get away for a time."

"Ah, and you'd be havin' some young girl after you I reckon?" Fitzpatrick asked with a laugh.

"You could send 'er my way, lad," one of the sailors joked, and the others laughed aloud. Calvin stayed silent.

The longboat scraped up against the side of the ship, and the jacob's ladder was dropped over. Calvin and the other men climbed aboard, one at a time, and stood in a loose group on deck. A moment later, a man came to speak to them. Calvin recognized him as the American ship's captain who had nearly started the revolution.

"Men, my name is Mark Costain, and I welcome you aboard the *Distant Star*. We are waiting for one more person to come aboard . . . a passenger of sorts . . . and then we get underway."

"Where are we bound, Cap'n?" one of the sailors, who had come aboard with Calvin, asked.

"Are you not satisfied with the wages we've offered?" Mark replied.

"Aye, Cap'n, satisfied enough," the sailor answered.

"Then don't be concerned with our destination. We've ample fare on board and the voyage should be an easy one. I'll promise you this, men. If we are successful, there will be a share for each of you at the end of the cruise. But for now, I'm afraid we must have a few secrets from you."

"That's fine by us, Cap'n," the sailor said. "A bonus can buy my silence."

"Good, good. Now, there's one more thing. The passenger we'll be taking aboard isn't exactly a volunteer, if you get what I mean. But you don't worry about that. The passenger is my responsibility. Are there any questions?"

There was a general murmur of acceptance from the crew.

"The officer who brought you here is Mike Fitzpatrick. Your first mate will be Ben Hall. You'll take your orders from them, as well as from me," Mark said.

"Cap'n, there's a boat approachin'," one of the sailors said.

"Mr. Fitzpatrick, see to our new crewmen," Mark said. "That'll be our passenger. I'll see to her."

"Her?" one of the new sailors asked.

"No questions," Mark warned sternly.

When the boat pulled alongside, the unconscious form of a girl was passed up.

"Is she all right, Mr. Hall?" Mark asked. "What have you done to her?"

"Nothing," the bald-headed man called up. He adjusted his eye patch and spit a stream of tobacco over the gunwales of the boat. "She's been given a dose of chloroform. She'll be out for a while, but she'll be fine."

"Good job, Mr. Hall," Mark said. "Now, secure the boat. I intend to get underway at once."

"Aye, sir," Hall answered.

The girl was carried across the deck, and down the ladderway through the forward hatch. In the light of the moon, Calvin saw her face.

It was Leilani.

Chapter Thirty-One

WHEN LEILANI AWOKE, she was lying in a bunk in a cabin she recognized as the one Rose McPheeters had used during the *Distant Star*'s earlier voyage.

Why was she here? What had happened?

Her head hurt, and almost immediately she remembered how she had been kidnapped. She had started into Beeker's Bar to see Milam, when someone grabbed her. She struggled, and something was held over her nose, and she passed out. But what was she doing here, on the *Distant Star*?

There was a knock at the cabin door.

"Yes," she called.

The door opened and Mark Costain stepped in.

At the sight of him a thrill coursed through her. All the passion she held for him seemed on the verge of exploding. She took a deep breath, controlling her feelings, and was able to speak in an even voice.

"Mark, what is this?" she asked. "Why am I on this ship?"

"We are going to take a little trip," he said.

"To where?"

"To the island."

"Yes, Mark, that might work," she said, her mind working fast through the mystery of being on board the *Distant Star*. "Perhaps if you returned to the island, you would regain your memory."

"I have regained my memory," Mark said.

"You have?" She laughed and threw her arms around his neck. Happiness pulsed through her veins, and she nearly wept in relief. "Then you do love me and everything is going to be fine."

Mark removed her arms carefully. "Leilani . . . I must be honest with you," he said. "I find you a very beautiful girl, and any man would be very lucky to have you. But I'm simply not the kind of man who can be tied down . . . or be satisfied with one woman."

The words hit her as surely as a cold slap in the face. "Then I don't understand. What am I doing here?" She slipped back on the bunk, as far from him as she could be. What sort of madness possessed him now?

"I must return to that island." His words came to her through the din of her own thoughts. "And only you can find it."

Again she felt as though he had struck her. She sat and regarded him coldly. All feeling seemed to leave her body as the icy truth grabbed her heart. She opened her mouth to speak, and the words seemed to come from far away.

"I see," she said tonelessly. "This has to do with the treasure Pugh was talking about, doesn't it? Well, I wouldn't help Dr. Pugh, and I won't help you."

"I think maybe you will," Mark said.

"And why do you think this?"

"Because, quite simply, you are my prisoner now," Mark said. "And you'll remain my prisoner until you agree to help."

She allowed the shadow of a smile to cross her lips. "Do you believe you can keep me a prisoner?"

"I will keep you a prisoner," Mark said. "I know of your tricks now, and I'm prepared for them. That door will be locked constantly, and there will be a guard outside at all times. There are bars over the window since that is the way you left my cabin on board the *Sea Eagle*. There is no way you can escape. This time, when I want to see you, you'll be here." He stopped, his fingers absently touching the spot on his shoulder. Then, distantly, he murmured, "You broke your promise to me on the island. You said you would be there when I woke up, but you weren't."

He felt a wave of dizziness, and again a memory tried to return to him and he tried to grasp it, but finally it slipped away.

"Mark, you do remember, don't you?" Leilani

said cautiously. His eyes looked glazed, and she searched in them for the Mark she loved.

"Remember? Remember what?"

"The island. My promise to you. I was gone when you woke because I went to pray for Kanole. But I returned . . . you must remember that I returned. And the other promise I kept, as well. I still loved you when you woke."

"I . . . I don't know what you are talking about," he said. He turned abruptly to leave then looked back at her with a pained expression clouding his face. "Believe me, Madam, I wish I did. You are a very beautiful woman."

Leilani looked away quickly.

"You'll be comfortable here, I'm certain."

As he left, she heard the locks fall in place. She returned to her bunk and lay down.

Did Mark remember, or didn't he? Why had he regained his memory in all other things, but not in this? Was it possible that he had spoken those words to her, but hadn't meant them? And now he refused to confess this?

No, that wasn't possible, she told herself. Mark loved her. She knew that he loved her. When they made love, it was unlike anything she had ever experienced before. And she knew that he had felt the same thing. Why, then, could he not remember?

An unwanted answer crept into her thoughts. Perhaps she had bewitched him. The sexual power of the Alii-Nui was great, and Mark might have come under this power. If so, then it would not have been Mark's heart which spoke of love. It would have been his body. And his body would have been under the enchantment of her sexual power.

It would be so much easier if she could fall in love with another. Perhaps someone like Milam. But though she had tried to forget Mark, she had been unable to. No one filled her heart as did Mark Costain.

Damn Mark Costain! Had he rendered her incapable of ever giving her love to another? Perhaps she was wrong. Perhaps she had not enchanted Mark Costain as much as Mark Costain had enchanted her . . .

She could hear the sounds of the sea rushing by the ship's hull. There were groans in the wood and creaks in the rope. Occasionally one of the sails would give out a thunderclap as the canvas spilled wind. There was nothing she could do now, and she knew it, so she closed her eyes and within a few moments, was sound asleep.

Milam Beeker did not know of Leilani's capture, because he was involved in the excitement over the near murder of Sarah. The would-be murderer was definitely identified as Calvin Grimsley, and now the police were looking everywhere for him.

Everywhere except the Grimsley home. That task fell to Milam Beeker.

Milam followed the directions he had been given to the house, and when he first saw it, he feared he had made a mistake. It was a small, grass house, held together with sticks and mud. He had seen more substantial-looking pigstyes. In fact, most of the native houses he had seen since coming to the island were better looking than this small hovel.

Milam knocked on the wooden frame of the door, then stood back a moment until the curtain was pulled to one side.

"Yes?" a woman asked. She brushed a strand of hair back from her face and stared at him with curious eyes.

"Are you Mrs. Grimsley?"

"Yes."

"Mrs. Grimsley, I'm looking for your son."

"I don't know where he is," Marcia said. "I'm a little worried about him. He should be here by now."

"Perhaps Reverend Grimsley knows?"

"The reverend isn't here either," Marcia said. "He had to go to Honolulu to check on our supplies. He is not likely to return for a week to ten days."

"And you have no idea where your son might be?"

"No, I'm afraid not. Why?"

"I'd rather not say just now," Milam said.

"Please, tell me," Marcia said. "Is anything wrong?"

Milam looked at the woman. There was a beauty to her which wasn't immediately apparent, but which could be found when looked for. There was more than beauty, however. There was gentleness and suffering. Most of all, there was suffering.

God, how could Milam add to her suffering by telling her about Calvin?

"I can't tell you, Mrs. Grimsley. Please, don't ask me to."

Inside the woman's eyes a light flickered, then went out. It was as if something, some hope, died.

"He isn't injured in some way?"

"No." Milam sighed. "Someone will tell you. It may as well be me."

"He has done something wrong, hasn't he?"

"I'm afraid so, Mrs. Grimsley."

"What has he done?"

Milam took a deep breath and steeled himself. "He's done murder," he said.

Milam couldn't get the thought of the woman out of his mind as he returned to town. He'd never seen such pain and anguish in a person's eyes. It was as if her eyes were windows which opened to the soul, and he could see all the demons of her private hell. But she didn't even shed a tear.

And that was what Milam found so distressing. Seeing those eyes . . . those magnificent, beautiful, soul windows that knew such pain without even the comfort of a tear. No woman had ever moved him so, and he knew he was going back tonight.

Jebediah had so dominated Calvin's life that Marcia felt like an outsider with her own son. The fact that she was Calvin's natural mother, while Jebediah was not Calvin's natural father, seemed to have no effect on her relationship with her son. When Milam Beeker told her that Calvin had done murder, the words were merely locks on a door which had been closed for many years.

But now something else bothered Marcia. Something had happened to her as she spoke with Milam Beeker. A resolution of sorts, a cry from some inner part of her, screamed for Marcia to find a new freedom. It was as if locking the old door on Calvin had opened a new window onto her life. And somehow, she knew this man—Milam Beeker—would be part of it. She was not surprised, then, when he came to her house again later that evening. It was predestined, and whatever happened, would happen. She knew she would have no control over it.

"Have you found him?" she asked.

"No," Milam said. "I thought perhaps you might have heard something. That was why I came back."

"I've heard nothing," she said. She was playing the game with him, though she knew it was but a game. And she knew that Milam knew it, too. She stepped back from the door. "Won't you come in . . . Milam?"

"Yes, thank you."

She looked at him in the failing light of the evening. He had a face weathered from years at sea, and there was none of the slim youthful grace of Joseph, her young lover of so many years ago. But Milam was a man, and he was the first man Marcia had looked at in such a way for over twenty years. She touched him on the cheek, then pulled her hand away.

"No," she said quietly. "No, I can't do this."

"Yes, you can," Milam said gently.

"I mustn't."

"Do you know a girl named Leilani?" Milam asked.

"Yes, I know her very well. She was a student of mine," Marcia said.

"That's interesting, because I was a student of hers."

"You were her student?"

"Yes. I learned that moments like this are too precious to allow them to escape. I'll not pass this moment by."

Milam put his arms around her and pulled her to him, pressing his lips against hers. Marcia returned the kiss with equal passion. Suddenly, as if struck by what she was doing, she broke away.

"Please, no," she said. She was trembling in his arms like a frightened bird. Tears streamed down her face. "Please, Milam, help me to fight this thing."

"Don't fight it, Marcia, be a part of it," Milam said. He tried to kiss her again, and when she turned her lips away to avoid him, he moved his kiss down to her neck. Her skin was incredibly warm, and the pulse in her neck was beating rapidly. For one instant she leaned against him, pressing her body against his, then she gasped for breath with a crying, pleading sound. "I beg of you," she said, "don't you know what you are doing to me?"

Milam broke off his kiss and looked down at her. "I can't help it," he said. "From the moment I saw you this afternoon, I knew I would be back. I was compelled by some force beyond my power. Marcia, I'm caught up in a whirlpool, woman, and I cannot get free. I must have you, can't you see that? I *will* have you!"

I will have you! The words burned themselves into Marcia's heart. They were the same words she had put on the lips of hundreds of men in thousands of nights of fantasies, while she slept cold and lonely, aching for a word of affection or a tender caress.

"I'm married," Marcia said, forcing the words out.

"That doesn't matter," Milam replied. "Your husband isn't here now. I am."

Milam's kisses came again, and he brushed back her hair to kiss her forehead, then her cheeks, and finally, her mouth again.

"Milam, we mustn't do this," Marcia said. Her breathing was very heavy now, and the words were spoken in a whisper of anguish. "It's not right. The reverend won't . . ."

"The reverend be damned. To hell with him, and to hell with his church," Milam said.

"Milam, please don't talk like that! I'm a Christian woman."

"No, by God, you're a woman!"

All the while he was talking, his hands were moving over her body. They were strong hands, warm hands, and they left their mark on her in a blaze of heat wherever they traveled.

She tried to fight against his words, but felt herself growing weaker and more confused. It was difficult to believe this was happening to her, and even more difficult to marshal her defenses against it. The warmth spread through her, carrying her away with dizzying speed. Milam continued to kiss her with open, hot lips, as confidently as if he didn't care if all Hawaii were watching.

Marcia had never been kissed by Reverend Grimsley. Not since she had tasted Joseph's lips as a young girl had she experienced a real kiss, and she had nearly forgotten how it could make her go hot and cold and shaky all at the same time. She surrendered herself to him then, unable to fight him and her own emotions at the same time. She fell to his will, eager to do his every bidding.

Milam bent her body backward and his lips traveled down to her throat where the first button fastened her blouse. His fingers opened up her bodice and moved underneath, across her scorching skin, and to her breast, warm and vibrant, straining to be touched. A soft cry of protest formed in her throat, but emerged instead as a sigh of ecstasy.

He moved her toward the bed and lay her on it. His hands were busy, here freeing a breast, there raising a skirt. There was a soft breeze blowing, and Marcia felt it caressing her naked thighs, making her aware of her nudity. From the waist down, she was as naked as the day she was born. It was a good feeling that she had waited to feel again for many years.

Marcia's legs were downy soft and milky white beneath the sea-browned, muscled legs of Milam. She looked at their legs as if to steady herself, and tried hard to fix the image of them in her mind, to catch up with events which were sweeping her along with dizzying speed.

Milam didn't wait but moved over her, then into her, and for the first time in over twenty years, Marcia was a woman being loved. She didn't care what happened after this.

She felt his weight and breathed the male scent of him, tobacco and leather, rum and the sea. She thrust against him, giving him the pent-up feelings of a lifetime. Then it started, a tiny tingling which began deep in her, pin-wheeling out, spinning faster and faster until every cell in her body was caught up in a whirlpool of pleasure. Her body was wound like the mainspring of a clock, tighter and tighter, until finally, in a burst of agony which turned into ecstasy, her body attained the release and satisfaction it had long yearned for. There were a million tiny pins pricking her skin, and involuntary cries of pleasure coming from her throat. She felt as if she lost consciousness for just an instant, and lights passed before her eyes as her body gave its final, convulsive shudders.

They lay together for several minutes while Marcia floated with the pleasant sensations which stayed with her like the warmth that remains after the fire has gone.

"Be honest with me, Marcia," Milam finally said. "Has your reverend ever made you feel like this?"

"I've never had sex with Reverend Grimsley," Marcia said quietly.

Milam sat up quickly and looked over at her. He was shocked. "What?"

"Reverend Grimsley swore an oath of celibacy before we were married. He has never violated that oath."

"But your son?"

"There was another . . . a boy I knew before I was married. Calvin is his son."

"And in all this time Reverend Grimsley has never touched you?"

"Never."

Milam stood up and took a few of steps across the room, then whirled around angrily. "By all that's holy, woman, what the hell kind of man is he? You are a woman, Marcia, with a woman's natural needs. To deny you all these years . . . it's inhuman and cruel!"

"He will deny me no more," Marcia said.

"Good. You've come to your senses then,"

Milam said. "You'll be leaving him, I suppose?"

"No," Marcia said. She smiled at Milam, then got out of bed and padded across the floor to kiss him. "No, Milam. I'll not be leaving him. But I will be prepared to leave him if I have to. I have been reawakened to what has been denied me all these years, and I will be denied no longer."

"I wish you the best then, Marcia," Milam said.

"Thank you. And thank you for coming into my life now, when I needed you. Forgive me please, dear Milam, for stepping back out of yours."

Milam smiled. "I'll tell you what, Madam. If that man of yours is so foolish as not to listen to you, then you'll always have a place with me. As my wife, if you wish."

Chapter Thirty-Two ───────────

No MATTER WHERE Mark positioned himself on the ship, his thoughts returned to the cabin where Leilani was. He couldn't understand why he couldn't get her out of his mind.

Surely there was nothing to the girl's claim that he loved her. Of course, he may have told her that when they made love. But he shouldn't be held accountable for words uttered during moments of passion. They were mere words which seemed to add to the woman's enjoyment. They had only a momentary truth at best.

There was one unusual aspect about this entire thing. He couldn't remember making love to her. He could remember that they did make love . . . but he could remember nothing about it.

And yet, perplexing as it was, he couldn't forget it, either.

Of all the women Mark had bedded, and once in a moment of satisfied reflection he figured that he had had sex with more than five hundred, there was none who had made enough of an impression on him to stand above the rest.

There was none, that is, until he met Leilani.

Mark went to her cabin and stood just outside her door. "Has she made any sound?" he asked the guard.

"No, sir."

"Unlock the door. I wish to speak with her."

"Aye, aye, sir," the guard said. He unlocked the padlock and Mark stepped inside.

Leilani was sitting on the bunk with her knees drawn up and her arms around them. She looked up as Mark entered.

"What do you want?" she asked, looking away.

"I want to talk to you."

Tears came to her eyes and slid down her cheek.

Mark felt guilty, and he sat beside her and wiped the tears away with a handkerchief.

"Leilani, we don't have to battle," he said. "There's enough treasure for us all to have a share. Why won't you join us?"

"What do I want with treasure?" Leilani said. "It means nothing to me."

"Well, it means something to me, and I aim to have it. And you are going to help me find it."

"Why should I?"

"Because I intend to keep you prisoner on this ship until you do."

Leilani laughed, a cold, ironic laugh. "Captain Costain, I shall remain a prisoner on this ship for only as long as I wish to remain prisoner. In the meantime I have no intention of helping you find your treasure."

"We'll see about that," Mark said.

"Tell me. What do you want with the treasure anyway? What will you do with it? Buy more whiskey, more girls?" she asked.

"No," he answered. "With this money, I can get a new start. I can give up my odyssey."

"No more sirens to tempt you?" Leilani said.

Mark looked at her with a puzzled expression. Again he felt a dizziness, an attempt to recall something just beyond memory. He put his hand to his head.

"Is something wrong?" Leilani asked.

"No, I . . . it's nothing. I was dizzy for a moment, that's all."

"Perhaps it's the malaria."

"No," he said. "Have you ever tried to think of forever?"

"What?"

"You know. The idea of forever . . . on and on without end. Have you ever tried to grasp it with your mind?"

"No," Leilani said.

"Try it sometime. There's no standard to gauge forever by, and it can make the mind grow dizzy by thinking of it. That was how I just felt. There was something my mind tried to grasp, but it was just beyond memory and I couldn't come up with it."

"It was my mention of sirens to you," Leilani said. She felt herself soften toward him, hoping. "When you came to the island you told me the story of Odysseus and the sirens. Then you called me a siren."

"Please," Mark said, standing and holding his hand out to stop her. "Enough of this. Why must you continue to do this?"

"Why? Because I must know, Mark. If you are suffering from some temporary affliction, then I would be untrue to you if I abandoned what we had. But if there is truly nothing there, then I am foolish for hanging on. I must know the truth."

"You won't like the truth," Mark warned.

"It doesn't matter whether I like it or not. It only matters that I know it. What is the truth?"

"The truth is . . ." Mark started. The wave of dizziness swept over him again, and he looked at her as if trying to focus on her. "God help me, Leilani, I don't know what the truth is."

He ran from her cabin with the questions pounding in his mind. What was wrong? Why did he have no memory of loving Leilani? Why could he not accept her now? Why could he not forget her now?

Chapter Thirty-Three————————————

"I DON'T SEE why we have the girl locked up," one of the sailors said. There were several men, including Calvin and Ben Hall, standing around the sail locker on the orlop deck, talking together.

Hall was looking under a coil of rope. "Now, where in hell did I put it?" he mumbled, more to himself than the others.

"You put it in a different place every time," one of the sailors said.

"Hell, yes, I do," Hall exclaimed. "That's to keep you bastards out of it. Ah, yes, here it is."

Hall got on one knee and pulled a jug from beneath the bed. The cork came out with a hollow sound, and Hall turned it up, taking several bobbing swallows before he began to pass it around. He handed it to Calvin first.

"No, thank you," Calvin said. "I don't drink.

Liquor is the Devil's agent, and those who drink it serve his will."

"Right you are there, lad," Hall said. " 'Tis the Devil's brew all right, 'n' you're right not to drink it. Besides, it leaves the more for us, right, mates?"

The others agreed with Hall and laughed uproariously, then each took the jug for a long swallow.

"What do you say about the girl?" the first sailor who spoke asked again. "Why do we keep her locked up in the cabin? Seems to me there'd be more use to her if we brought her out 'n' let the crew have their way by 'er."

"She's a purty'n, all right," Hall agreed. He rubbed himself, unaware that he was doing so. "But I just can't get the picture out of my mind of that girl standin' there in front of the powder locker, holdin' a burnin' brand 'n' about to touch off that explosion. I'd sure hate to see somethin' like that happen to the *Distant Star*. I don't rightly know what the cap'n's got in mind, but I hope it ain't nothin' that would lead to somethin' like that."

"You mean you think the cap'n's right, keepin' the girl locked up?"

"Aye, I do that, lads. That girl's near on ter bein' a witch, 'n' you can't always depend on what's goin' to happen." Hall punctuated his statement by sticking a large wad of tobacco in his mouth.

Calvin laughed. "She isn't a witch, or a spirit,

I assure you. I've known her for her entire life. She's but a girl."

"I tell you this," Hall said, switching the tobacco from one cheek to the other. "I 'low as how that girl has addled up Cap'n Costain's brains somewhat. He sure don't seem the same no more."

"What is your reckon on what we're about, Mr. Hall?" one of the sailors asked. "'N' how does this girl figure in?"

"I'll tell you my reckonin'," Hall said. "My reckonin' is that we're goin' to Africy for a load o' slaves. 'N' this here girl is what we're goin' to trade to one of them African kings."

"Slaves?"

"That's my reckonin' on the matter. The cap'n promised a bonus at the end of the trip. I don't know nothin' which pays a better bonus than slavin'. Nor more fun, neither."

"Have you been on one?"

Hall laughed and pulled his eye patch off, then stared at the men with a sightless puff of red where the eye should have been.

"Mind me to tell you sometime 'bout how I lost this here eye," he said. "'Tweren't so much the losin' of it that makes the good tellin'. Some nigger pulled it outten my head afore I could stick him with my knife. But the slaver ship I was on. That's what the good story's about. Well, now, lads, that was quite a cruise. We cut us out the comeliest lookin' wenches in the kaffle, 'n' there was some fine lookin' ones too,

I'll tell you. The crew had a fine time! We slept warm all the way home."

Hall chuckled, and in his one good eye, Calvin could almost see the reflection of the man's wicked past. He saw flames licking at the villages, the men and women running in terror, the groans and shrieks of agony of the slaves on the ship, and the soft, brown bodies, visited night and day by the sailors. It was like looking into the very depths of hell.

Even as Calvin's flesh crawled from the revulsion of it all, he felt the unmistakable urges of lust as he thought of it. For a moment he indulged his fantasy, and he thought of what it would be like to have the girls here, to lust on their bodies and then bring their souls to the Lord.

"I mind the time we set out from Coramantine," Hall started.

"Mr. Hall, the cap'n's compliments, and he wants all hands on deck. There's a storm comin' up," Fitzpatrick yelled from above.

The men started topside, but Hall stopped Calvin. "Boy, you go and relieve Wise as guard to the girl. Don't mean to offend you none, but you ain't worth a damn in the riggin' 'n' like as not you'll get yourself kilt up there. Wise'll do us more good."

"Aye, sir," Calvin said gratefully.

Mark was on the quarterdeck, and he saw Hall and others come topside. He had no idea

how they would react as a crew. Except for
Fitzpatrick and Hall, they'd been put together
on short notice, gathered from the rum shops
and whore houses. This would be their first
test.

"Mr. Hall, we're into heavy seas," Mark said.
"We'll be taking in sail."

"Aye, aye, sir," Hall said. "All hands, all
hands, turn to, turn to," he shouted.

The bowsprit of the ship dipped and poked
through a large wave. The wave broke over the
bow and threw its spray the length of the deck.

"Reef the topsails," Mark ordered, and the
order was repeated by Hall. A handful of sailors
scrambled up the mast. "Lads, see that there
is a proper furl," Mark called.

The wind was blowing with gale force now,
and the ship was crashing violently through
the waves. Mark steadied himself at the rail and
watched the men work. They furled the topsails
with enough authority to satisfy him, but the
wind continued to build until suddenly the
great mainsail on the mainmast ripped open
from top to bottom.

"Lay up there and furl that sheet before it
blows to tatters," Mark shouted.

Men climbed the mainmast and began working on the torn sail, but no sooner had they
finished with it than the main skysail tore loose
and began flapping in the breeze, threatening
to pull away and take with it the main royal
mast which was now moving back and forth
like a wand.

The rain began to come then, in large, heavy drops, blowing in sheets across the deck, mixed with the salty sea spray. Finally the ship was rigged for storm with special sails, smaller, stronger canvas, triangular in shape, and mounted close to the deck. But even with the ship so rigged, the danger was great, and Mark found it necessary to keep all hands on station to prevent the storm from dismasting the ship . . . or causing an even more severe problem.

Calvin had been to sea very little, and then only on the small boats which traveled from place to place among the islands. He had never been to sea during a storm. He gripped the stanchion tightly and looked at the door which led to Leilani's cabin.

Leilani was the answer to all his problems. It was she who first awakened the sin of lust in him. She, with her devil's beauty, who tempted him to the way of evil. And yet she had denied him her body . . . used her wantonness to drive him to the point of despair, then withheld her flesh from him.

Now Calvin had crossed the line. He was unable to return home because he had been found out. He was acting in the Lord's service when he killed, but no one would understand that. He would be taken to jail, and martyred. That would disgrace his father, and besmirch the name of the Lord.

Calvin knew that there was only one person

to blame for that. Leilani. She was responsible
for all his problems, and she must be made to
pay for it. Oh, yes, she with her beauty and
her wantonness . . . she was the handmaiden of
the devil and she must die.

But before she died, she must be saved. And
she could be saved only one way. By fornicating
with the Lord's messenger. It mattered not
whether she was willing. As the messenger of
the Lord, Calvin was infallible. He would save
her by knowing her flesh, and as the waters of
baptism erased all sin, so would the sanctified
seed of Calvin's sexual act cleanse Leilani's soul.

He felt a tremedous erection straining at the
front of his pants, and he knew that was a sign
that what he planned to do was right and
proper. He unlocked the door to the cabin and
stepped inside.

Leilani was sitting on her bunk, riding out
the storm. She looked up to see who had come
in, and was surprised at seeing Calvin.

"What are you doing here?" she asked.

"I have come to save you."

So that explained the missionary boy's
presence. "Yes," she agreed. "During the storm
would be a good time. But with everyone on
deck, how will we launch a boat without being
seen?"

She stepped up to Calvin, ready to leave with
him but she was totally unprepared for what
happened next.

He grabbed the lava-lava she was wearing
and pulled it apart at the shoulders, so that it

fell to the floor in a pool of silk. Leilani found herself nude and she looked at him in surprise.

"Whore!" Calvin said. "Slut . . . adultress . . . vile creature of the flesh!"

With each word, Calvin brutally slapped Leilani, all the while forcing her back toward the bed.

"Calvin!" she shouted, raising her arms to defend herself. "What are you doing?"

She tried to assume a stance to use her martial arts to fight him off, but martial arts depend on balance, not strength, and with the ship pitching so violently, she could not get her balance.

"You denied me before," Calvin said. "I will not be denied again, for truly I am the sword and the shield of the Lord!"

He slapped her again and the slap coincided with the roll of the ship so that she was knocked down on her bed. She fell across it.

"Yea, verily I say unto you," Calvin said, "you are the whore daughter of Satan, and with the wantonness of your womb have you come to tempt me! But it is the will of God that I accept the temptation so to cleanse your spirit of the weakness of your flesh."

All the time Calvin was talking he was removing his clothes, and each time Leilani tried to get up, he slapped her back down again. By now a cut had opened and blood was trickling from the edge of Leilani's mouth.

"And now I shall know you for the whore

you are!" Calvin shouted. He forced her legs apart, and poised just above her, was ready to thrust into her.

Suddenly she saw a blur and heard the smack of fist against flesh. Mark stood at the foot of the bed, his face twisted in rage, his eyes flashing in anger. He was the avenging angel, and with one blow, he had swept Calvin aside.

"You son of a bitch!" Mark shouted angrily. "You get out of here. I'll deal with you later!"

"You are interfering with the work of the Lord," Calvin shouted.

"Get out of here before I kill you on the spot," Mark said.

Calvin scooped up his pants and darted out of the cabin. Mark slammed the door behind him, then turned to look at Leilani.

"Are you all right?" he asked.

"Yes," she said, touching her lip.

"Here, let me look at that," Mark said. He crossed over and sat on the bed with her, then cradled her face in his hand. With his other hand, he took out a handkerchief and dabbed at the cut.

"This handkerchief is as soaked from the storm as I am," he said. "But that is good, because it'll clean the cut better. There, that doesn't look too bad."

Leilani looked into Mark's face with her large, brown eyes, and for an instant, Mark had a memory of love-making in the soft sand on the beach of the island.

"I . . ." he began.

"Yes?"

Mark touched the spot on his shoulder and looked at Leilani with an expression of wonder. "What is it, Leilani? What is it about you? What is bothering me?"

She sighed deeply.

"Mark, don't you know? Don't you realize yet?"

"Don't try to tell me again I've sworn my love for you. If I did say it, it was under the effect of a malaria attack, and you can't hold me to that." He stood up and took a few steps away from the bunk. "Don't you understand? You can't hold me to that!"

Leilani said nothing. She just looked at him, her heart again torn with her love for him, with his confusing words. He was in torment, she knew. Surely he must know that she, too, felt the same anguish. She felt helpless.

"And don't look at me like that!"

She shifted her gaze to the rumpled bed. Her heart was breaking now. It was true. He had been affected by a malaria attack. That was all. She couldn't hold him to the words he had spoken then.

Suddenly Mark was on the bed with her, and his arms were around her. He pulled her to him, and pressed his lips against hers, hard, so hard that she felt pain in the cut.

"Don't you understand?" Mark said, breaking off the kiss. "This is all you are to me. You are someone to make love to, but not someone to love."

"Then I'll not be made love to," Leilani said. She twisted away from him, miserable and empty.

"Yes, by God, you will be made love to," Mark shouted. He grabbed her again and pushed her down, then removed his wet clothes as he held her trapped on the bed. "You've been wanting this, haven't you? Haven't you begged me for my love?" he asked mockingly. "Well, girl, this is the only love Mark Costain ever gives!"

Mark was naked in an instant, and his smooth, hard-muscled body was wet from the driving rain on deck. Leilani stared at him, at the wildness in his eyes. Shocked and hurt by this cruel, mocking display, she shuddered and fought back the tears pounding behind her eyes. Yet, as he reached out and touched her, the love for him flooded her and she trembled at the nearness of his manliness. She was weakening and she was afraid. Even though he was mocking her, telling her he didn't love her, she felt her body yielding.

"No," she said, her resistance ebbing from her. "I want your love, Mark Costain, or I want nothing."

"You're going to get my love," he said. "The only love I can give to anyone."

He moved over her and thrust into her. It was wrong, and she knew it was wrong. He was using her. He held her captive like one of the warrior kings in the old days of her people, and he took her like a male animal takes a mate. He offered her no love, no apology, gave her nothing but the driving flesh which was the badge of his manhood: the symbol of *haole* authority.

Leilani wrapped her arms around him and felt the raindrops on his body. She closed her eyes and Mark became as a dolphin to her, the dominating ruler of the seas, mahimahi, came to claim that which was his.

Like an erupting volcano, Leilani felt a searing flash, and as it happened, she put her fingers on the spot on Mark's shoulder, bringing him along with her in a shattering explosion which swept both of them into an ecstasy more tempestuous than the raging storm which held the ship in its grip.

"Will you say it now, Mark Costain?" Leilani asked a moment later.

He sat up and looked down at her. He put his hand on the spot on his shoulder, and his face was drawn into a mask of confusion. "Who are you?" he asked. "What are you?"

"I am Leilani."

Mark stood up. He grabbed his clothes and backed away from her with the look of confusion on his face now changing to one of fear. "No!" he said. "No! You are a siren come to claim my soul!"

Tears sprang to her eyes. What had been a feeling of exultation and joy turned to the bitter ashes of frustration and pain. "Get out," she said quietly. "Leave me be."

Mark stepped out of the cabin and slammed the door, then locked it securely. He pulled his

clothes on quickly and had just dressed when
Hall came running up to him.

"Cap'n, on deck quick," Hall shouted.

"What is it?"

"It's the Grimsley boy."

"I'll attend to him," Mark said angrily. "He
has punishment coming."

"I guess he's way ahead of you, Cap'n."

"What do you mean?"

"He's climbed to the top of the mainmast. I
think he aims to jump. Fitzpatrick is up there
tryin' to talk him out of it."

Mark hurried on deck and saw a small group
of sailors looking at the topmost yard of the
mainmast. Calvin was standing on top, and Fitzpatrick was just below him, talking quietly to
him.

"Grimsley, come down here," Mark called.

Calvin looked down at him, then looked up
toward heaven.

"Into your hands, oh, Lord," Calvin called.
He leaned forward, then plummeted straight
down, falling more than seventy feet. He kept
his arms locked by his sides all the way down,
and when he hit the deck, Mark heard his neck
snap as loudly as a dry twig breaking on a cold
day.

Chapter Thirty-Four————————

Sailors are apt to be a superstitious lot. The lower the caliber of the sailor, the more superstitious he is likely to be. And the men of Mark's crew on board the *Distant Star* came from the lowest strata imaginable. All were there by virtue of desertion or dismissal from their original crews. Even the officers, Hall and Fitzpatrick, wouldn't have measured up to the caliber of the mess boys Mark had when he served on U.S. naval vessels.

Among men disposed toward superstition, any rumors, misunderstandings, and unusual events can be given special meanings. Thus it was with the storm, Calvin's death, and the presence of Leilani. So concerned and restless was the crew that Mark found it necessary to have a meeting of all hands on the morning after the storm.

The meeting was held aft of the mizzenmast,

which had been damaged in the storm. Loose rigging and smashed fittings hung in disarray from the large pole, which looked naked without the great puffs of sail.

Mark paced back and forth on the quarter-deck, looking at the assembled men. He could see fear in the faces of some, curiosity in others. He ran his finger along the scar on his cheek and remained silent for several moments. There was, during this time, only the sounds of the sails and the creaking of the ship's fixtures as she answered the wind. Two birds from the nearby island of Hawaii fluttered above the swaying masts and called to each other in shrill cries.

Mark looked up at the smashed rigging. "Some of you will no doubt be happy to hear that we are going to put in to Honuapo on the Big Island to repair damages done by the storm," he said.

"Aye, 'n' I'm for stayin' there, I'm thinkin'," one of the men shouted.

Mark looked at the speaker, then at Ben Hall. "Mr. Hall, I believe that was Tim Brown. Would you see to it that he remains ashore when we anchor?"

"Aye, Cap'n," Hall answered.

"Is there anyone else who wishes to stay ashore?" Mark asked. His question was much more of a challenge than an inquiry, and no one else took him up on it.

"Very well, then I am to assume that the rest

of you are going with me. I can tell you now that we are bound on a mission which has no danger . . . but a great chance for a sizeable bonus for all."

"Are we slave shippin', Cap'n?" Hall asked.

"Slave? No, certainly not," Mark said. "Whatever gave you that idea?"

"You promised us a bonus," Hall said. "Don't know of any easier way to make a bonus."

"There is an easier way, Mr. Hall. And, as I said, a way where no risk is involved."

"What would it be?"

Mark rubbed his scar. He wondered if he should tell them, then decided that it might make for a more cooperative crew if they knew what they were working for.

"We're going after treasure," he said.

"Treasure? What sort of treasure?" someone shouted. There was a general murmur of surprise and excitement among the crew at the announcement.

"Buried treasure. We've discovered where Drake buried the treasure he took from the Spanish ships. There's gold, silver, and precious jewels. In short, gentlemen, a king's fortune. Enough to pay a handsome share to each of you."

"You say there's no danger?" Hall asked.

"No danger at all," Mark replied. "We merely go to the island and dig it up."

"Suppose this here Drake gets wind of what we're doin' and shows up to prevent it?"

Mark laughed. "That's highly unlikely. Sir Francis Drake has been dead for over hundred and fifty years."

"Are you trying to tell us that treasure has just laid out there for a hunnert 'n' fifty years, 'n' nobody's took it yet?" Hall asked.

"That's exactly what I'm trying to say," Mark said. "You see, Drake mischarted the island, and it's been lost all these years. But I just came from there. I've seen it."

There was a buzz of excitement among the men, then Fitzpatrick spoke up. "Cap'n, we're all for stayin' with you."

"What about the girl?" someone shouted.

"What about her?" Mark answered.

"She be a witch, don't she?"

"She's jinxin' the ship," another said.

"I don't mind tellin' you, I'm afeared of her."

"There is nothing to fear from this girl," Mark said.

"Is it true she destroyed your other ship?" one of the men shouted.

"Aye, that's true," Mark answered.

"'N' is it true a musket ball passed right through her?"

"No, that isn't true."

"Ain't she one of them Alii-Nuis?"

"Yes."

"Then she is a witch."

"She is no such thing," Mark said. "She's a woman, and that's all."

"She put a hex on the boy, Grimsley," one of the men said. "We all seen it. He come out of that cabin 'n' clumb up that mast like as if he was transfixed. There ain't no denyin' that, Cap'n, 'cause we done all seen it."

"If you want to know what made Grimsley kill himself, it was his fear of me," Mark said. "I caught him in the cabin attempting to rape the girl. I stopped it. I imagine he was afraid of what I would do to him."

The sailors looked at each other. It was easy enough for them to buy that explanation. Most of them had served with captains who could conceive of punishments which were cruel beyond imagining. They didn't know that Mark didn't believe in that kind of command, but they knew it was possible. Fear of that sort of punishment could drive a person to desperate measures, even suicide.

"Cap'n, why do we have the girl?"

"It's not necessary for you to know that," Mark said. "I can only tell you this. It is important that she not escape. And it is important that she not be harmed in any way. But you can put everything else about her out of your mind. She is just a girl, no different from any other."

"Hell, I'm for stayin' with the cap'n. It sounds pretty good to me," one of the sailors said.

"Me, too," another answered, and pretty soon all the sailors were laughing and cheering about their prospects of finding buried treasure.

"Cap'n, I reckon I could come along with you," Brown said.

"Mr. Brown, I believe you've made your decision," Mark replied. "You'll stay in Hawaii."

Mark dismissed the crew and returned to his cabin. He glanced toward Leilani's door just before he entered his own cabin, and thought about what he had told the men.

"She is just a girl," he said again, to himself this time. "No different from any other."

But even as he said the words he knew they weren't true. Leilani was different from anyone he had ever met.

The Reverend Jebediah Grimsley was on board the *Mary Luck,* returning to Lahaina from Honolulu, by way of Hanuapo. He had gone to Honolulu to try to locate the missionary supplies which were nearly one month late in getting to him. It was a frustrating trip, because he had found no supplies there.

Captain Jason Roberts had been in Honolulu, and Jebediah had managed to book passage for the return on his ship. Roberts was still looking for Mark Costain, whom Jebediah had helped gain his freedom from Governor Kekuanna's prison. Roberts wanted Costain for mutiny, and ordinarily Jebediah would have told what he knew of Costain's whereabouts. But for some reason he didn't tell Roberts. In fact, when Roberts asked him if he knew where Costain was, Jebediah lied.

The fact that he lied bothered Jebediah a great deal. He had never told a lie that he could remember. And yet he told a lie to Captain

Roberts. Of course, the question didn't even come up until Jebediah had had a chance to measure the man's cruelty. Jebediah believed that he had never seen a man who took more pleasure in inflicting pain than Captain Jason Roberts. He didn't know the reason for Mark Costain's mutiny. But he felt that any mutiny against this man would be justified.

It was nearly noon when the *Mary Luck* dropped anchor off Hanuapo. The sun was merciless, and the breeze which spilled from the reefed sails was no more than a hot breath of air.

"Anchor's let go, Cap'n," Bell shouted.

Of all the men on the ship, Jebediah felt most uncomfortable around the first officer, Bell. Bell did the whipping, and there had been a number of men flogged during the last few days. Bell used his whip with obvious enjoyment, and he always smiled when he looked at Jebediah, as if he would like to whip him. Everybody was a potential victim to him.

"Very well, Mr. Bell," Roberts replied. "See to the shore party."

"Aye, Cap'n," Bell said. He looked across the water at another ship. "Hey, Cap'n, don't that be the whore ship?"

Roberts took a look and grinned. It was the first time Jebediah had seen him smile since he came on board, and even when smiling, Roberts looked evil.

"I believe you're right," Roberts said. "Mayhaps we'll bring the girls over for another visit."

"I'm not sure they'll want ter come over, Cap'n," Bell said. "You hurt that one girl the last time, somethin' fierce."

"Watch your mouth, Bell, or you'll feel the bite of your own cat," Roberts snapped.

"Aye, Cap'n. I didn't mean nothin' by it," Bell apologized.

Roberts sent the short party off with a list of supplies and retired to his cabin to think about the whores. Perhaps he had gotten a bit carried away with the injured girl. But she seemed to enjoy it when they first started. She liked it when he tied her to his bunk, and had even gone along willingly when he put the gag in her mouth. But she didn't share the fun with him after that, when the whip snapped against her flesh.

Perhaps this time he would be more careful. If only the girl hadn't angered him. After all, it was her own fault.

There was a knock at the door, and Roberts was startled from his reverie.

"Yes, what is it?" he called irritably.

"Cap'n, we've got a visitor on board."

"I gave no permission to allow a boarder," Roberts said angrily.

"No, sir, you didn't," Bell said. "But I figure you'll want to talk to this man. He knows where Costain is."

Roberts sat up quickly. "Bring him to me, Mr. Bell, at once," he said.

Costain, Roberts thought. At last, he was about to get his hands on the man.

"He's in there, Brown," Roberts heard Bell say a moment later. "And you'd best show proper respec' for the cap'n. We don't run a loose ship here."

"Aye, sir, I know how to give proper respect," Brown said.

Roberts heard a hesitant knock on the door.

"Come in, man," he said.

Brown entered cautiously, hat in hand. "Beggin' the cap'n's pardon, sir," he said. "I was wonderin' iffen I could sign on with yer crew, jes' long enough to return to Lahaina."

"That might be arranged," Roberts said.

"Tell the cap'n about Costain," Bell said. Bell had come in behind the sailor and stood watching him.

"Aye, sir. I know where he is."

"Where?" Roberts asked, leaning over the table and looking at him.

"Right here, sir," the sailor said. "In Honuapo."

"Where in Honuapo?"

"He's cap'n of the *Distant Star*," Brown said.

"We've got 'em, Cap'n," Bell said, smiling broadly.

"Not quite," Roberts said. He stood up and walked over to the cabin window and looked across the still water at the *Distant Star*. "This changes things a mite. If he's captain of that ship, we'll have his whole crew to go through to get to him."

"I'll be happy to lead a boardin' party to get to the bastard," Bell said.

Roberts looked at Brown. "Are there whores on board the *Distant Star*?"

"Whores, sir?" Brown asked in confusion. "What do you mean?"

"Dammit man, you do know what a whore is?"

"Aye, sir."

"Well, are there whores on the ship?"

"No, Cap'n. There's only the one girl, 'n' she's a prisoner. But no one is usin' her as a whore. Unless of course the cap'n is. I doubt that he is, though, 'cause of the treasure."

"The treasure?" Roberts asked. "What treasure?"

"That's what the *Distant Star* is goin' after," Brown said. "Cap'n Costain says he knows where there's a buried treasure. I think he found it when he was on an island somewhere, or somethin'. Anyway, this girl seems to be the key to it all, 'cause he's laid down the rule about her. She's to be kept prisoner at all times."

Bell laughed. "You don't expect us to believe that bilge, do you?"

"I don't know, sir," Brown said. "That was jus' what the cap'n told us. He promised a share to all of the crew. I spoke out of turn, and was put ashore."

"What, exactly, did he say about the treasure?" Roberts asked.

"He told us about a fella named Drake who buried a treasure on some island hereabouts. The island was mischarted so it's been lost for over a hunnert years. But the cap'n, he happened onto the island, and knows all about it."

Roberts rubbed his chin reflectively and walked around his cabin.

"Cap'n, you don't believe this swill?" Bell asked.

"Just hold on for a moment," Roberts said, raising his hand to shush Bell. "Costain might have found an island when he left our ship. It would explain what happened to him. And there are no islands charted in those waters, so if he found one, it would be one that's not known." He looked at Brown. "I'll take you on, Brown. Report to the boatswain."

"Aye, sir, thank you, sir," Brown said.

"Bell, bring the preacher to me," Roberts ordered after Brown left. "Don't say anything to him about finding Costain, or about the treasure."

"What you want the preacher for?"

"Just do it, Bell, and quit questioning my every word," Roberts ordered.

"Aye, sir," Bell said.

Roberts waited anxiously for Bell to return with the preacher. Roberts had no education beyond the sea, but he knew that the preacher had. The preacher might be able to answer a question for him.

"Yes, Cap'n?" Jebediah said as he ambled into the cabin.

"Reverend, you went to some school to learn preaching, did you?"

"I went to Harvard, sir," Jebediah said proudly.

"Did you learn anything more than preaching?"

"I took a regular curriculum in addition to my courses in theology," Jebediah said. "Why do you ask, sir?"

"Have you ever heard of a fella name of Drake who sailed in these waters?"

Jebediah smiled. "You must mean Sir Francis Drake. Of course, I've heard of him."

"Tell me about him."

"He was a privateer for Queen Elizabeth of England."

"Privateer? Don't that mean pirate?"

"Yes. But he was a pirate by commission of the Queen."

"Did he ever have any treasure?"

"Oh, my, yes. The *Golden Hind* was filled to capacity with treasure when he sailed through the Pacific. He was the first Englishman to sail in these waters."

"Preacher, have you ever heard anything about him maybe burying some of that treasure?"

"There are rumors to that effect, yes," Jebediah said. "What's all this about, Captain?"

"Was the treasure ever found?"

Jebediah vaguely remembered a discussion with Angus Pugh once, years ago, as they were crossing the Pacific en route to Hawaii for the first time. Pugh had spoken of a buried treasure and a lost island, and had commented in an off-hand way that perhaps they should look for it during their voyage.

"I can't be sure without further research," Jebediah said. "But as far as I know, the treasure wasn't found. It was buried on some lost island somewhere."

"Then it's true!" Roberts said, slamming his fist into his hand.

"Captain, may I enquire what this is all about?" Jebediah asked.

"No, preacher, you may not," Roberts said. "Now, if you'll excuse me, sir, I've work to do."

Chapter Thirty-Five ─────────

LEILANI HAD COME to accept the situation. Whatever it was that she had with Mark had been stillborn. If he insisted there was nothing between them, if he could remember nothing they shared, then there was no longer any reason to think that it might be otherwise.

It was difficult for her, because although she had been made love to by others, she had shared deep love with another. Love was a powerful emotion, and to an Alii-Nui, an emotion such as love was doubly powerful. But even the strongest emotion could be drained if there was no exchange to keep the heart full.

Leilani stood up and walked over to look through her cabin window. When she saw the ship *Mary Luck* arrive, she began to formulate a plan. Mark was ashore at a ship's chandlers, buying materials for repairs after the storm. This would be the best time for her to escape.

As she stood looking across the water at the other ship, she heard the door being unlocked, and when she turned around she saw the first officer, Ben Hall, bringing food to her. Perhaps this would be her chance.

"Thank you, Mr. Hall," she said. "I was getting hungry."

"I'll leave the food on the chest," Hall said. He put the plate down and started backing away. As he did so, his one eye darted about apprehensively.

"Why, Mr. Hall, are you frightened of me?" Leilani asked.

"Me, afeared of you?" Hall asked. "Why, no." He laughed uneasily.

"You mean you aren't afraid of my powers? My witchcraft?" She watched him carefully.

"You ain't no witch. You're just a woman," Hall said, though not with complete conviction.

"Then if I'm just a woman, why is it that you never look at me as a woman? You always look at me with fear." She took a calculated step toward him.

"You're the cap'n's woman," Hall said.

"Did he say that?" She stopped, studying his eyes.

"He don't need to say it. Hell, you can look at him and know it."

For a moment, she nearly gave up her plan to escape. Perhaps there was some truth in what Hall said. Perhaps everyone could see it but Mark, and he, too, would eventually recognize it. On the other hand, perhaps he would recognize it more quickly if he thought he was going to lose her. She quickly decided to continue with her plan. She smiled at Hall and moved toward him again.

"Maybe I don't want to be the captain's woman," she said. "Maybe I'd like to be your woman."

As she moved toward Hall, he started backing away. "Don't come near me," he said.

"Mr. Hall, am I as ugly as all that?" she asked innocently. She released the tie on her garment, slowly and purposefully then stretched her arms out so that the lava-lava was held wide open. The silk hung from her arms to the floor, spread like a brightly colored gossamer wing behind her.

"Ugly? No, you ain't ugly, you're . . ." Hall started, but the sight before him cut short whatever he was going to say, and he stood there with his mouth slack and his one good eye wide open.

Leilani moved to him. As she crossed the room, the air raised the silk, and she appeared to glide beneath it, as if flying, until she stood close to him. She put her hand lightly on his shoulder, moved her fingers across it quickly, then up the neck, around the ears, and finally to the jawline where she found a small spot which was giving off a tremendous heat. She pressed against it lightly.

"I aim ter have you, now!" Hall said thickly. He reached for her with both arms, but she was ready for him. Quickly, so fast that Hall had no time to react, she twisted the eye patch so that it covered his good eye. Then she ducked under his arms, and as he started tripping forward, groping about blindly, she stuck a foot in front of him and gave him a sharp blow behind the neck. He went down with a crash, and Leilani grabbed the key, then stepped outside and locked the cabin door behind her.

She was on deck and over the side before anyone else knew she was gone. A short, quick swim later she was climbing up the anchor chain of the *Mary Luck*.

She vaulted over the rail in front of the startled seaman who had the anchor watch. He stood rooted in shock as she untied the silk from her waist, then casually wrapped it around her naked body and secured it at the shoulder. She brushed the dripping hair from her face, then looked at the sailor and smiled. "May I see your captain, please?"

The sailor took a few, hesitant steps backward, then turned and ran, calling for the captain as he did.

"Leilani, could that be you?" a familiar voice asked. "Have you come to this ship to whore with the sailors?"

Leilani turned to see Jebediah Grimsley. He was looking at her sternly, accusingly.

"I am not a ship's whore, Makua Grimsley," Leilani said. "I have been held prisoner on the *Distant Star*. I have just escaped."

"You were being held prisoner? For what purpose?" Jebediah asked.

"Because Mark Costain wants me to lead him to an uncharted island, and its buried treasure. He knows that only I can find it."

"Then you did well coming to me," Captain Roberts said, coming up behind them at that moment. He smiled at Leilani, and she noticed with some surprise that the captain was much shorter than she was. "I am Captain Roberts, at your service," he said.

"My name is Leilani. I live on Maui."

"We are going to Maui," Captain Roberts said. "You, like the preacher, are welcome to take passage with us."

"Thank you," Leilani said.

"Mr. Bell, weigh anchor. We're leaving at once," Roberts ordered.

"Cap'n, we've a landing party ashore."

"That's their problem, Mr. Bell," Roberts said. "I intend to get underway immediately. Preacher, would you see to the comfort of our guest?"

"Yes, Captain, thank you," Jebediah said. "Come along, my dear. You may find privacy in my cabin until your clothes dry and you can make a more presentable appearance."

"Thank you," Leilani said. She suddenly remembered Calvin, "Would you stay with me for a moment? I have something I must tell you."

"It would not be proper for me to be alone with you in the cabin," Jebediah said.

"It is very important, Makua Grimsley. Please."

"Very well," Jebediah said. He led her to the

small cabin which was his, and when they stepped inside, she sat on the bed. He remained standing.

"Perhaps you should sit down," Leilani offered.

"I prefer to stand, thank you," Jebediah replied.

"Makua Grimsley, it is about your son."

"He has not lain with you?" Jebediah shouted, pointing an accusing finger.

"No," Leilani said.

"That is good," Jebediah said. "I feared the worst."

"Calvin is dead," Leilani said.

"Dead?"

"Yes."

Jebediah let out a long sigh, and put his hand to his forehead. He pinched the bridge of his nose and was quiet for several seconds before he spoke again.

"How did it happen?"

"He killed himself."

"My son committed suicide? Why would he do such a thing?" Jebediah asked in surprise.

"I don't know why," Leilani said. She felt that, under the circumstances, it would be best if she didn't go into Calvin's attempted rape of her.

"If he committed suicide, then I can only surmise that Satan moved into his heart. I should have known that blood would tell. I tried to raise him as a Christian, but in the end the Devil claimed his own."

The door to the cabin was suddenly slammed

behind them, and they heard a key turn in the lock.

"Here, what is this?" Jebediah shouted. He ran to the door and began shaking it. "What is happening here?" He turned to look at Leilani with a confused expression.

"They've locked us in," Leilani said. "I should have gone ashore. I'm no better off now than I was."

"But why have they done this?" Jebediah asked. "What is this all about?"

"They must have found out about the treasure."

"The treasure?" Jebediah asked. "Yes, that must be it. Captain Roberts was asking me questions about the treasure of Sir Francis Drake. But I'm not certain the story about the Drake treasure is even true."

"It is true," Leilani said. "After the wreck of the *Sea Eagle*, the seas swept me to an uncharted island, and I was there for several days. During that time, I found this Drake treasure. Somehow, Dr. Pugh has discovered that the treasure must be on that island, and he and Mark Costain have launched a joint search for it. Mark Costain kidnapped me and is trying to force me to lead him to it."

"Dr. Pugh is mixed up in this, too?" Jebediah asked. "A man who came to the islands to preach the word of God?"

"Yes," Leilani answered.

Jebediah walked over and sat on the bunk, with his head in his hands. He sighed. "I sometimes wonder if I have truly interpreted God's will," he said. "Despite my best efforts, I failed with Calvin. And Dr. Pugh, whom I took as my friend when we were missionaries together, has provided me with more disappointments than my soul can bear."

"I'm sorry about your son," Leilani said softly.

"He was not my son," Jeebdiah said.

"He wasn't?"

"Mrs. Grimsley was with child when she came to me. I tried hard to help the boy overcome this sin. But I failed. I don't know where I went wrong, but I failed."

"Makua Grimsley, I have tried to be a good Christian the way you teach, but there are some things which I cannot understand. Perhaps if I ask you questions, you would answer them for me."

"Yes, of course, child," Jebediah said. He looked around the cabin. "We are locked in here. Perhaps it is God's will that we should be thrown together like this so that I could teach you of His word. Maybe I can succeed with you, where I failed with Calvin."

"Why is love a sin?" Leilani asked.

"But it isn't a sin, child. It's a most noble emotion. Of all God's creatures, only man is capable of love. It is a gift from Him, and that is why it should be used to honor Him."

"Can we not love one another?"

"Of course. There should also be love of one's fellow man."

"And love of man for woman and woman for man?"

Jebediah cleared his throat. He perceived the direction the conversation was taking, and he didn't particularly like it.

"There is a place for love between man and woman," he said. "Provided they are man and wife."

"Is there no love allowed between men and women who aren't married?"

"No. That would be a sin," Jebediah said resolutely. "First, there must be marriage. Then there can be love."

"But aren't marriages performed by men?"

"Ministers may perform marriages, yes, in accordance with the laws."

"Man's laws?"

"Yes, through the blessings of a minister."

"That is what I do not understand," Leilani said.

"What is it you do not understand?"

"Why you must have man's blessing to use God's gift. If, as you say, love is a gift of God, then we should be able to use it just as we use His gifts of sun, rain, and air."

"It isn't that simple," Jebediah said, coughing defensively.

"You said Calvin could not overcome his sin of birth. But how did he sin?"

"By being conceived in the womb of an unwed mother," Jebediah said.

"But it was not his doing," Leilani said. "Why should it be his sin?"

They heard a sound at the door, and before Jebediah could answer, they looked up to see Bell coming in. The big, red beard was split by a wide, evil grin, and he looked at them, scratching himself obscenely.

"I didn't interrupt anythin', did I, Preacher? I mean you wasn't about to bed this little ole girl, was you?"

"Certainly not, sir," Jebediah replied in an offended tone.

"Too bad," Bell said. He laughed. "The cap'n's probably goin' to have some sport with 'er, and after he gets through with 'em, they ain't in much shape for another man's pleasure. The cap'n wants to talk to you now, girl. You better go on inter his cabin."

Jebediah started toward the door with Leilani, but Bell put his big hand on Jebediah's chest and pushed him back. "Where do you think you're goin'?"

"I intend to make my protest to the captain over our treatment," Jebediah said.

Bell laughed. "That's rich, Preacher. This here treatment's the cap'n's idea."

Jebediah sat on the bed and watched the door shut behind them. He was frightened for her and wondered what Captain Roberts intended to do with her. For that matter, he was frightened for himself.

As he sat on the bed waiting for Leilani's return, he thought of their conversation. In particular, he thought of the last statement Leilani had made when she said that the sin had not been Calvin's.

Leilani was right. It wasn't Calvin's sin, but Jebediah had perceived it as such for all these years. He had used it as an excuse for his hate.

His hate? Had he finally admitted it to himself? Now, after Calvin was dead, did he have the courage to face his own sins and shortcomings?

Jebediah lay back on the bunk and folded his hands behind his head. The chances were very good that he would be killed. He realized that and accepted it calmly. Now, with the thought of his death just around the corner, he wondered if he would have the courage to face the truth.

The truth was that everytime he had looked at Calvin, he had thought of how Calvin was conceived. He thought of Marcia bedding with another man, and the thought had eaten away at him for twenty years, infesting his soul like a disease.

Jebediah had taken a vow of celibacy, not from religious conviction, but from jealousy and anger with Marcia. The vow had been a rash act, but one Jebediah had been true to, though there were many times when he was sorely tested.

Marcia was an attractive woman, and there were many times when he would have liked to lie with her. During those times, he cursed himself for the fool he was, and he cursed Marcia for committing the act which had forced him into such a position. He came down with more than the required zeal on fornicators, because in fighting them, he was also fighting his own battle.

But it was a battle of jealousy, a sinful act of selfishness which drove him, not conviction. If he survived this trial, he would go to Marcia and ask her forgiveness.

He wanted her to forgive him, not only for what he had done to her, but for what he had done to Calvin, as well. For Jebediah realized with as much certainty as if the words had been carved in stone before him, that, somehow, he was responsible for Calvin's death.

He prayed for forgiveness.

And he wept.

Chapter Thirty-Six ─────────────

MARK WAS IN the ship's chandlers when the news was brought to him that Leilani had escaped. He immediately ordered all hands who were not engaged in repairing the storm damage to look for her. They searched every inn and public place, and sent runners into the villages with promises of large rewards for anyone who could find her. They even searched the place known as Sanctuary, a traditional hiding place for refugees from docking ships, but they had no luck.

Mark returned to the ship at midnight, discouraged and ready to abandon the hunt. It wasn't until then that he heard another ship had come and gone during the day. When he discovered that the ship had been the *Mary Luck,* he felt certain that Leilani must have escaped to it. He also reasoned that if Captain Roberts learned of the existence of the treasure, he would try to find it. So Mark ordered the anchor weighed at shortly after midnight, and the *Distant Star* cleared Honuapo Harbor.

Now, some five hours later, Mark leaned against the rail and watched the coming of dawn. They had sailed through the night with all the canvas they could carry, and were more than fifty miles to sea.

Mike Fitzpatrick handed Mark a cup of tea, piping hot from the galley.

"What makes you think she would tell Cap'n Roberts anythin', when she wouldn't tell us?" he asked.

"Captain Roberts will not put the questions to her as gently as we did," Mark said. "I'm afraid he'll get the information from her."

"Even if you're right, I can't help but feel we're on a wild goose chase," Fitzpatrick said. "We've been under full sail throughout the night, 'n' we never saw a stick of mast nor a flicker of light to indicate that we're behind her."

"We're going in the right direction," Mark said. "I'm not certain where the island is, but I know where I quit the *Mary Luck* and that's where we're headed."

"What do you aim to do when you find the *Mary Luck*?" Hall asked. He had just joined the two men in their conversation.

"I intend to take Leilani from it," Mark answered.

Hall rubbed his chin and looked out over the pearly water, lightening quickly now with the coming of dawn. "That'll mean a fight, more'n likely."

"It may," Mark agreed.

"You told the men there'd be no risk involved."

"There wouldn't have been," Mark said. "But the situation has changed now. You let the girl get away, you can answer to the men. The bonus will justify the risk. They'll go along with it."

"S'pose you catch up with the ship and we fight her. S'pose even that we win 'n' get the girl. There may be some of us kilt."

"That's the risk," Mark said.

"But s'posin' even after all that the girl still won't tell us where the island is. Then all that risk is for nothin'."

"That's true," Mark said.

"I'm thinkin' there's a better way," Hall suggested.

"What way would that be?"

"Let's just hang back a mite 'n' give Cap'n Roberts his head. That way he'll have a chance to get the information outta the girl. Then we can follow 'em to the island," Hall said.

"That might work," Fitzpatrick put in.

"No," Mark said.

"Why not? You said yourself that he'd be more likely to get the information out of her than you would."

"No," Mark said. "I don't like the idea."

"Cap'n, iffen you're gonna ask the men to risk a battle with the *Mary Luck*, then you gotta

give 'em somethin' worth riskin' a battle for. I
say we let Roberts get the information outta
her."

"I am the master of the vessel, Hall, and I'll
make the decisions," Mark said. "You don't know
Roberts and I do. I know the brutality he's
capable of. I'll not let Leilani be subjected to it."

"All right, Cap'n, if you think you can get the
men to fight," Hall said.

"The men'll fight for you, Cap'n," Fitzpatrick
put in.

"Thanks, Mike."

"Cap'n, are you in love with that girl?" Fitzpatrick asked suddenly.

"You gentlemen had better see to the changing of the watch," Mark said, not answering
Fitzpatrick's question.

Mark turned away and walked back to the
railing. He leaned over it and stared out over
the sea. The rising sun was a great orange disc
now, and before the sun, stretching all the way
to the *Distant Star*, was a great band of red,
laid out like a carpet on the sea. The few clouds
which dotted the eastern horizon were purple,
and the great white sails of the ship were
rimmed in gold from the sun. Flying fish broke
from one wave and propelled themselves by a
powerful beat of their tails over a long distance,
until they nosed down into another wave like
arrows launched into the sea.

The sea was like a tonic to Mark. It was not
surprising to seamen like him to discover that

the salt content of the sea and of human blood was exactly the same. For Mark, the sea was the stuff of life itself. And he knew that even if he found the treasure, he would not want to give up the sea.

He wondered how Leilani would like the sea. He had known merchantmen captains who took their wives with them. The great cabin was fixed up as living quarters, and the children, when they came, were born and raised on the ship. It was not unusual, but Mark sometimes thought it was a lucky man who could find a woman to allow him the freedom of the sea while also providing him with the pleasures of her bed.

He could not expect Leilani to do that, could he?

What was he doing? What was he thinking about? Was he seriously considering Leilani as someone to share his life?

There, as if floating just over the horizon, he could see her face, and he suddenly remembered a similar time of reflection on board the *Mary Luck*. He had been haunted by her then, too. Then he had vowed that he would see her again.

The spot on his shoulder began to throb, and he reached up and touched it without realizing why. And in that moment, he saw her before him on the island, holding her arms out to him, coming to him, and making love with him in the sand. From that instant, the veil of confusion fell away. Mark could then remember everything that had happened to him, including the voyage to the island and the love he felt for Leilani.

It was true! He did love her! What a fool he had been! How cruel he had been to her!

"The island!" Mark suddenly said aloud. "I believe I can find the island. Mr. Hall, Mr. Fitzpatrick, to my cabin!"

A few moments later, Mark had the chart rolled open on the table in his cabin. He weighted the corners down with mugs and pistols, and bent over the table to examine the map.

"I left the *Mary Luck* at this point," he said, putting a divider on the chart. "And I sailed for approximately"—he closed his eyes and computed—"forty hours, north, north west, with a slight westerly swell. I remember now gauging our speed at approximately three knots." He spread the divider, then put the other point down. "Here," he said. "A hundred thirty-nine degrees, thirty minutes west longitude. Eight degrees, thirty minutes north latitude."

"That's near a hundred miles off the shippin' and whalin' lanes," Hall said. "There wouldn't be no ships there."

"Exactly my point," Mark replied: "If the island were on the lanes, it would have been found by now."

"You think we should head right for there?" Fitzpatrick asked.

"Yes, Mr. Fitzpatrick, I do," Mark said. "Keep lookouts aloft at all times. Keep as much canvas spread as the ship will carry. With any luck we'll intercept the *Mary Luck* before she gets there."

Leilani was bound hands and feet and spread-eagled at the bowsprit. She was nude and the sailors of the *Mary Luck* were gathered at the bow, looking at her with leering eyes and drooling mouths. She saw bulges in the pants of many of them, and a few were openly and unabashedly rubbing themselves.

Bell had the cat-o'-nine laid out on the deck before him, and he chuckled under his breath as he straightened the lashes out. Finally he picked it up and flicked it toward her, allowing the strips to fall painlessly, but threateningly across her shoulders. He moved the whip down slowly, tantalizingly, and nine lashes tumbled across her bare breasts and nipples.

"The cap'n has a taste for this," Bell said. "And unless you tell him what he wants to know, you'll be feelin' the sting."

"He will do it anyway," Leilani said calmly. "I'll not tell him a thing."

Bell grabbed one of Leilani's nipples between his big thumb and forefinger. "You know I could bust this li'l ole' nipple here liken it weren't no more'n a grape iffen I was of a mind to. How would you like that?"

Leilani felt his fingers on her nipples. They were heavy enough to be uncomfortable, but not painful.

Bell let go, then jerked the whip back. He

flicked it forward again, then checked the swing at the last instant. The lashes popped wickedly, just short of her body, snapping against her skin with just a hint of pain the whip could bring.

"Maybe you ought ter give 'er one good 'un, so's she could see what it's gonna feel like," said one of the men, one who had been rubbing himself openly.

The men, many of whom had been flogged themselves, were now watching with sadistic delight as the show was being played out before them.

Bell brought the whip back over his shoulder, ready for one brutal blow. Leilani tensed her body, waiting for it.

"Here, stop that!" Jebediah yelled. The preacher had broken out of his cabin, and he had come up on deck just in time to see what was going on. He surprised Bell by grabbing the whip from him and tossing it overboard.

"Why, you little pissant!" Bell shouted angrily. He clubbed Jebediah on the head and the lean preacher collapsed on the deck.

Bell turned his attention back to Leilani and began removing his belt. "It don't matter none to you, girl. I'll just do with my belt what I was goin' to do with the cat."

Jebediah raised to his knees and shook his head to clear it. He looked up in time to see Bell about to swing the belt, and he jumped up and grabbed him.

"No," he shouted. "Leave her bel"

Bell pushed the preacher away from him. "Somebody grab this bastard," he said.

Two men grabbed Jebediah, one on either side, and dragged him to the foremast.

"Don't hurt him!" Leilani shouted.

An evil grin split Bell's face. "You don't want to see him hurt, huh?" He brought the belt around in a whistling arc, and it snapped against Jebediah's back. Jebediah screamed and jerked convulsively under the ropes that held him.

"No!" Leilani shouted. "Please, leave him alone. He doesn't know anything."

Bell laughed and brought the belt around in another wicked smash against the preacher's back. He looked at Leilani, smiling with evil, foul-smelling yellowed teeth. "Do you like to see this?"

"Please, stop," Leilani begged.

Bell slashed out again. "I think I'll just beat on this pissant preacher here, until I find out where the island is."

"But he doesn't know," Leilani said.

"That's my point," Bell said. "There ain't nothin' he can do to stop it. Only you can, girl. By tellin' us where the treasure is."

Another whistling blow, and Jebediah screamed out in agony again.

"How about it, girl? You want to see me turn this here skinny little runt into strips of shark bait? You just keep quiet a little longer, 'n' you'll see it done."

She knew the *haole* seaman had won.

"Don't hit him again," she said. "I'll lead you to the island."

"Well, now," Bell said, rolling the belt up. "That's more like it. I think the cap'n'l be pleased to hear that. One of you men, get him. It looks like we got us a guide."

Chapter Thirty-Seven ───────────

LEILANI WAS UNTIED, but Jebediah was kept lashed to the foremast.

Leilani leaned over the bow of the ship, reading the wave patterns and indicating to the helmsman which way to steer. She watched for the opportunity to speak with Jebediah, and when it came she moved closer to him. They spoke quietly so that none of the sailors would overhear.

"Makua Grimsley, I fear that when they find the treasure they will kill us anyway."

"I am certain you are right," Jebediah said. "I'm sorry my weakness allowed them to use me against you."

"I have a plan," Leilani said. "But I will need your help."

"I will do what I can . . . though under the circumstances, I don't know what it would be."

"I know that Mark Costain will be following

us," Leilani said. "I intend to help him find us."

"But you have just escaped from Captain Costain. Now you want to go back to him?"

"Yes," Leilani said. "Our fate is in much better hands with Captain Costain. Also, I realize that I cannot put him out of my heart. I love him, and I will make him love me."

"But he is *haole* and you are . . ." Jebediah began.

"Heathen?" Leilani interrupted.

"Forgive me, Leilani," Jebediah said. "I have made many mistakes, and I have much to think about. I will say nothing about you and Captain Costain. But how do you intend to help him find us?"

"I will build a fire," Leilani said. "One that makes much smoke. If Mark Costain is looking for us, he will see the smoke."

"How can I help with that?" Jebediah asked. "As you can see, I am bound by these ropes."

"Captain Roberts must not suspect that the true purpose of the smoke is to signal Mark. I am going to tell him that the smoke is to carry a prayer to my gods to help me find the island."

"Blasphemy," Jebediah said.

"That's right, exactly," Leilani said. "I want you to grow very angry. Say things about false gods. That will mask the true purpose of the smoke."

"But even in jest, to make a show before a false god is blasphemy," Jebediah said. "I will have no party to it."

"Makua Grimsley, you must. If we cannot signal Mark, we will surely die."

"Then I shall become a martyr, like the Christians of old," Jebediah said resolutely.

"And you will martyr me too?" Leilani asked.

"Leilani, you don't know what you're asking me to do. It goes against everything I've taught and stood for all these years."

"Very well," Leilani sighed. "I just hope I can do this work without you."

"I'm sorry," Jebediah said.

Leilani began gathering bits of rope and canvas, then dropping them in a bucket half full of deck tar. She took a burning brand from the firebox and dropped it into the bucket. Within a few moments, she had a column of smoke boiling up in a long plume.

"Here, what the hell is this?" Bell shouted, running over to the bucket.

Leilani was on her knees, chanting what sounded like a prayer to the gods.

Captain Roberts was on deck as soon as he heard the commotion. "Put that fire out!" he commanded.

"No," Leilani shouted. "If you want to find the island, you must let it burn!"

"Are you crazy?" Bell asked. "Any ship for fifty miles will be able to see that."

"I must say my prayers to Kane, the sea god, if we are to have any chance of finding the island," Leilani insisted. She was still on her knees and she bent her body forward so that her forehead was touching the deck. She began chanting her prayers again.

"I don't know," Roberts mused.

"Cap'n, it's some kind of a trick. She's tryin' to signal Costain."

"Signal Captain Costain?" Leilani said. "Why would I do that? I just escaped from him."

"Maybe now you think you'd rather be with him," Roberts suggested.

"You *haole* are all alike to me," Leilani said. "Captain, if you want me to lead you to the island, then you must not destroy the smoke which carries my prayer to Kane. For if Kane does not hear my prayer, he will not send the wind to take this ship to the island."

Captain Roberts stood there for a moment, listening to the warnings from Bell and the entreaties from Leilani. It was obvious he was struggling to make up his mind as to what he should do.

"Destroy that vile and evil image of a false god!" Jebediah shouted suddenly. "Captain, I warn you, if you don't toss that bucket overboard now, you will know God's wrath for participating in a pagan ceremony. For twenty years I've fought against these pagan rituals, and I'll not stand by and see one conducted in my presence."

Roberts looked at Jebediah and his mouth twisted in a mirthless smile. "You mean there really is such a god as Kane?"

"There is but one God!" Jebediah bellowed.

"Cap'n, you want me to throw the bucket over?" Bell asked.

"No," Roberts said, his eyes narrowed on Jebediah. "The preacher here made up my mind for me. He wouldn't get so riled up if the girl was tryin' to trick us." He looked at Leilani. "But you better get your prayers said in a hurry, girl. Bell's right. This is a clear signal to anyone who may be lurking about. And I don't relish company right now."

"Thank you, Captain," Leilani said. She touched her forehead to the deck and began praying again.

"Idolater. Worshiper of false gods! Desist at once!" Jebediah shouted taking an unexpected relish in his role.

"Cap'n Costain, smoke two points off the larboard bow!" the lookout sang down.

"Helmsman, take a bearing on the smoke and steer that course!" Mark called. He hit his fist into his hand and smiled. "I don't know how she did it, but Leilani is behind that."

"What do you think the smoke is?" Hall asked.

"I know what it is," Mark answered. "It's the *Mary Luck.*"

"You think she's on fire?"

"That, or a signal from Leilani."

"How could she do that, Cap'n?"

"You have to ask?" Mark said. "Don't I recall seeing you abandon the *Sea Eagle?*"

"Yeah, you're right," Hall said. "I'll be a son-of-a-bitch! You know, Cap'n, that's some woman."

"Yes, she is," Mark said.

"Cap'n, the mizzenmast riggin' won't hold," Fitzpatrick reported. "We didn't get a chance to finish the repair to it before we left the island. Were goin' to have to reef the mizzen royal, top gallant, and topmast sails."

"Dammit," Mark swore. "This takes away all hope of catching them before they make the island."

"What are we goin' to do now?"

"Keep men working on the rigging. Try to fix it," Mark said. "In the meantime, rig spinnakers and trisails. We'll spread as much sheet as we can."

"Aye, Cap'n," Fitzpatrick answered.

Mark strolled to the bow of the ship and looked out toward the horizon. "Hang on, Leilani," he said under his breath. "I'm coming for you."

Chapter Thirty-Eight

THE BAY OF Sleeping Lady Island, formed by the fish hook, opened to the south. Mark reckoned that the *Mary Luck* would anchor in the protected waters of the bay. With good fortune then, his approach from the north would be masked by the ridge of mountains.

With the ship carrying as much canvas as he could spread, the approach still seemed agonizingly slow, and he felt the tension building around him as the island grew larger.

"S'posin' they got lookouts up in the mountains?" Hall asked.

"If so, they will no doubt see us approaching and they'll greet us with cannon fire," Mark said. He raised the glass to his eye and looked at the island. He saw the water breaking on the shoreline, and the trees waving gently a few yards up the beach.

"Ship ahoy, sir!" the lookout called down.

"Where away?"

"Her masts, sir, showin' through the trees there," the lookout said.

"If we've seen them, they've seen us," Hall said. "Perhaps we should stand away and prepare a broadside."

"No," Mark said. "I'll not fire on that ship until I know that Leilani is safe."

"What do you propose to do, Cap'n?"

"I'm going to board her," Mark said.

"Board her?"

"Yes. It's my guess that most of the crew's ashore. A small boarding party could take her."

"And what then?"

"Use your imagination, Mr. Hall," Mark said. "If we have both ships, of what use is the treasure to them?"

"Good point!" Hall said, laughing. "You can count on me for the boarding party."

"I *am* counting on it," Mark said. "I'll leave Fitzpatrick behind to look after the *Distant Star*."

Mark closed the telescope and turned to look at his men. Those who weren't in the braces were huddled anxiously on the deck.

"Lads," he began, "this is what it's all about. The treasure's here on this island. But first, we've got to take care of a little business. Captain Roberts has won the race, but he hasn't won the battle. I aim to take his ship, and I'll be needing a boarding party. Double prize money to all members of the boarding party. Do I have any volunteers?"

Half a score hands went up. Mark thanked them, then told them to arm themselves with cutlasses and pistols.

"Mr. Hall, lower the launch. We'll sail across the bay with the launch hidden behind the ship. Mr. Fitzpatrick, you will make smoke on the ship, and we'll use the smoke to shield the launch. By the time the smoke has cleared away, we should be upon them. Close enough, anyway, so they'll have no chance to bring their cannon to bear."

"How is she armed, sir?"

"She has but eight twenty-four-pounders, four to each side. As I recall, the guns have no more than a ten-degree down deflection, which means once we're inside a hundred yards, we're too close for them to bear."

"I'll admit, Cap'n Costain, we've the advantage of your knowing the ship," Hall said. "You heard the cap'n, men, lower the launch."

The men worked hard until the launch was put over the side. The boarding party got into the launch, and as the *Distant Star* sailed across the open mouth of the bay, the launch was hidden behind it.

"Cap'n, they've seen us!" Fitzpatrick called down from the deck.

"Are they showing signals?"

"Aye, sir."

"What signals?"

"Party ashore for food and water," Fitzpatrick said. "They want to know our intentions."

"Tell them we're landing a party for food and water, too," Mark said.

"Aye, sir."

Pennants were run up on the *Distant Star* and they fluttered brightly in the crisp breeze.

Suddenly a cannon boomed and a black cannonball whistled over the bow of the *Distant Star* and landed a hundred yards beyond with a great splash.

"Cap'n, they've signaled for us to stand to," Fitzpatrick shouted down. "If we don't, they intend to fire on us."

"Make smoke now, Mr. Fitzpatrick," Mark said. "Mr. Hall, prepare to come starboard."

"Aye, aye, sir," Hall answered from the tiller of the launch.

Smoke began boiling from the several tarpots on the stern of the *Distant Star*, and the little launch cut hard to the right, plunging into the black, choking cloud. By the time it poked out the other side, it was only a hundred fifty yards away from the *Mary Luck* and heeled over under a brisk wind. It skimmed across the water, heading for the anchored ship.

"They've seen us, men," Mark shouted. "Keep your heads down!"

The four cannons on the seaward side of the *Mary Luck* belched flame and smoke, and the cannonballs splashed into the sea, close to the launch, drenching Mark and the boarding party.

"That's it, lads," Mark said. "By the time they get reloaded and run out, we'll be well inside their effective range! Prepare to board!"

The cannons from the *Distant Star* roared, and Mark saw the cannonballs smashing into the trees ashore. He knew then that Captain Roberts had been alerted and was trying to return to his ship. Fitzpatrick's fire was keeping Roberts' head down ashore.

The guns on the *Mary Luck* fired again, but as Mark had predicted, the launch was inside their range, and the cannonballs whistled harmlessly overhead.

A moment later, the jib boom of the *Mary Luck* loomed over them, and they were alongside.

"Grapnel!" Mark shouted. "Boarders away!"

Grapling hooks were thrown up to the deck of the *Mary Luck* and hooked onto the railing. Men jerked on the ropes to tighten them, then started climbing up the side of the ship.

Mark was the first one on deck, and he was joined quickly by the others. A pistol discharged from the after hatch, and Mark heard the angry buzz of the ball as it whizzed by his ear. From his left, someone lunged at him with a saber and Mark turned to meet him, blocking the saber slash with his own blade in a clang of steel.

"So, Mr. Costain, I'll be openin' up your gut after all," Bell said, smiling evilly through his beard and slashing wickedly with his sword.

"Where's the girl, Bell?" Mark asked. He parried a slash and a thrust, and the steel rang like bells.

"You've a taste for the girl? Maybe she means somethin' to you, eh, Mr. Costain?"

More clanging steel.

"Where is she?"

"Don't you worry none about her, Costain. She'll all tied up 'n' spread out waitin' for me. 'Course the cap'n gets first nibs on 'er, 'n' he don't normally leave much for others ter enjoy. I fancy I'll get some pleasure from 'er, though."

Mark was preoccupied as he fought Bell, and he looked anxiously around the deck for Leilani. Bell had talked about her to distract him, and suddenly the big, red-headed man thought he saw an advantage. He raised his sword high over his head and brought it down sharply, aiming for Mark's neck.

Mark saw the blade flash in the sunlight and he managed to parry the arc at the last moment. Even so, Bell's strength nearly overcame him.

"When you see ole' Big Pigg in hell, you can give 'em a hello from me," Bell said.

Mark fought against the strength of the man until he saw an opening. If he could twist his body to duck, the force of Bell's thrust would carry his blade on through to the deck and that would leave his side exposed. Mark tensed, then feinted a move to his left, drawing Bell more that way. Then Mark quickly slid out to his right and jerked his sword away from the blocking position. Bell had been maintaining steady pressure on his blade, and with the resistance suddenly removed, the blade slammed down and stabbed into the deck planking.

As Mark stepped to the right, he plunged his sword back over his left arm, cleanly, gracefully, like a matador's ceremonial execution of the bull. The long blade slipped easily through Bell's ribs and into his heart, and he tumbled forward onto the deck.

Cheering broke out then, and Mark looked up to see that his men had carried the fight. The other defenders of the *Mary Luck* had dived over the rail and were swimming for the island.

Mark didn't join in the celebration. He was too busy looking for Leilani. He saw Jebediah securely lashed to the foremast and he cut the ropes with his knife.

"Preacher, where's Leilani?" he asked.

"She's in the cabin, below decks," Jebediah said. He rubbed his wrists gratefully. "Thank God, sir, you've come, just as she said you would."

Mark jumped through the hatch, down to the between decks. The sun sent bars of light slanting into the darkened interior and he ran through the floating, sunlit dust motes, calling for Leilani.

"I'm in here," a voice came from one of the cabins. As it happened, it was the cabin Mark had used when he was on the *Mary Luck.*

He tried the door, and when he found it locked he kicked it open. Leilani was inside, tied, nude and spread-eagled on the bunk.

"My God, what have they done to you?" he asked. "Are you all right?" He quickly untied her. As soon as her arms were freed, she sat up and threw both arms around him.

"I knew you would come," she said.

"I've been a fool, Leilani. A complete and utter fool. I can't begin to make it up to you, but I'd like to try. For what it's worth, I love you."

"You have made it up to me," Leilani said, kissing him, and laughing and crying at the same time.

"I love you," Mark said again. "I love you, I love you, I love you."

"Cap'n," Hall said, suddenly appearing in the doorway. "The men want to know when we're goin' ashore after Roberts and the treasure."

"We aren't," Mark said, handing Leilani the lava-lava to cover herself.

"What do you mean we ain't?"

"I've been a fool," Mark said. "I've found all the treasure I want, right here in this girl."

"That's fine for you, but what about us?"

"You've got the ship. Use it to strike a bargain with Roberts," Mark said. "You'll be able to work something out, I'm sure. I'm taking Leilani back to Maui."

"You mean you aim to give up your share of the treasure?" Hall asked.

"I'm not giving up a thing," Mark said. He looked at Leilani. "I've had it before me all this time, and didn't realize it."

Leilani smiled and put her arms around him. "You really mean that, don't you?"

"Of course I mean it."

"In that case, I will share a secret with you.

I know where the treasure is. I'll take you there."

"You don't have to," Mark said.

"Cap'n, are you crazy?"

"I don't think so," Mark answered.

Leilani kissed Mark, then looked at him and smiled. "I know I don't have to," she said. "That's why I'm willing to."

One hour later, two ships lay side by side at anchor in the bay. Captain Roberts and all his men were standing on the deck of the *Distant Star*. Captain Roberts' crew had made a pile of arms on the deck, and Mark's men were busy collecting swords, pistols, rifles, and knives. All the cannons of the *Mary Luck* had been shoved overboard, and now lay on the bottom of the bay, an interesting new attraction for curious fish.

Roberts paced back and forth angrily.

"You can't turn us loose with no means of protecting ourselves," he protested.

"Why not?"

"Who knows what we will see in these waters?"

Mark laughed. "Your biggest danger, little man, is in having to face your men without Bell and his cat-o'-nine to back up your authority. You'll have no danger from passing ships, if you can survive your own crew. You'll be all right. I have no intention of arming you, only to have you jump us somewhere."

Hall squirted a stream of tobacco juice over

the rail in front of Roberts and looked at him contemptuously. "It's a fair sight more 'n I'd a' done for you," he said. "If it had been left up to me, you'd be feedin' the fishes now."

"There may come another time, Captain Costain," Roberts warned.

"We'll see about that," Mark said easily. "Now, Captain, we will give you a six-hour head start. If I see your ship between now and the time we return to Maui, I will consider it a threat, and I will sink you."

"But we are unarmed!" Roberts said.

"Then I should have no difficulty in sinking you, should I?" Mark looked at the ship's clock. "Your six hours have started. I would suggest that you weigh anchor."

"Very well," Roberts said, "we will return to the ship now."

The crew of the *Mary Luck* returned to their ship, amidst the deriding cries and jeers of the men of the *Distant Star*. Some of the *Mary Luck* men made gestures, and threatened to even the score if they ever met again, but for the most part, they seemed anxious to leave.

Sometime later when the *Mary Luck* was hull down on the horizon, Mark, who had disappeared with Leilani and the preacher, returned to the deck and addressed the crew.

"Men, you've done a fair day's work here, and you are going to be well paid. Leilani has told me where the treasure is, and she and I are going to recover it. Every man jack of you is in for a share. Including the preacher."

"No, I can't . . ." Jebediah started to say, then he stopped and smiled. "Yes," he said. "Yes, I can accept it. It's about time I made a few things up to Mrs. Grimsley, and my share of this treasure will help."

"Mr. Hall, keep a good watch. If Captain Roberts shows up again, sink his ship."

"Aye, aye, sir," Hall said.

Mark led Leilani to the rail and helped her climb down into the launch. We'll be back in the morning."

"In the morning?" Hall asked. "Is it going to take you that long to find the treasure?"

"Oh, no, not at all," Mark said with a smile. "We don't have to search for it. We know where it is. We have other plans in mind for the night."

Hall laughed. "Aye, Cap'n, I get you." He looked at the preacher. "Well, Reverend, ain't you gonna give 'em your hell and brimstone message?"

"Why should I do that, Mr. Hall?" Jebediah asked.

"Because they're goin' to be *fornicatin'*, Reverend," Hall said. Everyone laughed with Hall.

"That is their right, Mr. Hall," Jebediah said. "I just married them."

"You *what?*" Hall shouted. He turned to look at Mark, but the launch was already underway.

"No more ghosts, Captain Costain?" Leilani asked as the boat headed for the beach.

"None," Mark said. "No regrets, Mrs. Costain?"

"None," she said.

The sun was setting in a brilliant burst of color, and white birds flew up in welcome to their island. A distant star hung over its namesake, riding majestically at anchor now, after having brought the two lovers together.

Behind them was the tempestuous path of love's course run. Ahead, the golden promise of their future.